BOOK TWO IN THE PFEIFFERBERG CHRONICLES

OF KINGS
And
CHRONICLES

DALE R. PFEIFFER

Carpenter's Son Publishing

Of Kings and Chronicles

©2017 by Dale R. Pfeiffer

Published by Carpenter's Son Publishing, Franklin, Tennessee, in association with Larry Carpenter of Christian Book Services, LLC. www.christianbook-services.com

Edited by Robert Irvin

Cover and Interior Layout Design by Suzanne Lawing

Printed in the United States of America

978-1-942587-73-6

"With the publishing of the Pfeifferberg Chronicles trilogy, historical novels have entered a new era. By definition, historical novels have to rely on historical documents, and they must, if they are to claim any degree of accuracy, be faithful to the historical record. Dale Pfeiffer, the author of the trilogy, has certainly met that criterion, and he uses as his springboard the most ancient historical documents that have come down to us, namely the tenth and eleventh chapters of the Book of Genesis. It is a brave man indeed who takes that step in such an age as ours in which the Book of Genesis is held in such contempt. But because he has taken that step, Pfeiffer is able to build a credible sweep of history from those most ancient times up to and including his own Pfeiffer forebears. The Pfeifferberg Chronicles, I have no doubt, will often be imitated by future authors, and deservedly so. It has set an important benchmark."

—**BILL COOPER PhD, ThD**
Vice President, Creation Science Movement
Adjunct Professor Master Faculty
ICR School of Biblical Apologetics

For more about the author,
and the Pfeifferberg Chronicles series,
visit http://dalepfeiffer.com.

THE PFEIFFERBERG CHRONICLES

OF KINGS *And* CHRONICLES

DALE REYNOLDS PFEIFFER

Of Kings and Chronicles, Book Two of the trilogy, is the story of the war-weary sons of King Iobaath, sojourning in Assuwa, of the exploratory voyage of Captain King Alanus and his pioneering sons, and of the emerging romantic Celtic kingdoms of Europa.

The first three chapters portray life in Assuwa from 2500 BC to 1100 BC before Captain King Alanus, a spiritual man of great faith, makes his voyage from Alanya of Panphylia to Catalanya of Europa along familiar Ionian trade routes to the Great Sea of Tarshish.

The last four chapters portray tribal life in a young Europa through four successive cultures of Celtic expansion and development: the Tumulus, Urnfield, Hallstatt, and Le Tene cultures.

The story ends in a special period of history that Scripture terms in the apostle Paul's letter to the Galatians, "in the fullness of time": in the early days of the Roman Empire when Julius Caesar conquers the Galatian confederacy under the leadership of King Vercingetorix in central Gaul.

As with Book One, the chronicle is based on the genealogy of the early British kings, and the Latin text and translation of Nenniun 17 and 18 by Nennius, published in *After the Flood* by Bill Cooper (Appendices 5 and 7).

Book One: *Descent from White Mountains*
Book Two: *Of Kings and Chronicles*
Book Three: *O Foolish Galatians*

CONTENTS

THE DYING GAULS

After the death of the eight Great Flood survivors, the progenitors of all human beginnings, a once peaceful coexistence among the tribal nations turned violent. Nimrod, the Mighty Hunter and Dragon Slayer, became a mighty warrior and initiated an age of unrest, violence, and bloodshed that lasted for thousands of years.

ONE

THE CHRONICLES OF KING EZRA

(APPROXIMATELY 2500 BC)

A CALL FOR HELP and aid from the land of Kau and the kingdoms of Japheth provided great inspiration to my father, King Izrau, for my name, Ezra, which appropriately means "help" in the tongue of Eber. The tribal nations surrounding the Hospitable Sea of Gomer, along with the tribal nations surrounding the Khazar Sea of Magog who settled in the northern coastal regions, along with the tribal nations of Madai who settled in the southern coastal regions, formed a league of Kau nations to defend our God-given territories against greedy and violent Sumerians penetrating our southern borders.

Since the days of my youth, we have been engaged in perpetual warfare with the armies of the once God-fearing and noble Nimrod, King of Shinar. After the LORD God flooded the earth, Nimrod, born of the seed of Ham, built the great Mesopotamian cities of Nineveh, Babel, Uruk, Akkad, and Calneh.

Our native land of Sumer was once called "the land of civilized kings." But no more! After the nations received their unique and distinguished tongues from our Creator at the tower of Babel, the King of Shinar built other cities: Rehoboth-Ir, Resen, and Calah. Asshur, the second son of Shem, abandoned the Eber nation to assist Nimrod. All these Sumerian cities became great and are ruled by their builder, the mighty hunter, warrior, and apostate: King Nimrod.

On several occasions Shem and Japheth attempted to dissuade King Nimrod from his prideful and violent course. But like a stubborn auroch, the elated king did not heed the voice of wisdom. His iron will would not be smelted; his foolish heart would not be convinced. His wantonness for power found no comfort or respite in the way of the LORD God, nor in obeying God's righteous commandments, nor in the animal sacrifices of Noah, the Herald of Righteousness. Like the mighty Nephilim who perished in the furious floodwaters of God's judgments, King Nimrod ceased to fear the LORD God, creating idols of his own heart and imagination, and stood recalcitrant in opposition to our Creator, the Sovereign Ruler of the Universe.

Many have sourced King Nimrod's ambivalence to the way of our Creator to the human adulation he received among the sons of Ham and Canaan at our great two-thousand-year gathering and celebration, that renowned tribal assembly held before the death of Noah in the days of Japheth, the Great Voice. Who among men would not be tempted to be puffed up in spirit from such admiration from the kinsmen who, according to our tradition, loudly shouted, "Nimrod, like a mighty hunter before the LORD!" In those early days after the flood, even the sons of Kau praised him for his mighty deeds. They gladly made for him a copper crown, placing it upon his head.

As King Nimrod aged, the once young and mighty hunter became narcissistic. Nimrod's courage and mighty hunting skills in the days of his youth, displayed in the conquest of Rimmon, the monster of Mesopotamia, morphed, in his latter days, into the art of war against his own kinsmen. King Nimrod is recorded in the chronicles of Eber as the one who ended peaceful negotiations among the elders and wise men who represented each tribal nation. Full of greed, Nimrod yielded to the serpent enemy of mankind within the heart of every man. He became a violent dictator and introduced warfare into our once peaceful and unified kingdoms.

King Nimrod's obsession to be worshipped and served by the sons of Ham was met, embraced, and satiated by the idolatrous appetites among deceived men who desired to be ruled by a human king. The men of the land of Shinar became as cursed women whose desire is for their husband. The mighty King Nimrod became the husband of the people and was exulted as their functional god, a place of exultation that is reserved only for the LORD God of Noah.

Our Kaucasus Mountain mother between the Hospitable Sea and the Khazar Sea provided a natural hedge of protection from the hostile chariots and warriors intruding from the southern plains of Shinar. With the help of our LORD God and united in spirit, our league of nations built defenses in the southern mountains of Kau, the land of Magog in the north, the land of Meshech in the southeast, and the land of Tubal in the southwest.

Although the armies of King Nimrod ransacked the vineyards of Togarmah that Noah planted in the land where the Tigris and Euphrates rivers are birthed, they have not been able to storm our defenses and capture our cherished Kaucasus Mountain territories, the birthplace of the sons of Japheth.

Ashkenaz, Riphath, and Togarmah, the sons of Gomer, with all their bands, have united on the coastal territories of the Hospitable Sea and at Ilion, the gateway to the Chief Sea and the Great Sea, to push back the massive armies of Nimrod. The kingdoms in the west and northwest—Dodanim, Ashkenaz, Tiras, and Riphath—have united with the kingdoms of Kau in the east. All the sons of Japheth united and emerged as a powerful and prosperous league of nations.

The Riphean grandsons of Riphath from Skythia and the River Danu came to our aid and taught us to make leather boots using tanning methods invented by their grandfather in the mountains of Riphath in the west. The leather boots provide foot protection for our mighty men of great valor who defend our God-given territories.

Our Dodecanese kinsmen learned much from our industrious northern cousins. The expansion of Japheth continues in our day as our kinsmen intermarried with the seed (or germ) of Gomer, who expanded and colonized new frontiers in the northwest territories along the River Danu and toward the north in Skythia and Taurica.

We thank God for the Gomerites, our comrades-in-arms, for their factories in Asia that built weaponry to defend ourselves and aid the sons of Tiras against hostile and savage bands of Peirates on the Sea of Chiefs and the Great Sea. The Gomerites supply our battery at Port Io with weapons to defend ourselves against Nimrod's aggressive armies in the east.

We also thank our Creator for Ilion, the centralized headquarters of our league of Kau nations. In His strength we built a fleet of ships on well-equipped and armed ports on the Hospitable Sea to defend against hostile marine invasions. The Hospitable Sea is well defended by the able sons of Gomer, but our enemies found an approach on the eastern waters of Magog and Madai on the Khazar Sea.

King Dodanim, also called Rhodanim, discovered the island of Rhodes that bears his name; he provided Javanian leadership from his headquarters at Ilion. Dodanim assembled a fleet from among the sons of his older brothers Ellis, Tarshish, and Kittim. Since Dodanim's brother, Tarshish, built great merchant ships and controlled trade routes on the Great Sea, they enforced a strict embargo, preventing Nimrod from importing supplies and weaponry from his allies in Egypt by seas through the port at Sidon. Our Javanian kinsmen successfully prevented King Nimrod from building his own fleet of ships on the Great Sea.

Our cousins on the Island of Kittim and the Island of Kaptara came to our aid. And our kinsmen in the west sojourning on the twelve Dodecanese islands of Dodanim helped fortify our defenses at Port Io where King Baath, the firstborn son of King Iobaath, the son of Dodanim, was stationed and built a small colony. All of them provided aid to us at the port of Io and at our neighboring town, Iopolis.

The Median nations of Madai are greatly concerned with defending their territory and the trade routes in the east that were established by Japheth. King Nimrod seeks to control those well-trodden trade routes and the wealth of the kingdoms of the Far East and all the ancient world. So the nations of Madai, the Caspian nation in particular in the southwest quarter of the Khazar Sea, occupy themselves with unceasing warfare with King Nimrod. They were unequipped to flank our southeast borders or protect us from invasions. For all these reasons, our Median fortress on the Khazar Sea is well fortified by the armies of Magog, Meshech, and Tubal from the land of Kau.

In the later days of King Iobaath, the armies of King Nimrod seized Noah's precious vineyard, the land surrounding Endon Lake, and the mountainous land of Kau surrounding Mt. Ararat, where the ark was abandoned by Noah and his sons. King Togarmah, the son of Gomer, and his armies made every effort to route the hostile intruders, but did not prevail in battle against the well trained and equipped warriors of Nimrod.

It was during these destructive raids that a remnant of our kinsmen retreated from the Port of Io into western territories south of the mountains of Tiras in the former territory of Tarshish north of the Great Sea. There we found rivers, rich soil, and green pastures for our herds, timber for shipbuilding, and hydration for our orchards, vineyards, and produce. We named the territory (in southern Asia) Kilikia.

The mountains of King Tiras provided a natural barrier, a safe harbor from those wearisome and recurring battlefields in Elba and Haran in the east. The grasslands of Tarshish, the shipbuilder, were a nearly perfect habitat for our cattle ranches and farm-steads. We imported horses from the herds of Magog, our matri-archal father from the northern steppe lands east of Skythia.

Resting in our placid homeland in Kilikia, my grandfather, King Baath, the son of King Iobaath, provided instruction in righ-teousness to us and stressed the importance of keeping chroni-cles for future generations. He said that according to Japheth, we must maintain our faith and connection to the LORD God of Adam, Seth, and Noah. So as the firstborn prince, I suppose that this righteous archival duty has fallen on my head.

Before his tragic death in the mountains of Ararat fighting for our league of nations and being the first prince among sons, Izrau, my father, the son of King Baath, gave me his treasured copy of the stone chronicles of Japheth, the seven command-ments of Noah recorded by Eber, the son of Shelah, and the Book of the Chronicles of the Kings of Iobaath.

The honored body of Prince Izrau was brought back from the battlefield for a proper and noble burial in the land west of Mount Ararat, where we sojourned during the war and where we built a city to honor our fallen king. In the tradition of our people, we dug a deep pit for our deceased war hero and built a mound of dirt, a tumulus above the ground to identify his sacred burial ground. We buried our honorable prince with his weap-onry. Then, painstakingly and with bloody hands, I chiseled a marble stele with the inscription: "You are gods, sons of the Most High, all of you; nevertheless, like men you shall die, and fall like any prince."

My brothers wanted to bury the stone chronicles along with the decaying body of Prince Izrau, but I objected to that notion, arguing that my father, Izrau, would not have wanted our genesis tablets to perish with him. I told them our father's desire would have been to pass the cherished tablets forward to future genera-tions. My brothers argued that there was little value in maintain-ing ancestral records and the traditions of ancient men.

But thank God! My arguments prevailed! We retained the

chronicles. We honored our father as taught by our noble grand-father, King Baath, who though feeble in body, lives, functioning as both king and judge in our newly established judicial system in Kilikia. King Baath gave support to my minority opinion in this matter.

After the death and burial of Prince Izrau and as our tribal nation expanded, some of our people returned to Iopolis; others ventured inland toward the green pastures along the River Tarzu birthed in the mountains of Tiras, which flowed south to the Great Sea; others sought refuge sailing from Iopolis to the island of our cousins, the sons of Kittim, the son of Javan; others returned to the islands of the Dodecanese; and yet others to various regions in Assuwa, known to the Ionians as all territories east of the Chief Sea. It was a dangerous place, but I stayed in Elba with my many stone tablets.

In the days of his youth, King Baath established a linguistic training school at Elba near the city of Haran, where I was born, a location perfectly situated on the trade routes that connected the ancient east to the emerging western frontier. Elba was located southwest of the white mountains of Kau and northeast from coastal shorelines of Port Io. These were familiar trade routes that provided access for importing and exporting animals of every kind and other merchandise to and from many emerging tribal nations in the east and west. King Baath was wise and perceived that the many nomadic merchants would be advantaged by the linguistics instruction provided to them.

All of the major trading languages were taught at the picture graph literacy training school in Elba. Eber, the son of Shelah, who was the son of Arphaxad, who was the son of Shem, who was Japheth's brother, taught King Baath to speak in Hebrew, the tongue of his cousin, Eber. I grew up speaking in the tongue of Aram and King Baath.

I learned that the sons of Riphath, the son of Gomer, borrowed words from the tongue of Madai; words like Danu, the term for a swift-flowing river. Some of the words of the Ripheans and the sons of Magog sojourning in Skythia were difficult for us to speak, and we often got words and their meanings confused. Our kinsmen found the God-given tongues of Riphath and Magog challenging at times, but also extremely fascinating and humorous. So with all of the language barriers imposed by our Creator at Babel to divide us, we found it best to communicate in picture graphs as the Sumerians and Egyptians did. The picture graphs provide a universal method to communicate, one tribe with another.

While sojourning in Elba, I spent four years of my life learning the Hebrew tongue of Eber, where I was instructed by knowledgeable men. It was challenging to learn the tongue of Eber, but I successfully translated and memorized the generations from Adam to Noah in the tongue of our tribal nation. To assist with the memorization, I created picture graphs by cutting wedges in stone using common symbols utilized during trade negotiations. I learned much about our ancient history and traditions while translating our shared ancient verbal traditions. I was fortunate as my teachers were disciples of Eber, the Hebrew.

A great debate emerged in Elba among the nations of Noah as to what was the original tongue of Noah and the eight who survived the Great Flood of God's wrath and judgments. The descendants of Javan contended that the Ionian tongue was the perfect, original, universal language of Noah; but Reu, the grandson of Eber, and his bands believe that their Hebrew tongue was the one universal language before the confusion of tongues at Babel. Both sides, the Ionians and the Hebrews, presented strong arguments; this debate continues to this day.

However, it is my humble opinion that neither of the two ancient languages, Greek or Hebrew, or even the Armenian tongue of Aram, was the original universal language. I learned from our chronicles that the original clay tablets of Shem were destroyed by Noah and his sons, and that the ancient language of our forefathers is spoken no more. I believe that Noah, Shem, Japheth, and Ham took the original universal tongue with them to their grave.

The tradition learned from our chronicles and from my teachers in Elba made sense to me, but was not broadly accepted among the prideful tribal nations. Except for the word *halle-lujah*—which may be the one original word that survived—I am convinced the original universal language no longer exists among men. But it is my understanding that every man who was disciplined and memorized the verbal tradition before Babel retained those traditions in their new tongue afterward.

I am thankful to the God of Japheth that all the bands of Rhodanim were tutored well, were taught to fear our Creator, to remember the Great Flood, and to teach our children to recite the same genesis story throughout the earth.

*****

Ah, King Iobaath, the Chronicler, and the grand stories of the ancient world that he preserved for us. We can learn much about a person by investigating the root meaning behind his or her name. His very name, *Iobaath*, has great meaning to us today. The prefix, *Io*, in the Ionian tongue of Javan means "I am." The suffix, *baath*, means "resurrected." So the linked name of King Iobaath means "I am resurrected." Our great-grandfather's name speaks of one who was resurrected.

Iobaath was named after Job, a dear friend of the seven sons of Japheth, the man who was tested by the LORD God, reached the point of despair, and then was resurrected from his despair by being blessed with a double portion of wealth. I was told by my father that King Iobaath was named "I am resurrected" to remind future generations of the testing of Job and lessons learned from his season of testing.

King Baath tells many stories about his father, Iobaath. The young Dodecanese prince was renowned among the sons of men and also a gifted athlete, crowned with the victor's wreath at the great quadrennial race at Ellis Island where so many of the young princes raced for the coveted crown. The crowned prince was the pride of the Javanian nations he represented in the Great Race.

Then Prince Iobaath was the son of Dodanim sojourning in the merchant city of Ilion in the kingdom of Dodanim below the Dardanelles, the waterway between the Sea of Marmara surrounding Marmara Island, where he was reported to have discovered white marble and was also the first to behold the Chief Sea. Iobaath was known as one of the finest stonecutters in all the land. His precision-cut slabs of white marble adorned king's palaces throughout the world. When Iobaath was not building ships, he was cutting glistening white crystal from Marmara Island.

According to our chronicles, Prince Iobaath was best friends with Prince Regen, from the mountains, lakes, and rivers of the Riphean nation, the son of King Riphath, the grandson of the Patriarch Gomer. It was reported that the competition between the two young princes was ongoing. Their competitiveness and pride caused each of the athletes to practice more diligently. They buffeted their bodies daily to win the treasured prize. Each desired the praise of men and the coveted victor's wreath for completing and winning the Great Race at Ellis Island. Sadly, this is an event that has ceased to be in our day; today our young men compete in battle on the plains of Shinar with the kingdoms of Nimrod. Perhaps the Great Race will resume one day among the many tribes represented on the Chief Sea.

I learned from our chronicles that every two years Prince Iobaath visited Prince Regen in the Riphean Mountains; Prince Regen visited Iobaath on the year of the Great Race and again two years following the Great Race. The work Iobaath did during his visit with Prince Regen was a retreat from the business of shipbuilding and stonecutting. Prince Regen learned shipbuilding and stonecutting skills during his visit to Ilion.

At Regen on the River Danu, Prince Iobaath learned to fish in freshwater lakes and rivers, hunt with a bow and arrow in the mountains, and spent time in the famous vineyards at Regen.

It was reported that the young princes hiked through the white mountains and made several discoveries. Iobaath's visits usually took place before and during the annual smashing of the grapes and the great celebration that followed.

During an ancestral interview with King Baath, I learned that one year Patriarch Magog, the son of Japheth from the land of Kau, brought his granddaughter, Ileana, to the Great Race in the year of Prince Iobaath's victory. King Magog was looking for a righteous and God-fearing young man to be Ilena's husband and to be blessed by the LORD God with many sons and daughters.

King Baath observed that after the qualifying sprints up the mountainside, Prince Iobaath gazed intently upon the beauty of Ileana. During the race and at the victory celebration that followed, Iobaath's affections and desires for Ileana grew stronger. Likewise, the affections of Ileana grew stronger in her desires for the handsome Dodecanese prince. Under the watchful and protective eye of Magog the patriarch, Iobaath and Ileana became well acquainted with each other at Elis Island.

Prince Iobaath and Ileana loved one another. Ileana was weak-willed and wanted Iobaath to lay with her. Iobaath was handsome; his adolescent and fit body naturally responded to Ileana's beauty and seduction. But the noble prince was a godly man of proven character who feared God and practiced constraint. Though the young lovers burned in their desires for one another, they did not lay together until after they were united by covenant in marriage. They honored both their Creator and their parents. With great self-control and restraint, they entered the marriage bed undefiled as virtuous virgins with no regrets, as is the custom among our people.

After the Great Race at Ellis Island, the crowned prince returned with Patriarch Magog and Ileana to meet Ileana's father, King Fathochta, the youngest son of King Magog sojourning in Taurica, who was not in attendance at the Great Race. When Ileana's father became acquainted with the handsome and righteous Ionian prince, he blessed the intertribal union and made marriage arrangements with his cousin, King Dodanim. The sons and daughters of Japheth from the land of Kau continue to intermarry to this day.

So Prince Iobaath sent word to his father, King Dodanim, and appealed to his father that a marriage ceremony and celebration be officiated and executed at Ilion on the first anniversary after his victory at the Great Race. It was unconventional for a prince to make such a request, but when King Dodanim received word about the engagement, great joy filled his heart. The Ionian nations looked forward to the marriage supra feast at Ilion and made preparations according to his son's desires.

King Baath reported that the marriage supra of Prince Iobaath from the Dardanelles and Princess Ileana from Taurica was regal in every detail. Prince Regen, a gifted organizer, stood with his dear friend from Ilion assuming administrative duties on behalf of all the tribal kings and kingdoms. Regen made arrangements to bring the pfeifers of Morava and dancers of Media to provide the sound of music and celebration at the marriage celebration. Regen also supplied the beverage of angels and the finest of vintage wines for the wedding.

Prince Iobaath was musically inclined, well practiced, and skilled in playing musical instruments. At the celebration Iobaath danced merrily around while playing his treasured pfeife with the children as they followed in step. Iobaath also played his unique version of the ancient stringed lyre of Jubal. His six-stringed kithara resembled the stringed tar of Prince Caspi in the east. The kithara was handmade from the finest of hard woods from the Schwarzwald Forest, west from the kingdom of Regen. Iobaath enjoyed playing the pfeife and strumming his kithara with the pfeifers on the River Morava downstream from the River Regen, both tributaries of the great River Danu, the mother of many tribal nations.

The prosperity that existed among the expansion of Japheth was inestimable as all the nations owned much silver and gold mined from faraway lands amidst the Great Sea of Tarshish. In the days of King Iobaath, they were clothed in fine Egyptian white linen fabric made from flax. The wealthiest of nobility wore colorful purple linens and silk clothing from the Far East. They wore fine, custom-made leather footwear from Regen. And many of the princes wore wreaths and fine jewelry with embedded precious stones from the Kaucasus Mountain, diamonds mined from the southwest kingdom of Put, west of the land of Egypt, a two-year journey.

All the kingdoms of the world were invited to the wedding celebration in Ilion—except the kingdom of Nimrod. Nearly all the kingdoms of Japheth were represented as well as many of the nations of Shem and Ham. The Pharaoh of Egypt came from the south with gifts for the great Ionian prince. The kings of Media brought gifts from the East and Far East.

The wedding celebration continued for six days and ended on the day of Sabbath rest. In the traditions of Japheth, the celebration tables were continually filled with delicacies from all over the world. Food gathered from land and sea was prepared by the best chefs in Ilion. The smell of bread baking in the stone ovens and assorted familiar and exotic meats roasting on the gigantic Ilion grills filled the air during the celebration. Traditional baskets of fresh roses, fruit, and vegetables lined the covered linen serving tables. For the first time, the finest of chocolates were introduced to the guests as dessert after the feast, a special gift to the guests in attendance. All were served with great dignity and respect.

I learned that many guests, and Job in particular, brought lavish marriage gifts. Prince Regen gave the newly wedded couple one thousand pieces of silver as a gift. As in our day, pieces of silver were given as gifts on special occasions as a symbol of peace and goodwill among the tribal nations. After the LORD God tested Job and restored his wealth, King Baath reported that Job procreated and had three beautiful daughters, Jemimah, Keziah, and Keren-happuch. Job brought all three of his beautiful daughters to Ilion along with gifts of cattle from his well-fed herds.

However, King Baath reported that Job's cattle caused no small disturbance and distraction at the wedding feast, especially the restless bulls. And the mildly intoxicated Prince Iberus, the grandson of King Tubal, a good friend and second cousin of Iobaath and Regen, was spotted taunting the bulls with flax linen dipped in blood. A raging bull pursued Iberus; he was unable to escape the bull's furry. Iberus appeared fearless in his attempt to dodge the bull as the terrorized crowds in the immediate vicinity sprinted here and there on the chaotic streets. From this, Iberus returned from Ilion to the Iberian Peninsula with a new passion to tame insubordinate bulls. The symbol of an ox, *alpha*, and a home, *beta*, were the two most prolific picture graphs recorded in our day. Since that day our people in Ilion called Aurochs-ford *Alphabeta*, and later shortened the name to, simply, *Ox-ford.*

From Ilion as a married couple, Prince Iobaath and Ileana followed the pfeifers to their homeland, sailing west on the River Danu to the Riphean kingdom. Regen prepared a place for them to stay during their three-month visit, a secluded cottage near the vineyards of Riphath. Prince Iobaath desired to take Ileana to the Rhodanim Glacier that he had discovered with Regen, but they determined that the hike to the territory would take several months. So they decided against venturing deep into the Riphean Mountains. Regen and his kinsmen supplied all their needs according to their abundant wealth and provided a hospitable environment in every way for the radiant newlyweds.

Leaving Regen, the couple rowed downstream on the Danu to the Moravian tributary, where the sound of music filled the air as minstrels sang and gaily danced while playing their pfeifes and kitharas. The jubilant music of Morava was reported to have gladdened the hearts of men who frequented the quant riverside colony. (A cherished pfeife in my possession has been handed down from father to son and is said to have been crafted from a bone of a cave bear by Morava, the brother of Prince Regen, as a wedding gift.)

The sons and grandsons of Morava escorted the newlyweds

back to Marmara Island by taking an alternate route toward the south. The River Morava became a trade route as the river meanders south and through the land of Thracia toward the Peninsula of Haemus, where the sons of Tiras expanded and colonized, and then toward the Chief Sea, through a land where many sons of Dodanim expanded and colonized. Although the trip was long and challenging, the hospitable sons of Morava who escorted them made the trip as comfortable as possible for Iobaath and Ileana.

After their wedding retreat in the Riphean Mountains and, according to the traditions of Japheth and our people, Prince Iobaath left his father and mother in the store city of Ilion and set sail to colonize the Islands of Dodanim, located on the southeastern tip of the Chief Sea; these islands are equidistant between Marmara Island to the north and the Island of Kittim to the east on the Great Sea. The newlyweds traveled in springtime when the waters of the Chief Sea were negotiable; few captains dared to venture on the sea against the strong north head- and tailwinds during the cold winter months.

I learned that the resourceful islands of Dodanim were given to Prince Iobaath as a wedding gift. The main island of Rhodes is predominantly mountainous with peaks rising above the seas to approximately four thousand feet. The mountains of Rhodes were graced with pine and cypress trees as on the Island of Kittim. The Island of Rhodes is full of wildlife provided by the LORD God for enjoyment and sustenance; island deer are abundant there. The subtropical island is a veritable paradise blessed with citrus fruit trees and olive trees. In the course of time and in the tradition Japheth and Noah, Prince Iobaath planted large vineyards on his island paradise.

Ileana gave birth to a firstling, Prince Baath, on the Island of Rhodes. Prince Iobaath and Ileana had many other sons and daughters on the subtropical island. The Dodecanese children included Baath, Kos, Patmos, Astipalea, Kalimnos, Karpathos, Kasos, Leros, Nisyros, Symi, Tilos, and Kastellotrizo. Except for

Prince Baath, all of them sojourned on the Dodecanese islands that bear their names.

The Dodecanese Islands provided excellent commons for the many enterprises of the sons of Javan; the islands were a short voyage from Athens, from Ilion, and from the Island of Kaptara to the northwest, north, and southwest respectively. From the perfectly situated commercial epicenter on the Island of Rhodes, Prince Iobaath negotiated trade deals with the enterprising sons of Javan on the Peninsula of Haemus and the Ionian Sea, the sons of Morava on the Danu, the sons of Tiras in Thracia and Taurica, the Gomerites on the Hospitable Sea, the sons of Kittim to the east, and with the sons of Dikti (the oldest son of Kittim) on the Island of Kaptara.

Uncle Kittim, the youngest son of Javan, colonized a larger island toward the east adjacent to Iopolis, a small port established for commerce by the sons of Dodanim. Kittim and his sons built a great forestry enterprise on the wooded island. Then Prince Iobaath reasoned that he could learn to forest timber from cousin Kittim and his sons. So Prince Iobaath spent a season on the Island of Kittim learning forestry.

I learned that the relationships between the sons of Iobaath and the sons of Dikti was, and remains, hospitable. As first cousins birthed and bread in Ilion, Prince Iobaath and Prince Dikti developed a great friendship through the years. As their kinsmen enlarged, all made many recreational voyages to and from Kaptara and Rhodes.

Then, for a season, the sons of Prince Iobaath and the sons of Prince Dikti took up arms and defended the island of Kaptara from Caphtorim invaders who were attempting to colonize the northern coast. The ongoing conflict with Caphtorim, the youngest son of Egypt, united the sons of Iobaath and Dikti in securing commercial advantages and naval supremacy on the Great Sea and destinations amid the Sea of Tarshish in remote western waters.

When Prince Baath matured, he was commissioned by

King Iobaath to move with his young kinsmen to the Port of Io and build a colony there to aid the sons of Javan, who traded merchandise with tribal nations in Mesopotamia and the Far East. From the newfound city of Iopolis, Prince Baath attended the king's interests, negotiating trade deals with the descendants of Job as well as a prosperous city-state built by Prince Sidon, the firstborn of Canaan, the son of Patriarch Ham.

In those days and according to King Baath, the expanding kingdoms of Gomer, Magog, Assuwan Tiras, and Javan strengthened the blood-axis that united all the tribal nations of Japheth. This league of Kau nations extended from the Riphean Mountains in the west to the northern steppe lands of the Far East as far as the Great Lands. Their combined southern territories extended from the land of Madai in the east and southern steppe lands of the Far East to the Iberian Peninsula and to Sea of Tarshish, where it was reported that there was gold, and even to the shores of a new Atlantis, where it was reported that there was tin. The bands of Japheth expanded and grew strong in numbers and power. The sons of Japheth controlled all ports of call on the Caspian Sea and the Hospitable Sea, and most of the ports of call on the Great Sea.

After informing me of the wedding celebration of King Iobaath and their colony on the Island of Rhodes, King Baath recited stories from the chronicles of Iobaath about the great pilgrimage of Patriarchs Magog, Japheth, and Madai into the Far East. He told me about Prince Tutan, who settled there, the fourth son of the Patriarch Gomer; Tutan had an oriental complexion and a quiet and gentle spirit. He told me about our close tribal kinship with the sons of the Assuwan, Tiras, the Red Bull (the youngest son of Patriarch Japheth), and our challenges with Peirates, his unbridled and somewhat bombastic bastard son. King Iobaath warned me of the mischievous behavior of the so-called "Pirates" on the Chief Sea and the Great Sea, their looting and murdering and lifestyle given to much debauchery and wantonness. His lawless children exasperate the nations to this day.

In great detail and with conviction, King Baath recounted the legendary story of Job, the renowned trade partner of Patriarch Japheth. I was taught that Job was a wealthy herdsman and entrepreneur, a righteous and God-fearing man. And how the LORD God served Job's integrity, as on a banquet platter, to be tested by Satan, the unseen enemy of the all tribal nations.

*****

Revisiting the testing of Job, King Baath reported to me, saying, "A whirlwind of great strength and magnitude destroyed all his buildings and killed all of Job's beloved sons and daughters." How tragic, I thought to myself. King Baath continued: "Then, after the whirlwind destroyed his property and offspring, Job's body was stricken with boils and the company of fools who had little understanding of the ways of our Creator. His closest friends accused Job of sinful behaviors that consequently resulted in God's well-deserved judgment and punishment. At the end of Job's test, God rebuked the ignorant and misguided counselors but blessed Job for fearing the LORD God and standing in his faith."

All the tribal nations of Noah knew that Job was a righteous and God-fearing man. We understand this from the stories about Job recorded in our own stone chronicles and verbal tradition. Job was a man of noble character who was magnanimous and religious in his care for the disadvantaged of this world, the poor, the infirmed, and the widows. Job expressed the steadfast love and goodness of God in all the seasons of his long life.

King Baath went on, continuing the story of Job, but with good news, saying, "After Job experienced great tribulation, his kinsmen and wealth were restored to him." It was then that I realized that God works everything together for the good of those who trust in him.

I suppose that Job will be remembered forever as a man

who confronted his evil day with great integrity and honor. We learned from the testing of Job that God requires a man to do justly, love mercy, and walk humbly with the LORD, especially in the midst of great adversity and loss. We also learned that the LORD God is the Sovereign Ruler over the unseen evil forces of darkness. We never need to be afraid, for God is on the side of those who fear and obey Him.

King Baath shared about his frequent visits with Eber in Elba and learned to speak in the tongue of Eber. He translated Eber's eloquent and much more detailed account of the story of Job in our tongue. It took several years to complete the translation and create a picture graph guide. I have read these sacred picture graphs and often remind myself that the LORD God is in control of my everyday circumstances, that evil will not prevail, and that I need to be a humble man submitted to the government of the Almighty God, our noble king that God has raised up, and our appointed judges.

I will never forget one occasion during my interview with King Baath. The king stood and, in the tradition of Japheth, The Great Voice, recited from memory his favorite part of Job's story, when the LORD God appeared to Job. King Baath memorized the faith-building apolegetia, and encouraged me to do likewise for future generations.

Then, speaking as the sage that he is, King Baath recited:

"Then the Lord answered Job out of the whirlwind and said, 'Who is this that darkens counsel by words without knowledge? Dress for action like a man; I will question you, and you make it known to me.

'Where were you when I laid the foundation of the earth? Tell me, if you have understanding. Who determined its measurements—surely you know! Or who stretched the line upon it? On what were its bases sunk, or who laid its cornerstone, when the morning stars sang together and all the sons of God shouted for joy? Or who shut in the sea with doors when it burst out from the womb, when I made clouds its garment and thick darkness its swaddling band, and prescribed limits for it and set bars and doors, and said, 'Thus far shall you come, and no farther, and here shall your proud waves be stayed?

'Have you commanded the morning since your days began, and caused the dawn to know its place, that it might take hold of the skirts of the earth, and the wicked be shaken out of it? It is changed like clay under the seal, and its features stand out like a garment. From the wicked their light is withheld, and their uplifted arm is broken.

'Have you entered into the springs of the sea, or walked in the recesses of the deep?

'Have the gates of death been revealed to you, or have you seen the gates of deep darkness?

'Have you comprehended the expanse of the earth?

'Declare, if you know all this.

'Where is the way to the dwelling of light, and where is the place of darkness, that you may take it to its territory and that you may discern the paths to its home? You know, for you were born then, and the number of your days is great!

'Have you entered the storehouses of the snow, or have you seen the storehouses of the hail, which I have reserved for the time of trouble, for the day of battle and war?

'What is the way to the place where the light is distributed, or where the east wind is scattered upon the earth?

'Who has cleft a channel for the torrents of rain and a way for the thunderbolt, to bring rain on a land where no man is, on the desert in which there is no man, to satisfy the waste and desolate land, and to make the ground sprout with grass?

'Has the rain a father, or who has begotten the drops of dew?

'From whose womb did the ice come forth, and who has given birth to the frost of heaven? The waters become hard like stone, and the face of the deep is frozen.

'Can you bind the chains of the Pleiades or loose the cords of Orion? Can you lead forth the Mazzaroth in their season, or can you guide the Bear with its children? Do you know the ordinances of the heavens? Can you establish their rule on the earth? Can you lift up your voice to the clouds, that a flood of waters may cover you? Can you send forth lightning, that they may go and say to you, "Here we are?" Who has put wisdom in the inward parts or given understanding to the mind? Who can number the clouds by wisdom? Or who can tilt the water skins of the heavens, when the dust runs into a mass and the clods stick fast together?

'Can you hunt the prey for the lion, or satisfy the appetite of the young lions, when they crouch in their dens or lie in wait in their thicket?

'Who provides for the raven its prey, when its young ones cry to God for help, and wander about for lack of food?

'Do you know when the mountain goats give birth? Do you observe the calving of the does? Can you number the months that they fulfill, and do you know the time when they give birth, when they crouch, bring forth their offspring, and are delivered of their young? Their young ones become strong; they grow up in the open; they go out and do not return to them.

'Who has let the wild donkey go free? Who has loosed the bonds of the swift donkey, to whom I have given the arid plain for his home and the salt land for his dwelling place? He scorns the tumult of the city; he hears not the shouts of the driver. He ranges the mountains as his pasture, and he searches after every green thing. Is the wild ox willing to serve you? Will he spend the night at your manger? Can you bind him in the furrow with ropes, or will he harrow the valleys after you? Will you depend on him because his strength is great, and will you leave to him your labor? Do you have faith in him that he will return your grain and gather it to your threshing floor?

'The wings of the ostrich wave proudly, but are they the pinions and plumage of love? For she leaves her eggs to the earth and lets them be warmed on the ground, forgetting that a foot may crush them and that the wild beast may trample them. She deals cruelly with her young, as if they were not hers; though her labor be in vain, yet she has no fear, because God has made her forget wisdom and given her no share in understanding. When she rouses herself to flee, she laughs at the horse and his rider.

'Do you give the horse his might? Do you clothe his neck with a mane? Do you make him leap like the locust? His majestic snorting is terrifying. He paws in the valley and exults in his strength; he goes out to meet the weapons. He laughs at fear and is not dismayed; he does not turn back from the sword. Upon him rattle the quiver, the flashing spear, and the javelin. With fierceness and rage he swallows the ground; he cannot stand still at the sound of the trumpet. When the trumpet sounds, he says, "Aha!" He smells the battle from afar, the thunder of the captains, and the shouting.

'Is it by your understanding that the hawk soars and spreads his wings toward the south? Is it at your command that the eagle mounts up and makes his nest on high? On the rock he dwells and makes his home, on the rocky crag and stronghold. From there he spies out the prey; his eyes behold it from far away. His young ones suck up blood, and where the slain are, there is he.'

"And the Lord said to Job: 'Shall a faultfinder contend with the Almighty? He who argues with God, let him answer it.' Then Job answered the Lord and said: 'Behold, I am of small account; what shall I answer you? I lay my hand on my mouth. I have spoken once, and I will not answer; twice, but I will proceed no further.'

"Then the Lord answered Job out of the whirlwind and said: 'Dress for action like a man; I will question you, and you make it known to me.

'Will you even put me in the wrong? Will you condemn me that you may be in the right? Have you an arm like God, and can you thunder with a voice like his? Adorn yourself with majesty and dignity; clothe yourself with glory and splendor. Pour out the overflowing of your anger, and look on everyone who is proud and abase him. Look on everyone who is proud and bring him low and tread down the wicked where they stand. Hide them all in the dust together; bind their faces in the world below. Then will I also acknowledge to you that your own right hand can save you.

'Behold, Behemoth, which I made as I made you; he eats grass like an ox. Behold, his strength in his loins, and his power in the muscles of his belly. He makes his tail stiff like a cedar; the sinews of his thighs are knit together. His bones are tubes of bronze, his limbs like bars of iron.

'He is the first of the works of God; let him who made him bring near his sword! For the mountains yield food for him where all the wild beasts play. Under the lotus plants he lies, in the shelter of the reeds and in the marsh. For his shade the lotus trees cover him; the willows of the brook surround him.

'Behold, if the river is turbulent he is not frightened; he is confident though Jordan rushes against his mouth. Can one take him by his eyes, or pierce his nose with a snare? Can you draw out Leviathan with a fishhook or press down his tongue with a cord? Can you put a rope in his nose or pierce his jaw with a hook?

'Will he make many pleas to you? Will he speak to you soft words? Will he make a covenant with you to take him for your servant forever? Will you play with him as with a bird, or will you put him on a leash for your girls? Will traders bargain over him? Will they divide him up among the merchants?

'Can you fill his skin with harpoons or his head with fishing spears? Lay your hands on him; remember the battle—you will not do it again! Behold, the hope of a man is false; he is laid low even at the sight of him. No one is so fierce that he dares to stir him up.

'Who then is he who can stand before me? Who has first given to me, that I should repay him? Whatever is under the whole heaven is mine.

'I will not keep silence concerning his limbs, or his mighty strength, or his goodly frame. Who can strip off his outer garment? Who would come near him with a bridle? Who can open the doors of his face?

'Around his teeth is terror. His back is made of rows of shields, shut up closely as with a seal. One is so near to another that no air can come between them. They are joined one to another; they clasp each other and cannot be separated. His sneezing flash forth light, and his eyes are like the eyelids of the dawn. Out of his mouth go flaming torches; sparks of fire leap forth. Out of his nostrils comes forth smoke, as from a boiling pot and burning rushes. His breath kindles coals, and a flame comes forth from his mouth. In his neck abides strength, and terror dances before him. The folds of his flesh stick together, firmly cast on him and immovable. His heart is hard as a stone, hard as the lower millstone.

'When he raises himself up the mighty are afraid; at the crashing they are beside themselves. Though the sword reaches him, it does not avail, nor the spear, the dart, or the javelin. He counts iron as straw, and bronze as rotten wood. The arrow cannot make him flee; for him sling stones are turned to stubble. Clubs are counted as stubble; he laughs at the rattle of javelins. His under parts are like sharp potsherds; he spreads himself like a threshing sledge on the mire.

'He makes the deep boil like a pot; he makes the sea like a pot of ointment. Behind him he leaves a shining wake; one would think the deep to be white-haired. On earth there is not his like, a creature without fear. He sees everything that is high; he is king over all the sons of pride.'"

With this, King Baath finished his dramatic monologue and sat next to me. We sat quietly, reverently pondering the sobering message from Eber's chronicles. We often forget that it was the LORD God of Noah who meticulously and with great attention designed and created all things, visible and invisible, in Heaven and on earth. We forget that our Creator rules the universe with His Word and commands the course of the stars and the sons of men. Together we began to praise our Creator for all His mighty and marvelous deeds.

I ended my interview with King Baath with great joy and much knowledge about our ancestry. With much amazement we pondered the greatness of our Creator. I learned why I lived among the sons of Shem and Ham but was born of the seed of Patriarchs Javan and Magog, blessed sons of Japheth.

I reflected on the sage's apolegetia for days. Although the world was a little older than two millennia, that world, created by God, had disrespected Him and existed as if God was not present. God created man, and yet prideful men did not honor him as Creator. God provided His own defense, saying, "Were you there?" God was right to bring such a charge.

I personally had no plea before God except to bow and humbly respond: "I am guilty as charged, LORD Creator; I am a prideful man. I was not there when you created the heavens and the earth in six days."

*****

With a strong desire to learn more about myself and my ancestral roots, and while enjoying a time of peace from battle, I secured funding and passage to the great merchant city of our patriarchs at Ilion, the land of Dodanim, a great progenitor, and the birthplace of King Iobaath. Although the dialect of the people of Ilion was obscure, I was able to understand a few words in their tongue. My cousins confirmed our tradition. I learned much more about Dodanim and his strong relationship with the enterprising King Ashkenaz, prince of Gomer, the prince of Japheth.

While in Ilion I recalled that the records of Noah recorded by Eber attest to the enlargement of Japheth. We are all witnesses to the promise from the LORD God that was fulfilled before our eyes. All the tribal nations of Japheth were expanding and prospering wherever they sojourned, as God intended. The witness of God's enduring love was with them—as he is with us today and shall be with the sons of Japheth until the end of days. As it was recorded by Eber, so shall the Word of the LORD be accomplished forever. Eber lived a long life and is alive until this day through his chronicles.

As I matured and was encouraged by the faith of my fathers, I became a man of strong conviction. I knew for certain, and heralded often, proclaiming: "Our God was and is the Creator and Sovereign Ruler of the universe! He is the King of Kings and Prince of Princes! Just as the sons of Japheth, the Great Voice, taught us, we must always endeavor to keep the LORD God in his rightful, exulted place. We must resist the temptation to live by sight, judging circumstances empirically only by what we see with our natural eyes. Without faith it is impossible to please God; this is what Job lived out for all of us. And like Job we must believe that He is, and that He rewards those who diligently seek Him.

"Be it far from our people to ascribe glory and honor to created things: the sun, the moon, and the stars. Be it far from our people to ascribe deity to men like King Nimrod. Be it far from us to worship any other creature, as the Canaanites have, whether visible or invisible, save the LORD God of creation. And although the earth is wonderful, it is never to be seen as the sole habitat of God's persona. For God exists outside of time and space. God is not observable, but God is there.

"In everything, even in the midst of war, we must give thanks to the LORD God. For we know that God is good and that God is great! And our caring and loving God works all things together for good for those who put their faith and trust in Him. We must trust God and do the next right thing as God directs our steps, just as Japheth instructed our people in the days of Noah."

My chief desire in my proclamation was to glorify and honor God in my generation.

Back in Elba I learned that refugees from Armenia in the land of Kau were forced out of their homeland by King Nimrod. We warmly welcomed the God-fearing sons of Aram, the youngest son of Patriarch Shem, who formerly sojourned in Kau. Aram's seed settled in the neighboring land of Syroi, the Hebrew land of Aram, and among their kinsmen who migrated west into Panphylia. And some of Aram's people migrated to Kilikia and lived here among our tribes on the fertile plains between Iopolis and Tarzu.

When I was a learned man and capable of supporting offspring, my father, Izrau, sought out a wife for me among the daughters of Iobaath, among the Dodecanese on the Island of Rhodes. When I was introduced to the woman of his choosing, my desires for her grew within my soul. Her name was Marmara, and she was beautiful, like shimmering marble, to my eyes. One day, to my great surprise, my father announced the marriage celebration.

Marmara and I were married and celebrated for six days in the tradition of our people on the rhododendron-filled Island of Rhodes.

Within a few months, Marmara became great with child. Our firstborn was a son. I named him Rea. When my son was born, I proudly lifted him up to the LORD and announced in the presence of those surrounding us, praying, "May Prince Rea be a levelheaded man, a ram among the flocks of Iobaath."

As Rea matured I instructed my firstborn about our Creator and about the laws and promises of Noah. Rea was a handsome man and walked in the way of the LORD God. Rea did not turn aside to worship created things. Marmara and I procreated often, and God blessed us with many children. Marmara birthed many other sons and daughters to the praise and glory of the LORD God our Creator.

When Prince Rea was mature in body and soul, he married and was also blessed with a firstborn son. Rea named his prince Abir. Prince Rea announced, "He will be a man with a sweet aroma and fragrance in his soul." Prince Rea also had many other sons and daughters.

So after many years of instruction from wise men and at the academy at Elba, I, Ezra, the scribe and chronicler for my pedigree, sojourning in Haran, hereby preserve a record for future generations in *The Book of the Chronicles of the Kings of Iobaath* as follows:

Abir was the son of Rea. Rea was the son of Ezra. Ezra was the son of Izrau. Izrau was the son of Baath. Baath was the son of Iobaath. Iobaath was the son of Rhodanim. Rhodanim was the son of Javan. Javan was the son of Japheth. Japheth was the son of Noah. Noah was the son of Lamech, Lamech was the son of Methuselah, Methuselah was the son of Enoch, Enoch was the son of Jared, Jared was the son of Mahalaleel, Mahalaleel was the son of Cainan, Cainan was the son of Enos, Enos was the son of Seth, Seth was the son of Adam. Adam was the son of God.

TWO

THE CHRONICLES OF KING MAIR

(APPROXIMATELY 1900 BC)

I WAS TWENTY YEARS old, the age when young men dress for battle. So as a young first prince, I was commissioned by my father, King Ethach, to study the art of war. I began my learning experience by reciting tradition and later reading *The Book of the Chronicles of the Kings of Iobaath* and other stone tablets that King Ezra, the son of King Izrau, the son of King Baath, recorded concerning the life of Job and confrontations our people had with King Nimrod of Babylon.

King Ezra, born in Haran, and his second wife, Queen Zugalum, an Eblaite, lived a long life. By way of King Ezra's marriage to Queen Zugalum, and for many generations, King Ezra reigned over a league of tribal nations from Ebla that included Haran, from our southern Asian coastal territories of Iopolis, Kilikia, Panphylia, Lukka, and from Rhodes and the Dodecanese islands.

As the future warrior king of the Dodecanese sojourning in

Kilikia, I was commissioned to describe the property that our Creator assigned to tribal nations. Japheth, the Great Voice, instructed our people that our Creator predetermined the dwelling places for all the nations of the earth.

So I set forth to study our God-given territories as well as that of surrounding nations. I studied the dirt beneath our feet as well as the human characteristics of the tribal nations. When I studied the earth, my research focused on the God-given resources of a given territory: the landscape, access to water, weather, and other gifts from God providentially deposited within the soil, rocks, and waters. As I studied the tribal nations, my learning included humanity: its cultures, industry, politics, and the social characteristics of the nations.

During the season of research in Elba, I discovered thousands of clay tablets. I discovered that King Ezra engraved much about his queen. I was surprised that many of the tablets chronicled by the record keepers referred to Queen Zugalum. In our day it was rare to find a woman who was acknowledged and inscribed on clay tablets. From the beginning women were considered a man's helpmate. The deeds of women were rarely recognized or recorded. A woman's glory is that of her husband, who rules over her. I understood from our tradition that this was the way our Creator established the order of paternal headship in the Garden of Eden since the early days of Adam and Eve, the father and mother of us all.

I learned from my father that for hundreds of years, even since the days of Noah, the descendants of Tiras, our Assuwan cousins in the city of Çatalhöyük, located northwest of Tarzu through the Kilikian Gate, and southeast from Ilion, had been creating large maps just like me. So, encouraged by my father with firm instructions to guard my heart from idolatry, I planned a visit to the ancient city of Çatalhöyük. It was there that I learned more about mapmaking methods used in graphing the characteristics of our world.

While sojourning in Çatalhöyük, I observed that many of

the traditions of Japheth were maintained. Although men were recognized as the paternal heads of kinsmen, women were held in high esteem and of equal worth as observed among the Eblaites. Most believed in our Creator God, reciting stories about creation and the worldwide flood of Noah; however, some elevated motherhood to demigod status, insisting that Çatalhöyük, as all cities, was guarded by goddesses. So they created stele of durable stone in honor of motherhood and maternal goddesses. This distortion of the traditions of the Great Voice angered me, but this new tradition gained broad acceptance among the Assuwan bands of Japheth.

In Çatalhöyük I observed that fatherhood was also highly esteemed among our northern cousins as naked icons of fit men with large, erected phalluses were painted on their walls. In Çatalhöyük paternal fatherhood and procreation were most significant among the Assuwan bands, and they were exulted by many, to a place of gross idolatry.

When I was a young man, my father prudently provided instruction to me about the importance of marriage, procreation, and raising offspring to honor the Lord God by keeping his commandments. But I observed that many citizens of Çatalhöyük worshipped the creature, not their Creator.

As I pondered the porno-graphic paintings on their walls, I remembered the stories of Patriarch Tiras and his unbridled desires for the Assuwan virgins. I also recalled his many conflicts with his bastard son, Peirates, and his decadent followers. The Assuwan, as well as our kinsmen, are still at war with these scorpions that infest the Dodecanese Islands and also along our southern coastal territories on the Sea of Kilikia. I perceived that this saying is true: "The sins of the fathers visit their sons to the third and fourth generations." Evidences of Tiras and his bastard son were everywhere and lived on in the perverseness of their offspring.

I found the naked icons of men and women most disturbing. My father warned me. Conflicted in soul and spirit, I made every effort to resist lustful fantasies and desires while gazing upon sordid, vulgar images. I understood that procreation was the will of our Creator. Japheth taught us that the sexual body parts of men and women were intentionally covered by God in the Garden of Eden. I understood from the teachings of the Great Voice that Noah was modest in the extreme and the man-part was not designed as an object for public exposure, lustful desires or, God forbid, worship! Man's phallus was intended for practical, pleasure, and procreation purposes.

I understood that we were commanded to worship our Creator alone; so it was my strong desire to order the immediate destruction of the erotic idols. But after much contemplation, I determined not to anger the Assuwan sons of Tiras under our rule. For this would not be beneficial to the political agenda of our government or to the cause of our prospering kingdom. For our kingdom had expanded in the territories of Ashkenaz, the firstborn of Gomer, east of Ilion. Looking back on this decision, it proved to be one of my life's regrets. I should have feared God instead of men and ordered the abominable icons completely destroyed.

The traditions of Tiras, the Assuwan Red Bull, were still remembered and spoken in Çatalhöyük. The dark-skinned bull aurochs became a local symbol of King Tiras and depicted and idolized his well-known bullish and at times stubborn nature. Heads of auroch bulls hung prominently on plastered walls. And like the Hebrew shofar, the horns of aurochs were used as instruments for blowing, assembling the warriors, and initiating tribal warfare.

It was said that the sons of Gomer imported the bison of Tiras to the Riphean Mountains and Skythia. The bison of Tiras were used in trade, given to the sons of Ashkenaz for their ferry services at Ox-ford. Our kinsman in Çatalhöyük exported the bison of Tiras beyond Put and as far away as Tarshish and the Iberian Peninsula.

Toward the east and northeast of Assuwa and beneath the

Hospitable Blach See, I learned from the Assuwan in Çatalhöyük that the germ of Gomer, Ashkenaz, Riphath, and Togarmah were the first to settle in the metal-rich plateau territories. I visited the territory once, and afterward, I was surprised to learned that the seed of Eber agreed with our tradition in this matter.

In the ancient traditions of Japheth, and Tubal-cain, the forger of all instruments of bronze and iron, King Gomer, the firstling of Japheth, and his three industrious princes established ironworks in the ancient city of Tavia, where copper, tin, iron, and silver were mined in the nearby mountains. The Gomerites who settled in Tavia spoke of building a gigantic bronze colossus honoring Japheth, the Great Voice. Many among the sons of Tiras and Dodanim affirmed this colony of Gomerites; I was compelled to record this migration into Tavia for future generations.

When I returned to Elba from my geographic studies in Çatalhöyük and Tavia, I continued to learn more about our diverse culture. I learned from the tablets in Elba that King Ezra led the league of nations from his outpost in Haran. In those early days, trained warriors from the nations surrounding the hospitable Blach See of Gomer united their tribes to confront King Nimrod and his confederation of nations in the east from Nineveh to Babylon. I learned that King Ezra's confederation included kings, princes, and warriors from the plateau, from Kau in the northeast, an Assuwan league of twenty-two tribal nations including warriors from Lukka toward the south, Dodecanese warriors, Phrygian warriors, and Armenian warriors east of Haran and south from the Kaucasus Mountains of Japheth, the land where the River Euphrates and the River Tigris originate.

I learned that King Ezra established a merchant outpost in Haran with strong connections to the store city at Ilion that was established by Dodanim and by Ashkenaz, the progenitor of the Phrygian kings. With the great cities of Nisibis and Nineveh to the east, Haran was situated on the well-established trade routes of Tubal in the plains between the Euphrates and Tigris rivers on a routinely traveled road from Iopolis, our growing port established by King Baath on the Kilikian Sea with access to the Great Sea. Haran also was blessed with two prosperous royal highways to the sons of Madai, the Medes, in the Near East and the distant territories in the Far East, where silk and spices were, and still are, imported and exported to the nations as far as the distant territories amid the Sea of Tarshish in the west.

It was during my study of human affairs that I became aware that the original *Book of the Chronicles of the Kings of Iobaath* was in desperate need of addendum. I observed that several entire generations were missing from the recordings. So in the days of my youth, I, Prince Mair, assumed the role of the chronicler for our generation. I began my quest by gathering information by way of interviews, asking questions just as King Ezra had done in his generation, and as King Iobaath had done before him.

I discovered that our Creator blessed our kings and princes with prosperity and long life. Japheth taught us that we were to honor our father and mother from the heart, and that the LORD God is very pleased with obedience. I learned from oral tradition that our kings outlived their contemporaries. Four generations of kings survived battles that took the lives of many of our neighboring chieftains. I observed that cities, small and great, were named after prominent princes and kings. There was little disease among us, nor drought, which caused so many to perish or flee to Egypt, where there was an abundance of food. Some found refuge from drought in Panphylia, the land of mingled tribal nations, and Kilikia, where we were blessed with abundant harvest as in the flooded plains of Egypt. We expanded according to the blessings of Japheth and inhabited many territories in our God-given land. I believe that all this was due to the honoring of our fathers and mothers so that our kings survived, prospered, and outlived many other princes.

Although King Oth was weak and most likely in his final days, he still remembered the former years. We did not expect King Oth to be with us long. So, aware of the season, I began my interviews with our reigning king.

King Oth was the son of King Abir, who was the son of King Rea, who was the son of King Ezra. We understood from our tradition that King Ezra had a strong relationship with Eber, the Hebrew, and he worshipped the LORD God of Shem and Japheth. So I visited King Oth to learn more about the two mysterious ancestral kings, King Rea and King Abir, and our unusual ties with the Hebrew nation. Most of our kinsmen had no relationship or connection with the descendants of Eber in the east. King Oth was wise—and eager—to share his stories with me about our shared history with the Hebrews. He was one hundred and seventy-five years old at the time of my interviews.

I learned from King Oth that Abir, the son of King Rea, the son of King Ezra, did not walk in the way of the LORD. King Oth said, "Son, King Rea was not a levelheaded ram among the flocks of Iobaath. He was stubborn as the aurochs, a lunatic having multiple personas, and forsook the traditions of Japheth. King Rea built high places to Baal and various and sundry fertility gods. It was said that he even worshipped Rimmon, the Syroi god, the dragon pictured in our clay chronicles.

"And just as his father before him, King Abir also forsook the way of the LORD and worshipped the stone gods and goddesses of the cursed Canaanites. King Abir was not a sweet aroma and fragrance to King Ezra, but bitter." From this I understood that the name Abir literally means *bitter*. Sadly, Abir, the Bitter, died before he saw the birth of his grandsons.

King Oth continued, saying, "Prince Lukka was the younger brother of King Rea, and he settled the coastal territory which bears his name located east of Panphylia. Lukka was said to have been the friend of pirates and, like his older brother King Rea, forsook the LORD God of Japheth. Lukka did not fear the Lord and was not loyal to his kinsmen, but became a skilled warrior. Despite the obvious ambivalence among the nations, Prince Lukka and his bands were invited to join the Assuwa league of nations. The sons of Lukka are sea people who strangely valued negotiations with pirates. However, they also possess great nautical skills renown in Assuwa, Panphylia, Kilikia, and Iopolis, making a better ally than an enemy."

Prince Ecthet, the son of King Oth, the son of King Abir, would soon formally be installed as the king and lead the league of Assuwan nations. However, Prince Ecthet had been our functional king since my birth. Prince Ecthet followed in the footsteps of his father and worshipped the LORD God of Shem and Japheth. The relationship between King Oth and Prince Ecthet was admirable. They were both known to be men of integrity, full of wisdom, and with proven character; they were both wise judges with astute discernment on a number of matters. They discerned good from evil.

First I asked King Oth about the LORD God of Shem and Japheth and about the Hebrew nation of Eber that King Ezra wrote about. It seemed to me that affections of our kinsmen for the LORD God had subsided over the centuries. Although all the nations believed in the Creator and most upheld and enforced the seven laws of Noah and animal sacrifices, as well as appointing judges among our tribes, we abandoned the worship of our Creator with the sound of music: the pfeife and lyre. These wind and stringed instruments are still used today, but only in celebration of our victories in battle and at festive supra and wedding celebrations—rarely in worship to the LORD God of Shem and Japheth, the one true God.

My heart's desire is to worship the LORD God with the sound of music and jubilant dancing feet. I understood from our tribal theology that the chief end of every man is to glorify our Creator; men of every race were free to worship and enjoy their Creator as long as they had the breath of life within them.

I asked King Oth about the Nephilim titans, the Great Flood of Noah, the expansion of Japheth from Kau, and the unseen powers of good and evil, which manage the spiritual realms. But for many of our kinsmen, God was not a person who we naturally banter with, as King Ezra's tradition suggests. We seldom thought of initiating a serious conversation with our Creator.

At times of unbelief, I falsely presumed that the LORD God had created the universe and then disappeared, allowing His well-designed creation to self-manage itself. But when I came to my senses, I rejected these disrespectful speculations and returned to the LORD God of my fathers.

The LORD God of King Ezra was a mystery to me and foreign to my generation, but there was a strong desire within my spirit to learn more about our Creator, the creation story, and our connection with Adam and Eve. The traditions of our fathers seemed so much more realistic than the idolatrous and self-serving worship of created things, as observed among the people of Çatalhöyük.

Even as a young man, and in so many ways, I related to the story of Job, the forces of good and evil at war, the relentless testing of a man's character and integrity, the providential circumstances that men experience day after day, week after week, month after month, and year after year. I gathered great inspiration from the story of Job, but at the same time, great rebuke as I recited the sobering apologetia delivered to Job in direct address by the thundering Great Voice of our Creator. I was so intrigued by the detailed characteristics of our world expressed by God to Job that I was the first among the Dodecanese descendants to graph visual representations of our earthly sphere on plastered walls.

A few days later, after mentally processing the tradition of our fathers, I asked King Oth how it was that our tribal nation migrated into the land south of the Hospitable Blach See, at the mouth of the Euphrates River, north of Ur. He explained: "After King Nimrod died, Ur, the land of Eber and his grandfather, Arpachshad, became a well-managed city-state. When our kingdoms united in warfare to defend the land of Kau from Nimrod's armies, we built strong relationships with our comrades from other tribal nations. We intermarried with our kinsman-cousins, the descendants of Magog, and the descendants of Patriarch

Javan. We intermarried with the descendants of Patriarch Gomer, the tribal nations of Ashkenaz, Riphath, and Togarmah. We intermarried with the descendants of the Patriarch Tubal and the descendants of the Patriarch Meshech and also the descendants of Patriarch Tiras in Assuwa."

King Oth continued. "But sadly, a few of our kinsman intermarried with the descendants of Heth, the Hethites, one of the twelve Canaanite nations. Intermarriage with Canaanite tribes was discouraged among our people as it was with the people of Eber. The Canaanites were known as a grossly idolatrous nation who worshipped created things, like the people of Çatalhöyük. They did not worship the LORD God of Shem and Japheth."

I discovered that although all these tribal nations established their homelands surrounding the Hospitable Sea, there were small bands of ethnic communities within a dominating kingdom. I knew that our progenitor was Dodanim, the son of Javan, but during my interview with King Oth I learned that we are related to the kingdom of Magog by marriage. Since we had connections with the sons of Javan and the sons of Magog, many of our people colonized between the two kingdoms, one in the east and the other in the west, south of the Hospitable Sea and on the north side of the Great Sea. Our tradition called the far western extremities of the Great Sea in the midst of the land the Sea of Tarshish, which was named after Dodanim's older brother, who ventured far into the western waters.

It was explained to me that our colony of people in Haran were centrally located with access to all the major trade routes. Our kings and princes led a league of nations, which included the Dodecanese from the Island of Rhodes, the cities of Tarzu, Iopolis, and Elba in Kilikia, and territories surrounding the mountains of Tiras including the city-states of Çatalhöyük, Tavia, and other cities there.

Our tribesmen recognized that various nations in our midst were emerging in population and strength. At some point one tribal nation would prove superior in strength and bring the other tribal nations in the league and their territories into submission to their king.

I questioned King Oth, saying, "Who will become the dominant nation? The Gomerites from the north on the Hospitable Blach See in Skythia? Our very own people, the Dodecanese? The Hethites, the sons of Canaan? The Assuwans or Ionians in the west? Or perhaps the ancient kings and princes in the land of Kau, of patriarchs Magog, Meshech, Tubal, or Madai, the people of the grassy steppe lands surrounding the Khazar Sea?" King Oth answered my question in a general way, saying, "Son, any one or more of the surrounding tribal nations that you identified could emerge as a dominant kingdom and bring our people to submission to their crown, their traditions, and their gods."

King Oth continued and shared with me what he remembered about our cousins to the south and our well-established relationship with Eber, the Hebrew of Ur, saying, "Since the days of King Ezra, all the kings spoke Hebrew as well as our native Dodecanese tongue. We had an advantage over other tribal nations of Japheth, staying in close proximity to the Hebrew nation to their culture and to the LORD God of Noah. I became aware that the traditions and teachings of Iobaath, King Baath, and King Ezra helped us to be a people of distinction among the other nations of Japheth and Ham. We were tempted to depart from the faith of our fathers but stood firm and resisted Canaanite idolatry and fantastic Javanian myths which elevated and exulted the wicked Herakles as a demigod."

King Oth continued; he expressed gratefulness for our relationship with the Gomerites. "We were also profoundly influenced by the work ethic, industry, and hospitable lifestyle of the Riphean pfeifers sojourning in Tavia."

I was filled with gratitude that our written chronicles helped our kinsmen preserve our moral integrity among the emerging Kau nations. I was thankful to our Creator that we did not worship the goddess of the moon, Nanna, from the land of Ur, or Sin of Haran, or Rimmon of Syroi. But as for me and my house, we feared the LORD God and remained steadfast to the traditions and teachings of Shem and Japheth.

But as the tribal nations of Japheth prospered, many did not share my faith or convictions and drifted away from the LORD God of Creation, believing myths and the erroneous speculations of faithless men.

King Oth explained. "You see, son, the Hebrew nation was the last tribe among the sons of Noah to claim their inheritance. A man named Abraham was visited by the LORD God, who commanded him to go claim their inheritance that was still waiting for the sons of Eber."

King Oth told me that Abraham shared his birth year and that he had heard that Abraham recently died. I was surprised to learn that Eber also lived a long life and died at the age of four hundred and sixty-four. Since Eber lived a long life as our forefathers, he died in the same season of life as Abraham. The stories about Eber were incredible to me, that giant men like Noah, Japheth, Iobaath, and Eber lived such long lives and were so intelligent and productive in their generation.

I also was surprised to learn that Abraham married, but he was not blessed with offspring until very late in life. Like Noah, Abraham was advanced in years before having offspring. This seemed so strange to our kings, who procreated often and had dozens of children and hundreds of grandchildren. Some among us questioned whether the linage of Eber would ever develop; some thought that the seed of Eber would become extinct like the woolly behemoths of the sleeping lands and the endangered aurochs in Assuwa.

But these projections proved false when King Oth learned that the aged Abraham and his wife, Sarah, eventually fathered Isaac, who fathered Jacob, who fathered Judah and several other sons. I learned from King Oth that all of them are alive except Isaac, who died at a young age.

I was informed that the sons of Abraham inherited the land on the eastern shore of the Great Sea, north of the land of Egypt, and south of the land of Sidon; unfortunately, this was a land occupied by the idolatrous Canaanites. After many centuries the sons of Eber expanded as the nations of Japheth, but they had failed to extricate the cursed blood of Canaan from their homeland. I understood this tolerance from my experience when living among the idolatrous people of Çatalhöyük. My spirit was willing to eradicate the idolatry, but my will to do so weak. I suppose our weakness will prove costly to future generations for both our nations. Idolatry in all its expressions must be hated and eradicated, not tolerated. Warfare seems so cruel, but removing evil tribal nations that serve idols appears to please our Creator and honor Him. Concerning the holiness of God and His abhorrence of evil, I am completely without understanding, totally dumbfounded.

Still curious about the sons of Eber, I continued to interrogate King Oth about the Hebrew nation. King Oth remembered the day when he heard through the trade routes in Mesopotamia that Abraham was commanded by the LORD God of Eber to sacrifice his only son, Isaac, on an altar built for animal sacrifice. This was another incredible story to me, that the LORD God would request such a horrible thing from Abraham. Why would God command Abraham to sacrifice his only son? At first I became angry with God and strongly objected to such an outrageous request. I expressed my outrage to King Oth as he sat quietly and patiently waited for me to be still and come to the end of my human rationalizing.

Then in the stillness and quietness, King Oth smiled as the face of an angel and patiently continued telling the story. "That's not the end of the story, son! The LORD God prevented Abraham from sacrificing Isaac and provided an innocent lamb to be sacrificed in his place."

I was so ashamed that I rushed to such judgment so quickly. My spirit filled with joy when I head the end of the story. I then perceived that the LORD God was testing Abraham as He tested Job; as the LORD God tests the hearts of all men and women born of Noah who fear the LORD God. The test proved that Abraham had what it takes. Abraham was a man of great faith who spared not his only begotten son. Abraham believed God, and his faith in the lamb provided by God made him righteous. I learned that to obey is better than sacrifice and that our blessings are just beyond our obedience. We are to hear and obey the Great Voice of God rather than men. From that day forward, I asked about Abraham, Isaac, and Jacob wherever I traveled.

There was much about our own nation that I needed to understand, but as time passed, I was aware that the LORD God had put this desire in my heart to study the Hebrew people, the descendants of Eber and Abraham. I was quite interested in finding out more about the Hebrew-speaking nation, but realized this was a personal interest not shared by all of my kinsmen or the other surrounding tribal nations. So I continued my interviews with King Oth to learn more about our people.

In a subsequent interview, I learned from King Oth that while the Hebrew nation was engaged in constant conflicts with the Canaanites, our confederacy of nations was engaged in constant conflict with the Medes and Persians in the east and the Assyrians of Nineveh toward the southeast. The nations of patriarchs Meshech and Tubal moved their people from the land south of the Kaucasus Mountains to the land north of the Kaucasus Mountains to the steppe lands of Magog, the territory known as Rosch, where they established cities along the southern River Rha that fed into the Khazar Sea to the south. The three tribes united, all speaking the Scythian tongue of Magog.

Due to the growing hostilities in the east and southeast, some of our kinsmen migrated into the land of Gomer and united with the Cimmerian warriors north of the Hospitable Sea. Our confederation of tribal nations excelled in sowing and reaping, herding, ironworks, and warfare everywhere we migrated. Others among our people returned to Kilikia migrating south of the mountains of Tiras, south of Çatalhöyük and Tarzu, west of Iopolis, along the grassy plains and shores of the Sea of Tarshish.

Yet others returned to the Island of Rhodanim, the land of the Dodecanese.

When I interviewed my great-grandfather Prince Ecthet, he told me about his encounters with the Hebrews at Hebron while serving in the confederate armies of Gomer and Javan. Prince Ecthet explained: "Our tribal nation maintained our connection to the germ of Gomer in the west and north. Together our league of nations recaptured the land of Togarmah and the mountains of Noah that were seized by King Nimrod. Bethuel, the Aramean of Paddan-aram, led our league of nations in those days."

I learned later that Prince Ecthet was commissioned by King Oth to Hebron because he spoke in both the Aramaic and Hebrew tongues. After his commission at Hebron, Hebrew became his second language.

Prince Ecthet continued. "Under the leadership of King Bethuel, our league of nations prospered and expanded from Hebron southeast into the land of the Canaanites. For a season we cohabited land with the idolatrous sons and daughters of Heth, the second son of Canaan. Regretfully during this season, some of our people intermarried with the Hethites."

It was then that I understood that Prince Ecthet considered this comingling an unfortunate mistake as our people began worshiping idols and committing abominable acts before our holy Creator.

Prince Ecthet continued the story. "Now Abraham's wife, Sarah, died when she was one hundred and twenty-seven years old. Abraham came to Hebron seeking a burial ground; so he arrived at the gate of the city where prominent and wise men sat in conference. I was stationed in Hebron to ensure that no insurrection was being planned against the forces of our confederacy. Abraham addressed me and boldly appealed to me, saying, 'I am a sojourner and foreigner among you; give me property among you for a burying place, that I may bury my dead out of my sight.'

"Understanding that the sons of Shem were our allies, I was honored to meet Abraham, and granted his request with great respect. I said, 'Hear us, my lord; you are a prince of God among us. Bury your dead in the choicest of our tombs. None of us will withhold from you his tomb to hinder you from burying your dead.' I was amazed when this prince of God bowed to the ground before me and his people expressed a deep gratitude for providing Abraham a useless cave to bury his deceased wife, Sarah. We let Abraham choose from our finest caverns."

I learned that day that the sons of Abraham buried their dead in caves like the Hethites; our tribes buried our dead in the ground.

Prince Ecthet continued, saying, "Abraham was a very wealthy man and knew exactly which cave he wanted for Sarah's burial, saying, 'If you are willing that I should bury my dead out of my sight, hear me and entreat for me Ephron the son of Zohar, that he may give me the cave of Machpelah, which he owns; it is at the end of his field. For the full price let him give it to me in your presence as property for a burying place.'

"Then I motioned for Ephron the Hethite to come forward as he was sitting among the men of prominence at the gate. Then I made an appeal, saying, 'Since this property belongs to Ephron, who is now among us, let Ephron speak for himself about this matter.' I knew Ephron to be a gracious and just man of proven character. So I was not surprised when Ephron came forward and responded to Abraham's request, saying, 'No, my lord, hear me: I give you the field, and I give you the cave that is in it. In the sight of the sons of my people I give it to you. Bury your dead.'

"Yet again, Abraham bowed down to our people and wanted to pay for the field, saying, 'But if you will, hear me: I give the price of the field. Accept it from me, that I may bury my dead there.' From this statement we understood that Abraham wanted to purchase the field from Ephron; he was a wealthy man and refused to take possession of the field as a gift from a Hethite."

Prince Ecthet explained this. "Ephron the Hethite wanted to give the field as a gift, but did not want to offend Abraham, who was grieving the death of his wife. So Ephron made his offer while expressing great affection for Abraham; he wisely said, 'My lord, listen to me: a piece of land worth four hundred shekels of silver, what is that between you and me? Bury your dead.'

"Well, the elders at the gate of Hebron were astounded at the wisdom of Ephron the Hethite. Ephron shared his fair value of the field with Abraham so that he could pay for the property, but ended the disclosure with an expression of deepest brotherhood and endearment, saying, 'What is that between you and me?' Ephron valued their friendship more than silver coinage."

Prince Ecthet explained that Abraham listened intently to Ephron. He stood and watched as Abraham weighed out for Ephron the silver coins he had named, four hundred shekels of silver, according to the weights current among the merchants. Ecthet told me that this experience with Abraham was one of the greatest moments of his life and encouraged his respect for the Hebrew nation of Abraham. When Prince Ecthet returned to our people in Hebron, he immediately shared this story with others in our cities.

In the course of time, Abraham breathed his last breath and died. He lived one hundred and seventy-five years and was gathered to his people. Ishmael and Isaac, Abraham's sons, buried him in the cave of Machpelah, in the field of Ephron the son of Zohar, east of Mamre, the field that Abraham purchased from Ephron. There Abraham was buried with Sarah his wife.

Prince Ecthet admonished me, saying, "Son, know this! Those of the household of faith are the true sons of God and Abraham. And the sacred Hebrew Chronicles of Eber and Abraham, foreseeing that God would justify the Gentiles by faith, preached good news to Abraham, saying, 'In you shall all the nations be blessed.' So then, son, those who are of faith are blessed along with Abraham, the man of faith. Let us abide in the faith of Abraham.

"For we ourselves are witnesses and it is written in the sacred Hebrew Chronicles that Abraham had two sons, one by a slave woman and one by a free woman. But the son of the slave was born according to the flesh, while the son of the free woman was born through promise.

"Now you, son, like Isaac, are children of promise. But just as at that time he who was born according to the flesh persecuted him who was born according to the Spirit, so also it is now. So, son, we are not children of the slave but of the free woman, according to the promised Seed of Abraham, the One who is to come. Hold fast to the promise of Abraham, son, for your eyes may see the coming of the Glory of the LORD God."

I perceived that Prince Ecthet was a very wise man. I was captivated by his understanding mind and his insight into the promised Seed of Abraham and of the Lamb of God who is to come to redeem all the tribal nations of the earth. For many among the sons of Japheth were misinformed that God was against them from the start; but I understood that the LORD God of Noah, Eber, and Abraham loves all the tribes of the earth who call upon and believe in His holy Name. It was then that I too understood the promise and believed wholeheartedly in the One who was to come.

During a subsequent interview, I also learned from Prince Ecthet that Isaac was married and had twin boys: Jacob and Esau. When Esau was forty years old, he took Judith the daughter of Beeri the Hethite to be his wife, and Basemath the daughter of Elon the Hethite, and they made life bitter for Isaac and his first wife, Rebekah. Of course when I heard this, it was no surprise to me that, except for Ephron and his God-fearing kinsmen, the Hethite people brought much bitterness to all the sons of Noah.

Prince Ecthet reported that Esau and his wives settled in the land of Edom across the Red Sea from Egypt and were neighbors of the Midianites. The Midianites were the descendants of Midian, who was a son of Abraham through his wife Keturah. Esau took other wives from the Canaanites: Oholibamah the daughter of Anah the daughter of Zibeon the Hivite, and Basemath, Ishmael's daughter, the sister of Nebaioth. Ishmael was the older half-brother of Isaac.

When Esau took many wives, this outraged our kinsmen and caused no small conflict within our gates. Although multiple wives were accepted among the Hethite tribes, our people, the descendants of Japheth, believe that polygamy, or the marrying of more than one wife, is unwise and strongly discourage it among the sons of Japheth. Prince Ecthet insisted and told me that Japheth, the Great Voice, and Noah, the Herald of Righteousness, taught us that marriage was to be between one man and one woman, like Adam and Eve. This was God's standard, not ours.

In our tradition we were warned about Lamech, Japheth's father-in-law, who took two wives and perished in the world-wide flood. Some exceptions were allowed in rare circumstances where a man's wife could not conceive or bear offspring. In our civil laws, such a man was pitied, permitted procreation rights, and with the consent of his wife laid with a household concubine. But in the course of time, as with Abraham, this path often caused trouble and bitter jealousy between the wife and the surrogate. Again, the act of procreation and producing offspring was highly regarded among our kinsmen; so the practice of one man and one woman continues to this day.

Prince Ecthet shared sobering and tragic stories with me about the cities of Sodom and Gomorrah, and he warned me concerning the wicked practices of men who pervert the righteous ways of the LORD God of Noah and Japheth. I was warned and instructed that these cities were populated with adulterous, idolatrous men who subjected their bodies to unnatural affections and defiled themselves. He did not hold back details but fully disclosed to me that the men of Sodom and Gomorrah who lived in the southern plains near the Salt Sea were destroyed by an angelic messenger from the LORD God.

I was grieved when Ecthet told me that the old men of Sodom and the young men of Sodom were bold in the extreme, proud of their waywardness, demanding that the powerful messengers from God lay with them in an unnatural way.

But then I was comforted when I heard that by an act of great kindness, the seed of Lot, Abraham's brother, was spared from the wrath of God. As in the days of Noah, God removed the righteous believing seed before the destruction of the wicked unbelievers, who practice abominable acts that God hates.

Again, with great wisdom and understanding, Prince Ecthet reasoned and provided wise instruction to me, saying, "Son, for the wrath of God was revealed from heaven against all the ungodliness and unrighteousness of the men, like the men of Sodom and Gomorrah, who by their unrighteousness suppressed the truth and walk in unbelief. For what can be known about God was plain to the men of Sodom and Gomorrah, because God has shown it to them. For his invisible attributes, namely, his eternal power and divine nature, were clearly perceived, ever since the creation of the world, in the things that have been made. So they were, as we are, without excuse. For although the men of Sodom and Gomorrah knew God, they did not honor him as God or give thanks to him, but they became futile in their thinking, and their foolish hearts were darkened. Claiming to be wise, the men of Sodom and Gomorrah became fools and exchanged the glory of the immortal God for images resembling mortal man and birds and animals and creeping things like the rest of the cursed Canaanites.

"Therefore, God gave the men of Sodom and Gomorrah up in the lusts of their hearts to impurity, to the dishonoring of their bodies among themselves, because they exchanged the truth about God for a lie and worshiped and served the creature rather than the Creator, who is blessed forever!

"For this reason God gave the men of Sodom and Gomorrah up to dishonorable passions. For their women exchanged natural relations for those that are contrary to nature; and the men likewise gave up natural relations with women and were consumed with passion for one another, men committing shameless acts with men and receiving in themselves the due penalty for their error.

"And since the men of Sodom and Gomorrah did not see fit to acknowledge God, God gave them up to a debased mind to do what ought not to be done, practices forbidden by Noah. They were filled with all manner of unrighteousness, evil, covetousness, malice. They are full of envy, murder, strife, deceit, maliciousness. Though they know God's righteous decree that those who practiced such abominable things deserve to die, they not only did them but gave approval to and tolerated those who practice them."

I was sobered by the story that Ecthet shared with me about the effeminate men of Sodom and Gomorrah. I began to understand the holiness of God and the dire consequences of idolatry and unbelief and not obeying and fearing the LORD God of Japheth and Noah.

I confessed to Prince Ecthet: "Sometimes I am depressed about the way God fashioned my physical body and dream of being a mighty man that I am not. I often ask myself, 'Do I have what it takes to be a man?' I too have been tempted to idolize and worship men, made in God's image and after His likeness.

"But thank God the thought of sexual relationships with men found no footing in my heart. May I never submit my mind, will, and emotions to the lust of my flesh. Lust does not make me a man. Overcome with great conviction, I prayed out loud to the LORD God, saying, 'God, please help me to never submit my mind, will, or emotions to unnatural affections like the men of Sodom and Gomorrah, and in the appropriate season of life, help me to direct my sexual desires toward the woman that you have ordained for me to marry. Please help me to serve my natural affections, procreate, and provide offspring to the glory of God according to the teachings of righteous Noah and our forefathers. Show me what it is to be a son of God."

I am thankful for my God-fearing and faith-filled father, who taught me the laws of Noah and of the promised Seed of Abraham, to be married to one woman, procreate, and produce offspring according to the purposes of the LORD God. I was taught that the LORD God blessed Japheth and said that his germ would be enlarged. My desire is to cooperate with the source and sponsor of life, the LORD God, and be part of God's expansion project.

* * * * *

After several weeks, I completed my interviews with Prince Ecthet and was looking forward to my interview with my grandfather, Prince Aurthach. In the days of my youth, my grandfather taught me how to ride a horse and how to hunt. So we planned to erect a linen tent woven from the flax of Kilikia. We raised the tent for our hunting camp in the hill county west of Haran and south from the forested mountains.

I learned that it was there in the uplands that King Abir, with the help of the other descendants of Dodanim, regretfully built an enormous temple for the Hethites with huge pillars with glimmering and colorful terrazzo flooring constructed from chips of burnt lime and clay, colored from the pits of red ochre. When the terrazzo floor settled and dried, it was polished.

I learned that Prince Aurthach was and is a fearless warrior who informed me about the rise to power of one, King Anitta of Hattusa, who made the Hethite nation his slaves and led fourteen hundred foot soldiers, men armed with bronze daggers, and forty charioteers outfitted with teams of horses with iron oxcart chariots into battle against the city of Salatiwara. He perceived that the Hatti people were from the not-so-Hospitable Sea, wayward descendants of Gomer. He predicted that the Hatti nation was growing in numbers and strength and that the Hatti people would bring great violence to our people one day as they did to our neighbors in the city of Salatiwara.

During another interview, my grandfather told me that he was acquainted with Esau and Jacob, Abraham's grandsons. Prince Aurthach explained. "After Abraham purchased the fields from Ephron in Hebron, Isaac asked his father if he could hunt deer there with his son, Esau, with a bow and arrow. Prince Ecthet and Isaac, Abraham's son, became acquainted when Abraham buried his wife in the cave of Ephron. Isaac brought Esau to the cave of the field of Machpelah east of Mamre. Isaac and Esau helped prepare for Sarah's burial. Prince Ecthet and I offered to help serve Abraham with preparations and stayed for the burial of the body. As they prepared the cave for burial, Prince Ecthet and Isaac, both hunters, were impressed by the wild herds of deer in the area. Prince Ecthet was an experienced archer and offered to teach the Hebrews his sport. After Sarah was buried, Isaac and Prince Ecthet made plans to return to the field and take Esau and me on the hunt. We were so excited to go deer hunting!"

I learned that Isaac was forty years old when he took Rebekah, the daughter of Bethuel the Aramean of Paddan-aram, the sister of Laban the Aramean, to be his wife. And like his grandfather, Abraham, many years later, Jacob went on his journey to find a wife and came to the land of our people in Haran.

My grandfather explained: "As Jacob looked, he saw a well in the field, and behold, three flocks of sheep lying beside it, for out of that well the flocks were watered. The stone on the well's mouth was large, and when all the flocks were gathered there, the shepherds would roll the stone from the mouth of the well and water the sheep, and put the stone back in its place over the mouth of the well.

"Jacob did not know us that we went hunting with his brother, Esau. Jacob questioned us, saying, 'My brothers, where do you come from?' We said, 'We are from Haran.' He said to us, 'Do you know Laban the son of Nahor?' We said, 'Yes! We know him.' He said to us, 'Is it well with him?' We said, 'It is well with him; and see, Rachel his daughter is coming with the sheep!' Jacob said, 'Behold, it is still high day; it is not time for the livestock to be gathered together. Water the sheep and go, pasture them.' But we said, 'We cannot until all the flocks are gathered together and the stone is rolled from the mouth of the well; then we water the sheep.'

"Then while Jacob was still speaking with us, Rachel came with her father's sheep, for she was a shepherdess. Now as soon as Jacob saw Rachel the daughter of Laban his mother's brother, and the sheep of Laban his mother's brother, Jacob came near and rolled the stone from the well's mouth and watered the flock of Laban his mother's brother. Then Jacob kissed Rachel and wept aloud. And Jacob told Rachel that he was her father's kinsman, and that he was Rebekah's son, and she ran and told her father.

"As soon as Laban heard the news about Jacob, his sister's son, he ran to meet him and embraced him and kissed him and brought him to his house. Jacob told Laban all these things, and Laban said to him, 'Surely you are my bone and my flesh!' Jacob stayed with Laban several weeks.

"Then Laban said to Jacob, 'Because you are my kinsman, should you therefore serve me for nothing? Tell me, what shall your wages be?' Now Laban had two daughters. The name of the older was Leah, and the name of the younger was Rachel. Leah's eyes were weak, but Rachel was beautiful in form and appearance. Jacob loved Rachel. And he said, 'I will serve you seven years for your younger daughter Rachel.' Laban said, 'It is better that I give her to you than that I should give her to any other man; stay with me.' So Jacob served seven years for Rachel, and they seemed to him but a few days because of the love he had for her.

"Then Jacob said to Laban, 'Give me my wife that I may go in to her, for my time is completed.' So Laban gathered together all the people and made a feast. But in the evening he took his daughter Leah and brought her to Jacob, and he went in to her. And in the morning, behold, it was Leah! And Jacob said to Laban, 'What is this you have done to me? Did I not serve with you for Rachel? Why then have you deceived me?' Laban said, 'It is not so done in our country, to give the younger before the firstborn. Complete the week of this one, and we will give you the other also in return for serving me another seven years.' Jacob did so, and completed her week. Then Laban gave him his daughter Rachel to be his wife. So Jacob went in to Rachel also, and he loved Rachel more than Leah, and served Laban for another seven years.

"When the Lord saw that Leah was hated, he opened her womb, but Rachel was barren. And Leah conceived and bore a son, and she called his name Reuben, for she said, 'Because the Lord has looked upon my affliction; for now, my husband will love me.' She conceived again and bore a son, and said, 'Because the Lord has heard that I am hated, he has given me this son also.' And she called his name Simeon. Again she conceived and bore a son, and said, 'Now this time my husband will be attached to me, because I have borne him three sons.' Therefore, his name was called Levi. And she conceived again and bore a son, and said, 'This time I will praise the Lord.' Therefore, she called his name Judah. Then she ceased bearing." My grandfather completed his story.

Later I learned that my father, Prince Ethach, son of Aurthach, and Judah, son of Jacob, were born in the same month in Haran. Judah had three older brothers at the time. Reuben was the firstling, then Simeon, Levi, and Judah. They were all the sons of Leah, Laban's oldest daughter. Prince Ethach and Judah were well acquainted. When they were twenty years old, they interacted as trade partners, Prince Ethach representing the interests of the league of nations, Judah representing Shechem interests. Shechem was renowned for its exporting of grapes, olives, wheat, livestock, and pottery.

When I finally interviewed my father, Prince Ethach, he recalled his visit to Shechem, where the gods Min, Oetesh, and Resheph were held in high esteem among the Canaanite tribes there. He observed that like the Hethites and the misguided descendants of Tiras in Çatalhöyük, the Canaanites also were an idolatrous people who forsook the LORD God of Noah, replacing the God of creation with Min, the Egyptian god of fertility; Oetesh, the Canaanite female goddess of sensual desires; and Resheph, the Egyptian god of war and disease. Prince Ethach purchased a limestone picture graph of the false, triune god with silver coins, and brought it back to Haran as a specimen of their apostasy and ignorance.

My father was deeply troubled by the depiction of our holy Creator. With great conviction, my father questioned, "How could such brilliant, engineering, scientific Egyptian minds be so misguided in their spirits?" Instead of worshiping our holy Creator, the Syroi men worship Rimmon-like creatures, hideous mutant hybrids, part man and part beast. The notion that baals are depicted as part human and part animal degraded the spirit of life and dignity that our Creator breathed into every son of Adam, who God meticulously created in His own image from the dust of the earth. The sons of Adam did not evolve from beasts of the field as these legends appear to suggest.

I was disturbed that the legend of Rimmon was reported in our tradition. I have trouble believing this beast ever existed. We have not found skeletal evidence of any such creature as Rimmon, pictured as a dragon with feathers. The Oracles of Eber do not record Rimmon as a real creature. So I concluded that this is mere Babylonian nonsense and fiction. Like Japheth, the Great Voice, I believe that man is devolving, not evolving. This devolution of men is evidenced in the degrading glory of mankind.

Sadly, one night I sat behind the plastered walls, eavesdropping on my father as he drank the wine of Shechem with a few of our kinsmen. Intoxicated from the wine and lacking sober judgment, my father showed the men the abominable idol that he purchased in Shechem. I listened as my father described Min as vulgarly and graphically pictured on the left standing sideways and totally naked with an erected man-part; Oetesh pictured in the center, nude, standing on a lion holding wheat in her right hand and a snake in her left hand; and Resheph pictured to the right, appearing to be gazing at Min's erected man-part. The men mocked and laughed at the outrageous depiction of Canaan's so-called fertility gods and harshly jested saying, "The perverted men of Sodom and Gomorrah probably worshipped Min too!"

As the other men continued to drink wine, my father was prudent and began to drink water. He became sober-minded and did not participate in the foolish camaraderie of his guests. My father spoke up and redirected the course of the conversation, commenting on how far men had fallen from a sound, understanding mind.

My father explained, telling them, "Noah and Japheth taught us to avoid such practices and said that it was idolatry. The clay picture graph was concrete evidence that revealed the distortion of truth and the depraved nature of sinful man. God created men and women for procreation. It was an abomination that men, made in God's image, exulted male and female reproductive body parts to be objects of devotion and worship. Men, some of us are becoming infatuated and obsessed with procreative body parts!" Father continued to admonish the men, saying, "God is a holy Spirit, and men must worship God in spirit and in truth." He encouraged the men to avoid all manifestations of Canaanite idolatry.

In that season of my life, my spirit was entertaining lust and my body craved gratification. Although I knew these practices were forbidden by the LORD God and our people, I was curious to see the naked picture graphs that my father described to the men. So later that night when my father had fallen asleep, I located the idol and gazed on it. With lust in my heart as I was gazing at the pornographic naked bodies of Min and Resheph, my imagination partnered with the enemy within. My maturing body responded to the stone picture graph as if I was gazing upon a living virgin.

After those erotic experiences, I realized that the evil my father spoke about is present in my own heart and the heart of every man. In the darkness of the night, I was much aware that the sin of idolatry, the sins of King Rae and King Abir, were visiting me. There was a struggle going on inside of me. Part of me was humble and honored God; part of me wanted to be free and indulge my carnal desires. I was conflicted within. I desired to do the right thing, but unfortunately, I practiced those things I did not want to do.

The following day when my father was sober and of sound mind, the fear of the LORD God overcame my weakness. I chose to be humble, confessing to my father in great detail what I had done and how I had been deceptive, eavesdropping on his conversation, locating the idol in the night while he was drunk with wine, my lustful imaginations, and spilling my seed on the ground. Expecting condemnation and reproof, instead my father was gentle and encouraged me with much care and affection to not look upon tawdry Canaanite picture graphs. He told me to commit my body parts to purity and practice self-control. My father instructed me that the sons of God save themselves for the women of God's choosing. He encouraged me to live by the objective truths from our Creator instead of the subjective lies pulsating from our sinful hearts.

My father was humble and apologized for purchasing and bringing the idol into our home. He also apologized for drinking too much wine and for his drunkenness. He destroyed the icon, extremely remorseful that he had engaged in such an evil and deceptive mission. I look back and cherish those corrective days with my father and future King Ethach. Without a father to provide guidance during my times of testing, my story might have been much different.

We both agreed it was time I find a wife.

* * * * *

On one of my father's visits to Shechem, he learned that the sons of Jacob were filled with jealousy and hostility toward their younger brother, Joseph. Jacob loved Joseph more than the rest of his sons and made Joseph a coat of many colors. My father reported that matters grew worse when Joseph prophesied outrageous stories about his older brothers bowing down to him. The brothers, full of bitter jealousy and selfish ambition, conspired against their little brother. Judah told my father that the brothers wanted to murder Joseph, but Judah persuaded them to sell Joseph into slavery instead.

* * * * *

After learning the art of war and documenting our ancestral history, I was commissioned to Timnah to purchase wine from the Canaanites, who sojourned there. It was there that I met Perez, the son of Judah, who was laboring in the vineyards. As we sat and shared a skin of their finest vintage, I learned from Perez that he was born at the time that Judah went down from his brothers and turned aside to a certain Adullamite, whose name was Hirah. There Judah saw the daughter of a Canaanite, whose name was Shua. Judah took her and went in to her. They procreated, and Shua conceived and bore a son. Judah called his name Er. Shua conceived again and bore a son, naming him Onan. Yet again Shua bore a son, and she called his name Shelah. Judah was in Chezib when she bore him the sons: Er, Onan, and Shelah.

Perez reported that his father, Judah, sought out and took a wife for Er his firstborn when he was of age. Her name was Tamar, a familiar name to me from tragic tales of Endon. But Er, Judah's firstborn, was exceedingly wicked in the sight of the Lord, and the Lord put him to death. Perez did not tell me how God put Er to death. I was curious to find out more about the life and death of Er.

Next Perez told me that Judah encouraged Onan to lay with his sister-in-law, saying, "Go into your brother's wife and perform the duty of a brother-in-law to her, and raise up offspring for your brother." But Onan knew the offspring would not be his. So whenever he went in to his brother's wife he would waste his seed on the ground so as not to give offspring to his brother. Onan did not want to redeem his brother's estate. What Onan did was wicked in the sight of the Lord, and the Lord put him to death as well.

Afterward I sat and pondered yet another amazing Hebrew story. I was very much aware of the wandering of the sons of Ham and Japheth, but I was surprised to know that the chosen offspring of Abraham disobeyed the teachings of Noah just like the sons of Ham and Japheth. As someone once said: "We all like sheep have gone astray." Every man walks in his own way. While pondering the life and death of Onan, I realized the importance of executing the role of redeeming a kinsman and guaranteeing the offspring and estate of an older brother. This notion of a redeeming kinsmen revealed to me the importance of a man's seed and bloodline from God's perspective.

It was then that the Lord God gave me an understanding mind. I began to understand that one day a preordained Kinsman-Redeemer would be provided by the LORD God of Noah through the promised Seed of Abraham, Isaac, and Israel to redeem Adam's race, atoning for the sin of Adam and the sin of all men so God could manifest the sons of God once more in all the earth. I perceived that God was superintending the Seed of Abraham until the promised Redeemer was born among men. A second Adam was to come. I connected the story that King Oth told me about Abraham, who was told to offer up his only son on the altar. The Kinsman-Redeemer, the Son of God and Man, would be sacrificed for Adam's sin and bring redemption to mankind from every tribe and nation. And I connected the tradition of Noah and Japheth that a Redeemer would one day bruise the serpent's heel. That day I had an understanding mind with respect to our future redemption—and by faith I began to long for the Day of the LORD.

Perez continued his report, saying that Judah, his father, said to Tamar his daughter-in-law, "Remain a widow in your father's house, until Shelah my son grows up"—for he feared that he would die like his brothers. So Tamar went and remained in her father's house. In the course of time, the wife of Judah, Shua's daughter, died. When Judah was comforted, he went up to Timnah to his sheepshearers, he and his friend Hirah the

Adullamite. And when Tamar was told, "Your father-in-law is going up to Timnah to shear his sheep," she took off her widow's garments and covered herself with a veil, wrapping herself up, and sat at the entrance to Enaim, which is on the road to Timnah. For she saw that Shelah was grown up, and she had not been given to him in marriage. When Judah saw her, he thought she was a prostitute, for she had covered her face.

Then, Judah, filled with a spirit of lust and selfish ambition, turned to her on the roadside and said, "Come, let me come in to you," for he did not know that she was his daughter-in-law. Pretending that she was a prostitute, Tamar said, "What will you give me, that you may come in to me?" He answered, "I will send you a young goat from the flock." And she said, "If you give me a pledge, until you send it—" He said, "What pledge shall I give you?" She replied, "Your signet and your cord and your staff that is in your hand." So he gave them to her and, unbeknown to him, procreated with his daughter-in-law. Desperate for offspring, Tamar deceived her lustful father-in-law, Judah, and conceived by him. Then she arose and went away, and taking off her veil, she put on the garments of her widowhood.

When Judah sent the young goat by his friend the Adullamite to take back the pledge from the woman's hand, he did not find her. And he asked the men of the place, "Where is the cult prostitute who was at Enaim at the roadside?" And they said, "No cult prostitute has been here." So he returned to Judah and said, "I have not found her. Also, the men of the place said, 'No cult prostitute has been here.'" And Judah replied, "Let her keep the things as her own, or we shall be laughed at. You see, I sent this young goat, and you did not find her."

About three months later Judah was told, "Tamar your daughter-in-law has been immoral. Moreover, she is pregnant by immorality." And Judah said, "Bring her out, and let her be burned." As she was being brought out, she sent word to her father-in-law, "By the man to whom these belong, I am pregnant." And she said, "Please identify whose these are, the signet and the cord and the staff." Then Judah identified them and said, "She is more righteous than I, since I did not give her to my son Shelah." And he did not know her again.

When the time of her labor came, there were twins in her womb. And when she was in labor, one put out a hand, and the midwife took and tied a scarlet thread on his hand, saying, "This one came out first." But as he drew back his hand, behold, his brother came out. And she said, "What a breach you have made for yourself!" Therefore, his name was called Perez. Afterward his brother came out with the scarlet thread on his hand, and his name was called Zerah.

I learned that Shelah, Perez, and Zerah had a difficult time following the ordinances of the LORD God. But the sudden and swift death of their brothers, Er and Onan, caused them to be soberminded and fear God. Perez confessed that it was challenging living in the midst of the idolatrous Canaanites. I thanked Perez for sharing such an intimate story with me. I could tell he felt uncomfortable disclosing such personal details about himself.

Later I learned from Perez of the sons of Judah according to their clans; these were of Shelah, the clan of the Shelanites; of Perez, the clan of the Perezites; of Zerah, the clan of the Zerahites. The LORD God had mercy on them and did not destroy them or their seed. I was thankful that God had been merciful to me as well.

I told Perez that our people lived among the Hethites, who were also an idolatrous nation, and also the sons of Canaan. I confided with Perez that it was difficult to live with neighbors and relatives who intermarried and abandoned the LORD God for icons and idols.

I understood from the life of Judah that where there is bitter jealousy and selfish ambition, there is every evil practice. But I understood that selfish ambition was present in my heart too. I cried out: "Oh wretched man that I am! Who will deliver me from this death?"

After meeting with Perez, I had a change of heart. I began to practice self-control as my father had wisely instructed me. I stopped feeding idolatry and spilling my seed on the ground. I sought and found a wife.

Before King Oth died, Prince Ecthet became our tribal king in Haran and lead our league of nations. King Oth lived a long life and died of natural causes when he was two hundred and fifty years old. He lived to see five generations of the sons of Iobaath. The wise sage held my firstborn, Simeon, whose name means "God has heard," on his lap in the year that he died. King Oth was delighted to know that God heard his prayers for god-fearing offspring.

* * * * *

So after many years of research, I, Prince Mair, the scribe and chronicler of the sons of Iobaath, sojourning in Haran, hereby preserve a record for future generations in *The Book of the Chronicles of the Kings of Iobaath:*

Simeon was the son of Mair. Mair was the son of Ethach. Ethach was the son of Aurthach. Aurthach was the son of Ecthet. Ecthet was the son of Oth. Oth was the son of Abir. Abir was the son of Rea. Rea was the son of Ezra. Ezra was the son of Izrau. Izrau was the son of Baath. Baath was the son of Iobaath. Iobaath was the son of Rhodanim. Rhodanim was the son of Javan. Javan was the son of Japheth. Japheth was the son of Noah. Noah was the son of Lamech, Lamech was the son of Methuselah, Methuselah was the son of Enoch, Enoch was the son of Jared, Jared was the son of Mahalaleel, Mahalaleel was the son of Cainan, Cainan was the son of Enos, Enos was the son of Seth, Seth was the son of Adam. Adam was the son of God.

THREE

THE CHRONICLES OF KING FETEBIR

(1500 BC)

MANY CENTURIES HAD PASSED when I, Prince Fetebir, updated *The Book of the Chronicles of the Kings of Iobaath.* Reviewing our ancestry, I observed that life appeared to be so peaceful in the days of King Mair. Since those days when King Mair made his entries, our people and allied league of nations endured much hardship, violence, and bloodshed. Our Dodecanese ancestors on the Island of Rhodes find themselves weary in the midst of constant mayhem inflicted upon them by the terrorist bands of Peirates and the orphaned Sea People from Lukka.

As the chronicler for my generation, I learned that King Simeon, the son of King Mair, married young but tragically died in a pitched battle with King Alluwamna of Hattusa in the north defending the Assuwan league of nations against aggression. King Simeon's younger brother, Pilliya, gave seed to Simeon's widow in the tradition of our kinsmen and redeemed Simeon's inheritance and offspring. Pilliya represented our league of nations until Prince Boib, the son of Simeon by redemption, was old enough to be our sovereign. It was then that Pilliya signed a treaty with Idrimi of Alalakh, allying our people with the Mitanni empire in the east. He also made peace with King Zidanta II of Hattusa. In those days our leagues of nations were referenced as *Kizzuwatna*, first by the Egyptians, then by the Hethites, and then by the Mitanni.

After Haran was razed to ashes by the chariot armies of King Piyashshili of Hattusa, and in the course of the conquest of Mitanni, our people and warriors retreated back to Kilikia on the coast with access to the Great Sea. We were forced to abandon the contested trade territory in Haran and return to our people in the homeland of our forefathers; we again sojourned in the fertile lands between our two rivers in Kilikia and between the ancient cities of Iopolis and Tarzu. We returned to the place where we were sheltered by the mountains of Tiras on our northern border and the Kilikian Sea on our southern border.

According to the traditions of our people, the Port of Io was the ancient port that our Ionian forefathers established for importing and exporting commodities from Mesopotamia to and from Ilion, a store city near Marmara Island amidst the Sea of Marmara in the land of Progenitor Dardanus and our Dodecanese ancestors from Rhodes. The Port of Io had been quite busy with commerce over the centuries and expanded into a major port with access to the Great Sea.

It was great to reunite with our tribal nation in Kilikia once again. The demographic populations of Kilikia and Panphylia had changed considerably as uninvited Philistine, Sicilian, Tyrrhenian, Etruscan, Sardinian, and Lukka sea peoples overran our fertile plains. Many of the Hurrian sons of Patriarch Meshech that resided peaceably among our people in Kizzuwatna deserted the area and moved northeast away from the sea people beyond Tarzu, passing through the Kilikian gates, where they settled in Çatalhöyük and in Kappadokia east of Asia.

But fortunately, before the destruction of Haran, my father, First Prince Ougomun, and I were able to secure *The Book of the Chronicles of the Kings of Iobaath* and many other stone chronicles. During our time in Iopolis and while my mind served me well, I updated the ancient records delivered from king to king since the days of Progenitor Japheth. Our cherished written tradition etched in stones has been passed along from one generation to the next when the firstborn was mature and literate. I followed in the footsteps of the prince chroniclers who had gone before applying their traditional research practices by interviewing and questioning our reigning king and his princes.

Our noble, redeeming King Pilliya, the second son of King Mair, the son of King Ethach, was aged and feeble but easily recalled his former days. Our kinsman-redeemer and peacemaker reminisced and spoke of the days of the great famine in Canaan when the sons of Jacob sought aid and refuge in Egypt. It was reported that Perez, the son of Judah, the son of Jacob, a close friend of King Mair, the uncle of Pilliya, along with his two sons, Hezron and Hamul, were taken to Egypt during the famine.

The pharaohs of Egypt prospered in those days from the rich soil that emerged after an annual flooding of the River Nile. The Egyptians produced an abundance of flax, wheat, and barley. Like their Canaanite and Hethite cousins, the Egyptians acknowledged our Creator but sadly drifted far from the righteous instructions of Noah and attributed their prosperity to their highly exulted pharaoh-gods and their many powerless baals.

It was reported to me by a Phoenician merchant visiting Iopolis that Joseph, the beloved prince of Israel, was sold into slavery to traveling Egyptian merchants by his jealous brothers. But Joseph, a man of great integrity, rose to prominence in the courts of Pharaoh. Many years later Joseph proved magnanimous, forgiving the vile actions of Judah and his brothers.

But after the death of Joseph the descendants of Israel were enslaved and forced into making bricks under cruel taskmasters supervising Pharaoh's many building projects. The enslaved tribal nation of Shem shed much blood, sweat, and tears in Egypt under the rule of their cruel taskmasters.

While the sons of Israel were subjected to slavery, making bricks for Pharaoh's pyramids, our kingdom of Kilikia fought against the advancing chariots of Egypt in Canaan in the plains of Megiddo along the trade route that connected Egypt to Mesopotamia. To avoid becoming slaves of Pharaoh Thutmose III, the Mitanni confederation reluctantly partnered with the Canaanite kingdoms to defeat the Egyptian armies who were taking advantage of the famished and disadvantaged tribal nations there.

So the King of Kadesh built a fortress, as did the King of Megiddo. This defensive strategy angered Pharaoh Thutmose III, so with 15,000 chariots and foot soldiers, the Egyptian armies entered the valley of Jezreel and stormed the ancient walls of Megiddo that rose high above the fertile plains of Jezreel. Jezreel means "God sows" in the tongue of Eber, and in the valley of Jezreel, God sowed and authorized conflict as the armies of Pharaoh beat their swords into plowshares.

The Egyptian armies of Pharaoh Thutmose III were successful during the reign of King Pilliya and ruled over the southern Levantine Sea territories in Canaan. But King Pilliya sought support from our allies in the west and led our armies in resistance against Pharaoh's chariots. With strength from the LORD God of Japheth and aided by God-given resources, our brave hearts were successful and kept the Egyptian warriors from invading Kizzuwatna.

I learned from King Pilliya that the predictions of King Aurthach were accurate concerning the Hatti people growing in numbers and power to our north. The king reported that the tribal nation of Hattusa destroyed the Amorite people, the descendents of Togarmah, the younger brother of Riphath, the youngest son of Gomer. The sons of Riphath and Ashkenaz came to the aid of their Amorite cousins but were unable to conquer the well-armed Hethite armies of Hattusa. The once hospitable

Blach See of Gomer was now in the hands of the inhospitable Hethite sons of Canaan.

King Pilliya reported that after the Hethites destroyed the Amorites, the kings in the east, the sons of Patriarch Madai made an unholy alliance with the blood-thirsty pharaohs of Egypt and with the kings of Assyria headquartered in the city of Washukanni on the headwaters of the River Khabur. It was from their ruling seat in Washukanni that the Mitanni confederation reigned over our people from the Great Sea to Endon in the southern White Mountains of Kau. The Mitanni confederation waged war against the iron chariot people of Hatti in Hattusa. During the war between the Mitanni and the Hatti, a remnant of the Amorite sons of Patriarch Togarmah sought refuge with our kinsmen in Kilikia and Panphylia. Renowned as a God-fearing nation, we welcomed their arrival and granted them land for homesteading.

The pharaohs of Egypt and kings of Assyria had much to be concerned about. The Hatti people of Hattusa gained control of our well-established ancient trade routes, the Riphean mines of Tavia, and the coastal cities along the Aegean Sea in the west, including our great mother city of Ilion. The tribal nations of Hatti were industrious, renowned ironworkers, herdsmen, and warriors. They sacked the Riphean germ sojourning in Tavia and seized the ironworks there. They devoted little time for merriment or the sounds of music; neither did they seek after godly wisdom or an understanding mind as was the practice of our kinsmen.

Since the days of King Aurthach, we perceived that our season of peace and prosperity in the fertile plains of Kilikia were at great risk. The Hatti people of Hattusa have swift charioteers. Although the Hethite tribes lost their connection to Noah and were ignorant about the Way of the LORD God of Ham, they maintained a belief in their Creator and remained an innovative and industrial tribal nation. They engineered iron chariots with lighter wheels holding four spokes in the wheels with a third wheel in the middle. The innovative chariots from Hattusa provided their armies advantage over the Egyptians as their chariots were engineered to carry three armed charioteers with bows and arrows while the chariots of pharaoh carried only one armed charioteer.

During my ancestral research, I learned that Prince Boib, the son of King Simeon, the son of King Mair, and our people established the merchant village of Bottia on the outskirts of Iopolis on the eastern plains of the River Typhon. The village of Bottia was strategically located. The Port of Io to the west provided access to the Great Sea. This newly colonized territory was naturally protected from hostile invasions from the south, and allowed for excellent enterprise, especially with the Phoenicians in Sidon, Tyre, and Byblos, who emerged as super shipbuilders and trade negotiators and carriers throughout our world.

I learned from Prince Boib that for a season our people lived in seclusion and peace under the distant rule of the Mitanni confederation. But in the course of time our people enlarged and prospered from our lucrative trade relationships with the confederation and our Phoenician trade partners at sea as far as the remote and distant territories of Tarshish, in northern Afri, southern Iberia, and on the Great Isles of Atlantis.

As the village of Bottia prospered, Prince Thous, the son of Prince Boib, was able to travel extensively on the Great Sea and negotiate trade agreements with other developing nations and city-states. Prince Thous secured shipments of cypress logs from our ancestors on the Island of Rhodes and with our tribal cousins on the islands of Kittim and Caphtorim.

The River Typhon was of little use for navigation or irrigation but provided a river valley fit and profitable for travel and trade. The River Typhon was unusual and flowed north from the Springs of Labweh in the south, then through a rocky gorge dropping two thousand feet into the heart of the lake at Homs, where Prince Boib and our people also built a dam and colonized the surrounding areas. From Homs the River Typhon flows north through the plains of Bottia.

Prince Thous reconnected with our people living in the land of Tiras in the southern plains in the mountains of Tiras in the north and with our kinsmen in the great Asian cities of Ilion and Apasa, the capital of the Hethite kingdom of Arzawa in the west. With aid from our Dorian and Dodecanese kinsmen, our mother city of Ilion emerged from the ashes and was rebuilt. But unfortunately, the great city of our forefathers was once again destroyed by an earthquake. The city of Apasa to the south of Ilion became a prominent city benefiting from Ilion's frequent seasons of tribulation.

Like Dodanim, Prince Thous was a great leader and ambassador for our kingdom. It was reported that while rebuilding Ilion, Prince Thous visited Marmara Island in the midst of the Sea of Marmara. Prince Thous and his crew boarded a well-preserved ship that King Tarshish, the brother of King Dodanim, gave as a wedding present to his nephew, our epic King Iobaath. This well-crafted vessel built by hands of Tarshish provided for Iobaath's voyage from Ilion to the Island of Rhodes many generations ago. It was my understanding from the traditions of the merchant sailors that Prince Iobaath was originally commissioned by the Dodecanese sons of Javan to the Port of Io, but after his marriage was gifted with the Island of Rhodes. The sailors also told me that the ancient vessel was one of the first merchant ships that Tarshish built. Often moored at Ellis Island during the first quadrennial games, the colossal titan ship was admired by all who attended the games. I marveled at the brilliance and, particularly, the engineering skills of our forefathers after the flood of Noah. The buoyant vessel was a magnificent relic of our ancestors' superb craftsmanship, more brilliantly crafted than the Phoenician ships of our day.

Like Javan and his enterprising Ionian sons, Prince Thous and his sons sailed to Ilion with cedar logs, horses and oxen, ironworks, leather footwear, handcrafted musical instruments, finished linen tents, raw flax from our fields for producing linen clothing, and other cargo. Prince Thous reported that navigation through the Aegean Sea was difficult, but they were blessed with an excellent crew of merchant marines and oarsmen who provided the crew and cargo safe passage along the Asian coast by way of Apasa to their final Marmara destination.

Returning from Ilion, Prince Thous and the crew visited emerging ports of call on the Chief Sea. They visited the Makednoi nation along the northern coast to the west of Marmara Island. Then they traveled south along the coast to Athens, and then on to the lands of the mighty Spartan warriors. Thous was quite fortunate, and thankful to the LORD God, that they did not encounter the ships of Peirates on their voyage along the Aegean coast.

Prince Thous reported that he visited the seven islands of Iobaath in the Ionian Sea. He learned from our kinsmen there that the great Dodecanese Prince Iobaath, during the Great Race on Ellis Island, was tempted to swim the mysterious waters between the Peninsula of Haemus and the Italos Peninsula. Encouraged by our Dodecanese ancestors from Argos, Prince Iobaath swam across what was afterward named the Ionian Sea. This achievement embarrassed the mocking Spartan spectators. And thus, a feud began between the Dodecanese of Argos and their Spartan cousins on Ellis Island. Prince Thous also established trade with our Heptanese kinsmen who sojourn on the islands of Iobaath.

* * * * *

It was during this season of travel that Prince Thous learned about a Hebrew named Moses, a man of great faith, like Abraham, who was chosen and empowered by the LORD God of Noah to deliver the sons of Eber with signs and wonders from their bondage in Egypt. We learned of one, Aaron, the older brother of Moses, who took as his wife Elisheba, the daughter of Amminadab and the sister of Nahshon. Elisheba bore him four sons: Nadab, Abihu, Eleazar, and Ithamar. Amminadab, who was the son of Ram, who was the son of Hezron, and his son, Nahshon, died in the wilderness along with this entire generation, but Nahshon was numbered among the tribe of Judah on the east bank of the River Jordan before his death.

It was reported that thousands of unbelieving Hebrews perished in the wilderness without returning to their homeland. It was amazing to me that the LORD God of Noah had been so patient with the tens of thousands of rebellious Hebrews during their extended forty-year march from the Red Sea to the River Jordan.

During my interview with my father, Prince Ougomun, the son of Prince Thous, I learned that the sons of Abraham were once encamped on the east bank of the Jordan River. I was told that they appeared in number as the sands of the sea. I learned that Moses died there and did not enter the land of promise. However, one named Joshua was anointed by Moses to lead the armies of Israel and finally drive out the Canaanites from their land.

The LORD God of Shem was with Joshua in a mighty way. It was reported that the Israelites became ruthless warriors, killing men, women, and children, along with their herds. In the days of Prince Ougomun, we were fearful that the sons of Israel under the leadership of a trustworthy and faithful Joshua might invade and destroy the village of Bottia, the city of Iopolis, and seize the Port of Io and even venture as far as Tarzu in Kilikia.

But we were fortunate; our God, the LORD God of Shem and Japheth, gave Joshua a clear mandate, a detailed survey of their territory. I learned from Prince Ougomun that the God of Abraham was very specific about the geographic boundaries of their promised land. They inhabited the land between the Great Sea as their western boundary and the Great River Euphrates as their eastern boundary. The Red Sea was their southern boundary, and the ancient city of Laish and the southern mountains of Lebanon defined their northern boundary. I praised God that our bands were safe outside those God-ordained parameters. To this day the Hebrew nation sojourned within their borders and have never advanced into our homeland in Iopolis and Kilikia.

In those days, Prince Ougomun did not know our fate and wisely prepared our young men over the age of twenty for battle. But instead of becoming our enemy, Israel became a strong ally and trading partner. Our fear of invasion subsided. After recapturing their homeland, the God of Abraham raised up judges in the land to lead His people as Noah instituted after the flood, and as our kings had done since the days of Japheth.

During this season I established trade relations with Salmon, the son of Nahshon in Judah. The tribe of Judah emerged as the largest tribe in Israel. Salmon was wealthy and prospered. Salmon had a son named Boaz who married a widowed women named Ruth, a Moabite who was reported to have suffered great loss.

It was in the same year that Boaz married Ruth that I met and married Olive, named for the lucrative olive orchards of Panphylia. I named our firstborn son Alanus. Since his youth I taught Alanus about his noble heritage dating back to Japheth. I instructed my son about creation and the seven commandments of Noah. Even as a young child, Alanus romanticized about the ancient days and idolized Javan and his sons, the titans who lived for hundreds of years and accomplished the marvelous and seemingly impossible. Those men were titans in his eyes.

When Alanus was a young adult, he would often be seen loafing around the village square in Iopolis bantering about with the old men, asking questions about their origins. In those days many described my son as an idler, but I knew that Alanus was far from that description. Alanus was a born adventurer who simply enjoyed learning about ancient history and great men who feared God and kept His commandments. Alanus reported that in the village square he discovered that tribes from every tongue recalled the same creation and flood stories as written in our chronicles.

Influenced by his great-grandfather, Prince Thous, Alanus

persuaded us to move to Iopolis, where he could train to be captain of Prince Thous's ancient ship and where there was a larger market at which he could learn more interesting stories about our past.

My son Alanus and I had a warm father-son relationship, both fascinated by and somewhat fixated on our noble ancestry and heritage. It was there at the Port of Io that Alanus and I worked hand in hand repairing Prince Thous's ancient ship, the envy of all the merchant marines who moored there. At night Alanus amused himself by associating with the men of wisdom at the marketplace in the center of the city as he did in Iopolis.

As an advantaged Dodecanese prince, I sought after knowledge and wanted my maturing prince to have the best education in the world; so our people established schools with large libraries in Iopolis and Tarzu. The LORD God had prospered my way and provided abundantly for the building projects. As the nations migrated westward, the literacy center of our world shifted from Elba to the more central island of Kaptara. So upon completion of his home-based education in Kilikia, I made arrangements for Alanus to attend the best schools of knowledge in Knossos on the island of Kaptara, where Alanus could complete his tertiary education and learn even more ancient stories.

It was in Knossos on the island of Kaptara that my son mastered tribal languages and became an ethnologist. Desiring to organize the Greek tongue for writing purposes and using the familiar Phoenician alphabet, Alanus and his colleagues successfully created an alternative phonetic-based Knossos Greek language. Alanus reported that the Mykēnē world was resistant and did not quickly embrace the new Phonetician-based Knossos Greek alphabet. But the linguists correctly predicted its future acceptance among the nations.

My son spoke of one Aeolic-speaking fellow, Homeros, a master of linguistics and ethnology who was also a minstrel and poet. It was reported that Homeros drew inspiration from a copy of an ancient twelve-tablet Akkadian version of the *Epic of Gilgamesh* that recently arrived in Knossos from a library in Nineveh. Our people were very familiar with these oral and written traditions that spoke of the musicality and poetic nature of the sons of Patriarch Madai, where the inspiration for the ancient epic poem originated.

Homeros and Alanus were kindred spirits and romanticized often about the ancients. However, Alanus was more given to theology and historical facts while Homeros, influenced by Greek mythology, was given to historical fantasy. While in Knossos, Alanus encouraged Homeros to write poetry, and Homeros encouraged Alanus to pursue the adventurous desires of his heart and maintain his ancient historical chronicles for future generations.

While sojourning on the island of Kaptara, Homeros invited Alanus to help with the geographical and ethnic research required for one of his books. The envisioned manuscript would be a catalogue of the Aeolian league of nations on ships filled with warriors waiting on orders from the titan gods to attack Troy in Asia. Homer and Alanus understood that Troy was the great ancient store city of Ilion.

My son was the perfect choice for this assignment as he had been studying tribal ancestry for many years and knew the peculiar characteristics of various Aeolian and Asian tribes. Alanus told me that he felt honored to share in the project and pleased that at least one of the Homeros's books was rooted in tribal history and not fantasy. Homeros appreciated the believable, historical perspective that Alanus provided to his novel.

After Alanus completed his linguistic studies in Kaptara, and while sojourning at the Port of Io, great tragedy visited our people in eastern Kilikia. While the Israelites were possessing their God-given territory, our people remained caught between the chariots of the pharaohs of Egypt to our south and the chariots of the kings of Hattusa to our north.

In the days of King Ougomun, the Assyrians, Hurrians, and Egyptians resisted Hethite aggression, but the Hatti people persisted and eventually ruled our lands and all of Mesopotamia. Then under King Suppululiuma, the chariots of Hattusa clashed with the chariots of Egypt in Kadesh on the southern shores of the Typhon River beyond Homs. It was reported that five thousand chariots converged there and thousands died in the pitched battle fought in Kadesh.

King Pilliya died at the age of one hundred and thirty. Prince Boib and his son, Prince Thous, and his son, Prince Ougomun, were all killed by the advancing armies of the Hatti, fifty thousand strong, en route to Kadesh to wage war against the chariots of Egyptian Pharaoh Ramesses II. The aging princes foolishly attempted to prevent the Hatti from trespassing on our trade routes and were cut down in Homs, where our brave men, both young and old, fearlessly resisted the well-armed northern warriors.

We grieved and mourned the loss of Prince Boib, the warrior, and those who fought and perished in brutal warfare. Alanus and I might have perished in the resistance like the others if we had not relocated to the Port of Io and occupied ourselves with academics and seafaring activities. Alanus and I felt as if God had a greater purpose for our existence. We felt a strong sense of destiny, as though our circumstances were about to change. We saw this tragedy as an opportunity to change what was about to come.

It was after the battle in Kadesh that our desires grew stronger to migrate to the land of Dodanim. Our kings reasoned that Ramesses II would come back our way one day after the Eyptians defeated the confederate Levant armies at Megiddo. But it was many centuries later, in Kadesh, that the advancing chariots of Egypt clashed with the chariots of the powerful Hittite nation to our north. Although we were sheltered from direct attacks in Kilikia, we were weary of constant conflict, surrounded by violence all around us. We longed for a more peaceful environment for our kingdom.

Twenty-five years had passed since the pitched chariot battle in Kadesh when the highly anticipated war broke out between our Aeolian cousins and our Assuwan allies in Troy. I learned from Alanus that the Aeolian sons of Javan sailed to Ilion to recover one, Helen, who lived there. She was the beautiful wife of Menelaus, the king of Mycenae, who had been abducted by Paris, the son of Priam, the reigning king of Troy. Alanus reported that his friend Homeros was obsessed with writing about the conflict mustering in the Chief Sea.

After ten years of failed attempts to capture the ancient and great Asian city founded by Rhodanim, Homeros reported to Alanus that the Aeolians achieved final victory by erecting a mammoth wooden horse that housed warriors. Once the horse was received within the walled city, the Aeolians leapt from the decoy and torched our ancient Ilion to ashes. Without their great Etruscan city, the sons of Tiras left Asia, sailed toward the Sea of Tarshish, and relocated to the peninsula of Italos, where it was reported by many that they built cattle ranches and planted vineyards.

As Dodecanese we struggled in our allegiances, being ancient allies with the Etruscan Trojans of Troy but also ancestral cousins of the Mycenaean sons of Javan. Our hearts were torn and greatly conflicted in the whole matter. This circumstance also encouraged the change that we so desperately desired.

After the third destruction of Ilion, Alanus, now in possession of and captain of Prince Thous's ships, finally persuaded me for adventure. Captain Prince Alanus was a peacemaker and convinced me to move away from Kilikia, Tarzu, Iopolis, and the village of Bottia. He argued that we had seen enough of war, bloodshed, chariots, war horses, Aeolian battleships, Sea People, and piracy. We were also weary of the idolatry and debauchery of the Hittites, Canaanites, Egyptians, and the Hebrews, who all seemed to have abandoned their Creator in times of peace. With fear in his heart, Prince Alanus argued that if our people stayed in Kilikia, we might cease to exist as a nation.

My young beloved prince desired to explore the ancient

world of Japheth, Javan, and Dodanim. My son wanted to fulfill the call of God spoken by Noah to Shem, Japheth, and Ham after the great worldwide flood, saying, "Be fruitful and multiply and inhabit the earth." The passion to go grew strong in his heart. Captain Alanus was blessed with an understanding mind and so made the fulfillment of the Word of God his greatest priority, quest, and soul ambition. Prince Alanus grew intentional about fulfilling the great commandment of the LORD God to spread the glory of God to the nations. My son sought the Lord daily for faith and guidance.

So preparing for our migration, we gathered our people, our cargo, and our herds. After warning our people of the dangers, but also the opportunities of migration, we set sail for the ancient land of Dodanim that Prince Thous had told us about.

We questioned the merchant marines about passage from Iopolis through the Aegean Sea. They warned us that sons of Peirates remained a threat, were hostile, and invaded ships passing between the Island of Rhodanim and the mainland. They also warned us about nor'easters and treacherous north winds that drove many large merchant ships off course; some of them capsized. Understanding that we might encounter adversity, we chose to be patient, agreeing to continue plans avoiding stormy seasons.

During our voyage from Iopolis to the Balkan territories of Dodanim, Prince Alanus and I had long talks on dark starry nights. One night Alanus shared his desires to marry among the daughters of Dodanim and to have a fruitful kingdom with many sons and grandsons. I encouraged my son, affirming his natural desires to marry, procreate, and, like Abraham, be the father of many nations. According to our tradition, I prayed for my son, Alanus, just as Japheth prayed over his firstborn, Gomer, that the LORD God would bless and expand his seed.

Leaving the Kilikian Sea, we carefully traveled along the northern coast of the Great Sea, but we never reached our desired destination port in Apasa on the Aegean Sea. During our journey we prudently sent scouts before us. They returned with news that the feared sons of Peirates were encamped in coves where the Tiras Mountains end in the west, adjacent to the Island of Rhodes, just as the merchant marines warned. We did not want a conflict that would endanger our people, so we committed our desires to the LORD God and waited patiently for His timing.

Although discouraged in spirit, we wisely suspended our journey, postponed our pilgrimage to the land of Dodanim and Morava, and established a colony along the coastline in Panphylia that would serve well as a port for high adventure on the Great Sea while providing protection from aggressors. We also reasoned that we were not too distant from our ancient homeland between Tarzu and Iopolis where we could learn more about the landscape of our world in the ancient city of Çatalhöyük to our north.

Like King Mair, Prince Alanus spent much time in the city of Çatalhöyük, studying drawings of the known world. It was thought by some in the city of Çatalhöyük that the Great Isles of Javan could be reached by river. Some proposed the notion that the River Danu of Riphath that flowed west connected somewhere with another river that flowed north to a northern sea. And from that northern sea, the Great Isles could be approached.

We informed the geographers that the River Morava flowed south from the Danu into the Balkans, avoiding the Cimmerian and Scythian armies of Skythia, who invaded the northeastern territory above the Danu. Knowing that navigating such a large ship upstream would be tedious, we were persuaded of a surer route that Prince Thous used on his trip to the Ionian Islands that Iobaath discovered beyond Ellis Island. From the Ionian islands, we were informed that our ships could cross the Ionian Sea to the great island of Syrakousai in the Sea of Tarshish.

So while Prince Alanus waited on the Lord, we built the Port of Alanya below the Mountains of Tiras in a rural territory west from Kilikia. Alanus reminded me that the coastal land was named Pamphyloi by our Dorian kinsmen because so many tribes migrated to the bay area seeking refuge. Between the mountains and the Great Sea, we rediscovered above the plains a forest of cedar trees, evergreen scrub, fig trees, and black pine. Since the cedar was ideal for shipbuilding, we reasoned that God seemed to be encouraging our vision and leading us to this territory. In those days we bred and exported horses and also cedar to the Phoenicians.

We discovered that we were not the first to discover this hospitable land. There was evidence all around us that ancients, perhaps even Tiras, the Red Bull, the youngest son of Japheth, harvested cedar from this very place. We pondered that perhaps the ship of Tarshish that we refurbished at the Port of Io was built from trees harvested from these ancient cedar forests.

Once we were settled into our new homestead, we traveled back to Iopolis. We told our people in Iopolis about the newfound territory that we had rediscovered and encouraged them to join us there to escape danger. We reestablished a naval trade route along the southern coast of Kilikia from the Island of Rhodes in the west, to the Port of Call in Alanya, to the Port of Call in Iopolis, including the Island of Kittim in the east.

Alanus understood that the descendents of Rhodanim established settlements in the Dodecanese islands in the days of Iobaath and aided Tiras in the capturing of Peirates. Rhodes was the largest of the Dodecanese islands. So as his heart desired, and as God satisfies the desires of our heart, Prince Alanus sought out a wife in the city of Rhodes.

Alanus was so excited when he met Alexis. As her name seemed to foretell, he believed Alexis would be the helpmate for whom his soul longed. Alanus reported to me that Alexis was the keeper of the beautiful rhododendron gardens that graced the island. The lovely flowering rose trees reminded Alanus of the rose gardens at Endon Lake recorded in our tradition. Alanus imagined a romantic life of wine and roses just like the life of Japheth and Naamah. Alanus presumed that her name and her rose trees were a sure sign from God that Alexis was meant to be his helpmate. Of course Prince Alanus had my consent to marry the young virgin from Rhodes, for I trusted his judgments better than my own!

Within a few years, I announced the wedding celebration, and Alanus and Alexis married. They had two sons who Prince Alanus named Hessittio and Armenon. Both learned the ship-building trade of their father and myself. They also helped harvest wood and metals from the forest and mountains. Alanus was proud of his strapping young sons. It reminded him of days of old, of Javan and his four shipbuilding sons. The home of Alanus and Alexis was surrounded by tranquil rhododendron gardens; their life was full of romance and hospitality. All were welcomed at their homestead in Alanya.

Alanus desired more sons and daughters, but the wife of his youth, Alexis, died prematurely, tragically bleeding to her death in childbirth. Everyone was amazed when Negue, their third son, survived the breech birth, but he was denied his mother's breast milk. My heart was full of compassion for my grandson, Negue, who was birthed without a mother's nurturing.

Prince Alanus became a widower and never married again. For a season the spirit of Alanus was crushed and filled with great despair and sorrow. The rhododendron gardens of Alexis were a constant reminder of their short married life together. He grieved the loss of Alexis for many years and occupied his remaining days with great adventure. It was during this season of mourning that he made up his mind to migrate away from Alanya and the memories.

God blessed and prospered Prince Alanus and his three sons. They all became wealthy from their trade industry. As Hurrians from the east migrated into our ancient homeland in Kilikia, our kinsmen from Iopolis and Tarzu migrated west to Alanya in Panphylia, and there we grew in numbers. As homesteaders we were greatly encouraged by their knowledge in husbandry.

The LORD God multiplied the seed of Captain Alanus in Alanya. Hessittio, his firstborn son, was nicknamed Hesse. Hesse was a tall, handsome man who married among the daughters of

Kittim, the son of Javan, sojourning on the Island of Kittim. They had four sons and four daughters. In the course of time, all of their children married and had sons and daughters. I was blessed to have fifty-six great-grandsons and granddaughters through the germ of Prince Hessittio. They all sojourned in Panphylia.

Armenon, the second son of Prince Alanus, married a Phoenician woman who claimed to be a descendent of King Iobaath. Armenon and his Phoenician wife had five sons and seven daughters. In the course of time, all their children married and had sons and daughters. I was blessed with sixty-eight great-grandsons and granddaughters from the germ of Armenon. They also sojourned in Panphylia.

And Negue, the third son of Prince Alanus, married the youngest daughter of King Boib. Negue and his wife, Adana, had three sons and five daughters. All of their eight children married and had sons and daughters. I was blessed to have forty-seven great-grandsons and granddaughters from the germ of Negue. They too sojourned in Panphylia.

After our people expanded and colonized Alanya in Panphylia, the sons and able grandsons of Alanus helped me build a port in a cove on a small peninsula that jetted out from the mainland in Lukka on the coast to the west of Alanya and adjacent to the Island of Rhodes. The territory was known by the Dodecanese as Telmessus, but Alanus honored me and named the cove city Fethiye.

The views from the rugged mountain ridges of Fethiye overlooking the mysterious waters of the Great Sea were majestic. These eyes had never seen such a beautiful place. It was there in the easternmost peeks of the mountains of Tiras beside the land of Lukka that I retired from shipbuilding and high adventures.

Prince Lukka, the son of my cousin, Finike, also helped us build Fethiye. Finike survived the battle against the Hattusa armies, escaping their chariots hiding in the waters of the river Typhon. Our numbers expanded under the leadership of Lukka, who led our warriors in resistance against the Hatti peoples who still troubled our coastal kinsmen on the Island of Rhodes, in Lukka, in Panphylia, in Kilikia, and on the Island of Kittim. Lukka and his navy also routed and cleared the vermin sons of Peirates from the coastal mountain coves.

I learned that a band of our Dodecanese ancestors from Rhodes and a band of their cousins from Crete united with the marines of Lukka. This hodgepodge of sea people invaded Egypt and the eastern coast of Canaan where they recruited other orphaned sea people. Lukka and his league of sea people captured several of the coastal towns south of Sidon and north of Egypt in Canaan.

Prince Lukka, the captain of the sea people, was well known and feared for his violent ways among the Hatti nation, among the Egyptians, among the Israelites, and among the coastal nations of the Great Sea. Upon hearing these reports, I boldly rebuked Lukka and expressed my opposition to his imperial and violent nature. On several occasions I appealed to Lukka to pursue the path of righteousness and peacemaking men, but my words fell on deaf ears.

From Lukka I learned that there was a growing desire among the sons of Abraham in Canaan for a king. For hundreds of years after their deliverance from Egypt, Israel was united under titan-like judges that arose among the people. The Patriarch Noah instructed the sons of Shem, Ham, and Japheth to appoint judges wherever they settled. So this practice was rooted in all tribal nations of the earth. However, our people maintained respect for our ancestors and the orderly succession of kings from Japheth until this day.

For hundreds of years the sons of Abraham seldom desired a king, instead proclaiming the LORD God of Noah as their Sovereign King. This news brought great sorrow to me that they would desire a man to rule over them, abandoning such privilege as the chosen race that would bring forth the promised Seed of Abraham who was to come. I have learned from history that most governments of men drift from great benevolence toward great tyranny, expanding government, and lording over its citizens with burdensome regulations and taxation.

As the king of our kingdom in Panphylia, I know no other government save the government of God. I have come to the conclusion that all governments are on His shoulders. Kings and kingdoms, they all pass away, but the Name of the LORD is from everlasting to everlasting. His kingdom knows no end. My desire is that the whole earth be ruled by the glory of the LORD God of Noah and Abraham. Our people feel secure when they know and observe that my trust is in the government of God. They understand that God and I, his humble servant, are working all things together for the good of those who put their trust in His statutes and obey His righteous way. With all that abides within me, I long for the government of God to rule and bring lasting peace to this violent, sin-laden world.

* * * * *

While sojourning on the rocky clefts of Fethiye, news spread about the Etruscan sons of Tiras who discovered gold in Iberia on the remote seas of Tarshish. Gold was a most coveted resource in our day, and I suppose that it will be forevermore. Prince Alanus was most interested in this news about finding gold, which motivated him even more to leave Panphylia to explore the world. My son had been patient for many years waiting for the right season. Alanus was eager to follow his heart and find his destiny. He had great vision and foresaw great opportunity in providing goods and services to the expanding and prospering Etruscan nation in the west.

Prince Alanus and I spent many days discussing his strengthening desire to explore the Iberian Peninsula with his Etruscans friends. I observed that the anticipation of discovering gold mines and other precious metals elated the heart of Prince Alanus. My three grandsons were also excited about the news. I reasoned that it was just a matter of time before Prince Alanus and his sons would put feet to their great expectations.

Negue and his band visited me regularly in Fethiye. Negue confided in me and shared his own migration plan from Panphylia to Iberia. Preferring land routes to waterways, Negue desired to take a more familiar route by land and water to their Iberian destination. He proposed traveling by sea from Alanya to Rhodes, then by sea from Rhodes to Apasa, then by seas from Apasa to Ilion, then by seas from Ilion along the coast of Thracia, by seas from Thracia to the territory of Dodanim, from Dodanim by land travel northward along the Moravian River Valley, then by land from the Moravian River Valley to the River Danu of Riphath, by river to the mountains of Riphath, and finally by land across the mountains of Riphath to Iberia.

Although Negue's travel plans were well established in our tradition and made great sense, I consoled and reminded him that his father, Captain Prince Alanus, and both of his older brothers, Hessitio and Armenon, desired to make the voyage on the Great Sea away from Alanya to Iberia from Ellis Island to Syracuse. Negue was discouraged but submitted to his father's desires. Negue made a vow, saying, "As the Lord lives and as the Lord leads, I will to follow my heart and migrate from Alanya to the Riphean Mountains and to the glaciers and rivers of Rhodanim one day! But first, I will honor my father and travel with him and my brothers to Iberia."

Prince Negue also had a desire to find gold and argued that the Riphean Mountains might be filled with the sparkling treasure. Like his father, Negue had a heart of adventure. He knew he had a destiny, a purpose for being, and he refused to give up until all the desires of his heart were fulfilled in the Riphean Mountains.

After many years of research, I, King Fetebir, sojourning high above the cove at Fethiye overlooking the Dodecanese islands, the scribe and chronicler of the sons of Iobaath, hereby preserve a record for posterity in *The Book of the Chronicle of the Kings of Iobaath*:

Francus was the son of Hessittio. Hessittio was the son of Alanus. Alanus was the son of Fetebir. Fetebir was the son of Ougomun. Ougomun was the son of Thous. Thous was the son of Boib. Boib was the son of Simeon. Simeon was the son of Mair. Mair was the son of Ethach. Ethach was the son of Aurthach. Aurthach was the son of Ecthet. Ecthet was the son of Oth. Oth was the son of Abir. Abir was the son of Rea. Rea was the son of Ezra. Ezra was the son of Izrau. Izrau was the son of Baath. Baath was the son of Iobaath. Iobaath was the son of Rhodanim. Rhodanim was the son of Javan. Javan was the son of Japheth. Japheth was the son of Noah. Noah was the son of Lamech, Lamech was the son of Methuselah, Methuselah was the son of Enoch, Enoch was the son of Jared, Jared was the son of Mahalaleel, Mahalaleel was the son of Cainan, Cainan was the son of Enos, Enos was the son of Seth, Seth was the son of Adam. Adam was the son of God.

FOUR

THE CHRONICLES OF KING LATINUS

(1200 BC)

ALANUS AND HIS SONS were weary from centuries of tribal warfare. In pursuit of academic achievement, they had little interest in the bloodthirsty conquests of their cousin, Lukka. The sons of Captain King Alanus were enlightened adventures, a band with strong desires to boldly venture westward on the Great Sea toward Tarshish in the west to the new Etruscan frontier, where there was gold, and toward the ancient Great Isles of Javan, where there was tin. Like the pioneering sons of Japheth, they desired to explore the ocean of Atlantis and become masters of their God-ordained destinies.

My great-grandfather, Captain King Alanus, was a well-educated first prince who adhered to the traditions of his father, King Fetebir, the chronicler in his generation who kept and made entries in our incredible record of ancestry. He was a seasoned linguist and ethnologist who educated his princes well in the traditions of our fathers as recorded in *The Book of the Chronicles of the Kings of Iobaath.*

Captain Alanus believed in God, feared God, and sought guidance from God in all his affairs. He understood the spiritual realm as our tradition teaches about the epic Job, how Satan desired to dissuade Job from faith in our Creator and how the LORD God honored Job's faith. Our noble king from Alanya desired to please the LORD God of Japheth, and like Abraham he walked by faith in the way of the LORD.

Grateful for the many chroniclers who had gone before him, Alanus understood that his divine purpose was to go into all the earth and be enlarged, just as Noah prayed, and as God had directed his steps. He understood that this was God's plan for mankind since the arc of time began.

When the princes of Alanus were about twenty years old, I learned that he laid hands on his three sons and prayed the blessings of Noah and Japheth over his seed: "God Almighty, I present these sons to you to fulfill your desires in them to enlarge the tribes of Japheth. May they forever fear you and worship you alone. I also pray for peace over the Hebrew nation, the sons of Abraham, Isaac, and Jacob."

They all had an understanding mind and desired to populate the earth according to the Word of the Lord. The sons born in Panphylia were educated in the Way and possessed with a peacemaking, God-fearing, pioneering mindedness. None of the sons or grandsons of Captain King Alanus sought out violence or concerned themselves with warfare, although Alanus, the Peacemaker, prepared all of his princes for battle in the event that Panphylia was attacked by hostile intruders by land or sea. Like the great Etruscan Patriarch Tiras, King Alanus was endowed with great protective instincts and wisely instituted a strong defensive-based strategy for guarding his colony in Alanya.

After relocating to Fethiye in Lukka, King Fetebir granted all governing authority to his able son. The peaceful tribal kingdom of Alanya was well managed and exuded integrity and strength. Captain King Alanus instituted a judicial system as recommended by Noah according to our tradition. He appointed judges who enforced works of righteousness and moral ethics among our people: civic, ceremonial, and religious duties. They enforced the seven laws of Noah, teaching: "My sons, keep your father's command, and do not forsake the law of your mother. Bind them continually upon your heart; tie them around your neck. When you roam, they will lead you; when you sleep, they will keep you; and when you awake, they will speak with you."

Like his fathers before him, Captain King Alanus instructed his generation in the seven things that God hates. He often quoted the Hebrew proverb, saying: "These six things the LORD hates, yes, seven are an abomination to Him: a proud look, a lying tongue, hands that shed innocent blood, a heart that devises wicked plans, feet that are swift in running to evil, a false witness who speaks lies, and one who sows discord among brethren."

Captain King Alanus discouraged being unequally yoked with unbelievers, those who denied the Creator-God of Noah and Japheth. King Alanus forbid the worship of idols and all immoral sexual behaviors. Although I was but a youth in those days, I remember that we all felt secure, well protected, and cared for during his benevolent reign. Panphylia was a safe haven to our spirits; we walked in love and in faith, fearing no man, only our LORD God. Captain King Alanus was a man of great courage and proven character in his generation, respected by all his peers in Panphylia and surrounding nations.

I remember when Captain King Alanus was saddened by the news that Lukka and his armies had waged war against the sons of Abraham, Isaac, and Jacob. Although Lukka believed in our Creator, he forgot his noble roots, lost all discernment, and treated the blessed sons of Shem, Eber, and Abraham as the cursed sons of Canaan. He did not fear God Almighty, but was seduced by the animism of Manu, who spent too much time with Canaan, subjecting himself to the sensuous deities of the damned.

Once, returning from the vineyards of Timnah, we learned from the sea people that one named Samson was born of the

Hebrew tribe of Dan and had married a Philistine woman from Timnah, the vineyard city that King Mair visited many years ago. They told us that the Philistines ruled over all Israel and that Samson was as the Nephilim, a giant among men with the strength of Herakles. It was reported that Samson ripped a lion apart with his hands, destroyed a grainfield by tying torches to the tails of three hundred foxes, and slew one thousand Philistines with the jawbone of a donkey. It was reported that Samson was raised up by the God of Abraham to defeat the Philistines, and he did so single-handedly.

* * * * *

The day finally came when Captain King Alanus and his princes made the difficult decision to leave their beloved city of Alanya and their homeland in Panphylia to relocate to Iberia, where they had confirmation there was gold. I learned that King Alanus purchased Etruscan gold from a merchant in Iopolis. While holding the Iberian gold he had purchased, he made the decision—one he had thoroughly thought through—to make preparations for our long and dangerous voyage.

So with God Almighty as his Sovereign, Captain King Alanus, his three princes, and their familia boarded vessels and navigated westward with plans to stop briefly on the Island of Rhodes and the nearby Island of Kaptara, which our dear friend, Homeros, renamed Crete. Afterward they continued on to ancient Ellis Island, where the mighty Spartan warriors sojourned. They all prayed to the LORD God for safe passage, carefully navigating on the lee of the islands to shelter their vessels from heavy north winds. God answered their prayers; they safely moored without incident at Argos on the east facing the ancient Peloponnesian peninsula.

I was instructed that Captain King Alanus wanted to learn more about the mysterious Atlantis frontier. So after brief visits in Korinth and Sparta, he sought mooring at the ancient port at Ellis Island in Olympia, where our tradition teaches that Rhodanim, progenitor and son of Javan, competed and was victor at the quadrennial games hosted there.

Hearing about the homecoming of the sons of Dodanim the Runner, the sons of Elishah (the son of Javan), on the west coast of Ellis Island, greeted the noble Dodecanese from Panphylia with great joy and celebration. We discovered that the Olympic athletes in Ellis believed in our Creator, but at the same time idolized our common ancestry in their distorted traditions, telling fantastic stories of one, Zeus, who our people call Japheth, the Great Voice. The symbols of Zeus include the thunderbolt, the eagle, the bull, and the oak tree—all symbols of power and strength in the heavens and on the earth.

Tiras, the youngest son of Japheth, they called Taurus, and he was a magnificent white bull of a man who abducted the Phoenician Princess Europa. From our own traditions, we confirmed that Europa, the wife of Tiras, was no myth. And of course the legends about the exploits of the antediluvian titan Heracles abounded in our chronicles. We presumed that the white bull represented the white Asian auroch that Tiras herded and domesticated. Our people understood Heracles as being a misguided, demon-possessed Nephilim from before the great flood of Noah, when the mysterious first earth was completely destroyed by waters that reached beyond the clouds.

There were rumors among the Ionian Olympians of resurrecting the ancient competitive titan games in honor of Zeus, but no one was found among their people who was administratively charismatic enough to take on the challenge of organizing and promoting the epic games. Plus, there was much tribal conflict in the world. We did not live in a peace-filled time. I ascertained that the Olympic games would never be reinstituted as the sons of Javan continued in civil wars among themselves, one kingdom waging war with another.

Our people and our forefathers were well acquainted with the great Etruscan traditions. The mountains of Taurus abide as the northern border of Kilikia, and they are also home to King Fetebir on the cliffs of Fethiye in Lukka. The name of Taurus, the Bull—whether red or white—was so famous that it was used to name one of the first constellations identified in the heavens. And as I recall, the first letter in our *alphabeta* was the symbol of Taurus. It then occurred to me that the Etruscan sons of Taurus have been allies of the Dodecanese since our genesis.

From our copy of the *Epic of Gilgamesh* that I have read several times, I learned that the goddess, Ishtar, sent Gilgamesh to kill Taurus, the Bull of Heaven, for spurning the lustful advances of Ishtar. The Bull of Heaven is closely associated with Nana, the goddess of sexual love, fertility, and warfare. We were also accustomed to sordid tales about the lustful days of Tiras and Europa, but also reports of their recovery, fertility, and war against the pirates of the highly contested trade routes on the Aegean Sea.

Many of our people have been seduced by these Olympian myths, but a few tribal nations held to the sound traditions of Japheth and Noah. Like the Hebrew nation, a remnant of our people hold fast to their traditions and reject idolatry along with their high places. Except for a few apostate kings, the sons of Iobaath rejected the things that God hates, the numerous baals and titans and goddesses of the Canaanites, Egyptians, Etruscans, Hatti, Iconiums, Ionians, Syroi, and Phoenicians.

After our lengthy visit on Ellis Island, where we visited the sacred high places where Japheth preformed animal sacrifices to the LORD God of Noah with his seven sons, we returned to Alanya again, stopping briefly in Crete, where they had also built altars to our Creator.

The vision of traveling to Atlantis grew large in the heart of Captain Alanus. He shared his ideas often with kinsmen that he desired to visit Tarshish, the newfound region of our Etruscan neighbors, and the Great Isles of Javan. Captain Alanus desired to explore the northern regions of the river that Rhodanim discovered and return to the northern frontier of Dodanim by way of the River Danu and the River Morava of Riphath.

At first the sons of Captain Alanus believed that their father had gone mad, and in jest they mocked their father's desires. But in the course of time and as Alanus patiently waited, God changed the hearts of Alanus's sons and grandsons. With wild adventure calling the heart of every man with great abandonment, we all finally embraced the vision of our beloved Captain King Alanus, and in one accord, we all desired to make the great journey to destinations beyond the new Etruscan frontier.

Captain King Alanus was encouraged by one, King Nemedius, a Skuthai kinsman-chronicler from Skythia. King Nemedius was a distant relative and close friend of King Fetebir. King Fetebir reported that King Nemedius was about to travel to the Great Isles of Javan. But before King Nemedius left on his long journey to the Great Isles, King Fetebir appealed to him to correct the misinformation that had been recorded in their chronicle of kings. But King Nemedius was convinced that their record was accurate, that Patriarch Magog was the progenitor of our people and not Patriarch Javan. Although King Fetebir understood why King Nemedius would think that Magog was his progenitor, the granddaughter of Magog being in the maternal ancestry of the kings of Rhodanim, King Alanus was confident that the paternal seed within his loins was that of Javan.

To continue the ancestral argument that his father began, Captain King Alanus desired to find the Skuthai king and chronicler on the northernmost island of the Great Isles, which was said to have been colonized by the Skuthai tribe of King Nemedius. Like his father, King Alanus was convinced that King Iobaath was the son of Javan, the son of Japheth. According to the record of our Skuthai kinsmen, recorded in their *Book of the Chronicles of the Skuthai Nation*, Patriarch Magog from the land of Kau was the father of King Jobhath, who we know as King Iobaath. King Baath, the son of Iobaath according to our chronicles, was recorded in the Skuthai chronicles as the brother of Jobhath. King Fathochta was recorded as the son of Patriarch Magog; our tradition also records Fathochta as the son of Magog. Although they did find many areas of agreement in their ancient chronicles, this matter caused no small conflict among the descendants of King Nemedius and the descendents of King Fetebir, especially by my grandfather, Hessittio, the firstborn of Captain King Alanus, who insisted that Japheth was the progenitor of the Skuthai nation.

* * * * *

It was during this time that I attended school in Crete, as was the tradition of our kings, as I continued my tertiary education. Like my great-grandfather I became a linguist and studied ethnology in Knossos on Crete. I loved to read the ancient chronicles and took advantage of the thousands of papyrus scrolls and ancient stone chronicles of kings in the libri where they were archived. I also read some of the newer literature including the books of Homeros.

One day I longed to develop our own tribal language rooted in Knossos Greek by using the phonetic alphabeta. But in those days I wrote lyrics, mostly psalms, and music, while learning to play the pfeife. After my schooling was completed in Knossos, I returned to Panphylia and our people in Alanya where we awaited our much-anticipated launch date. As we waited I was much aware of the great patience of King Alanus as he waited on the Lord.

My cousin, Elishah, the son of Britto, married in his youth. After the birth of his son, Dardanus, he left to aid the defense of the great city of Ilion. Elishah feared no man, and with great courage he returned to Ilion to stand with the men there who were under siege. After the city was destroyed, Elishah survived and returned to Alanya with a discouraging report. Upon his return Elishah suffered from memories of the battle and the bloodshed. He lost many friends in the gruesome combat and felt guilty that he survived while others had their flesh torn asunder. When Elishah returned from Ilion, we were all ready for the anticipated launch date.

With a great sense of destiny and guidance from the LORD God of Japheth, Captain King Alanus boarded vessels with his sons and grandsons along with all their wives, daughters, and household servants.

King Fetebir was very wise, a wealthy man with much gold. He often told us, "It is not the profit you make from a covenant; it's what you save afterward. It is the gold and silver that you keep and do not squander of depreciating assets and worthless amusements. That is what measures the wealth of a man!" So spending his accumulated wealth, King Fetebir purchased three of the swiftest of Phoenician vessels and hired the most experienced crew from Byblos. Although I reasoned that ships are depreciating assets, I understood that our king was being generous. I discovered that King Fetebir paid oarsmen double wages to motion our vessels.

So with the oarsmen and other essential crewmen recruited, we loaded our cargo on three well-crafted ships and set sail toward the Sea of Tarshish, westward on the well-trodden trade routes of King Thou.

In jest and complete mockery of Greek mythology, Captain King Alanus named his three ships Europa I, II, and III; Europa is the name of the moon of the planet Jupiter, who was named after Japheth. The Olympians spoke of Europa as a Phoenician noblewoman who was courted by Zeus and became Queen of the Island of Crete, where the Phoenician sons of Sidon also built a colony. Alanus named our ships Europa I, Europa II, and Europa III, one for each of his three beloved princes. The *familia* of Prince Hessittio boarded Europa I. The familia of Prince Armenon boarded Europa II. And the kinsmen of Prince Negue boarded Europa III.

Before we ventured westward, Captain King Alanus charged me, Latinus, the son of Romanus, the son of Hessittio, with protecting and maintaining the treasured *Book of the Chronicles of the Kings of Iobaath*. Although I thought others were much more qualified for the task, I counted it an honor to be chosen by our king. I had spent much time with King Fetebir in Fethiye as the king's scribe, recording the traditions of our people in Knossos Greek as he dictated. The others entertained no selfish ambition or jealous spirit, but instead expressed encouragement to me and support of our captain's choice in word and deed.

I was not a social spirit, but a man who spent much of his time alone focused on developing a new written language that I termed *Latin*. I was also not as anxious about finding a wife as my cousin, Elishah, had been. Like Captain King Alanus, I had great expectations and believed that my new written language would replace all other written languages, and that one day it would simplify the communication of arts and sciences among all our tribal nations. Our kinsmen were not a people who embraced new ideas readily, but I believed in them and in the LORD God, who authorized ethnic diversity in all its expressions by *genos, glossa,* and *topos.*

So as the distinguished chronicler for our people, I was granted a private quarter aboard Europa I. Captain Alanus considered my role as the recorder for our kinsmen an honorable calling. Above the cabin entrance I placed a cedar board etched with the name *Libri.* It was there in the Libri cabin on Europa I that I made entries in our ancient chronicles and collected manuscripts from the various ports of call we visited. I read, wrote, and conferenced much in those days aboard Europa I.

Before we launched on our lengthy voyage, our three ships moored in a large cove beneath the rugged cliffs of Fethiye. Disembarking from the ship, we visited our humble king so that we might honor him. King Fetebir had strong desires to quest along with his beloved *familia,* but our kinsmen dissuaded him from making the long and challenging voyage westward. We all convinced our king to complete his time on earth overlooking the Great Sea from the cliffs of Fethiye. We were all encouraged by the faith and financial support of our beloved chieftain. Over the years I often recalled the wisdom of my great-great-grandfather. I admired King Fetebir, and I made it my aim to be a

God-fearing man like him in spirit and in truth.

Before we departed, King Fetebir officially installed his cherished son, Alanus, as king of our tribal nation. After the casual ceremony high above the Great Sea, one by one we embraced and kissed King Fetebir. We were doubtful we would ever return to the cliffs of Fethiye or embrace our noble leader again. So with great sadness and many tears, we boarded our three awaiting vessels. King Fetebir stood far off on the cliffs, his arms and face raised to the heavens, a signal to us that he was surrendering our destiny into the hands of our faithful Creator. We will always remember that day when we departed from Fethiye and our much loved King Fetebir.

On our short voyage from the cove at Fethiye to the Island of Rhodes, I reread through our ancient manuscripts about the kings of Rhodes, Kilikia, and Panphylia. I loved history and learning about the creation story as described by Iobaath, as well as about the Satanic Nephilim on the earth before the Great Flood. I read about the wisdom of the Great Voice. I discerned that the LORD God of Japheth was one God with three personas, and that this is unlike the many gods of the Egyptians and Canaanite descendants of Patriarch Ham.

I learned from our chronicles that the tribal nation of Abraham was chosen among the tribes of the earth as a special people of God, a race from whom the promised Seed of Abraham would appear one day on the earth, a Lamb of God, one who would save all mankind from sin and death. This good news was a great mystery to me, but I embraced the prophesy in my heart and longed for the Day of the LORD's appearing. King Fetebir was not ashamed of the good news about the redemption of all tribal nations, and when we communed he shared this blessed hope with me often.

After our brief stay in Crete, we sailed to the island of Ellis; from that most ancient of ports we sailed to the port at Ithaca, passing by the Ionian islands of Iobaath. In Ithaca Prince Hercle, the son of Boguarus, the son of Negue, shared with me his desire for knowledge and an understanding mind in the Way of the Lord. So after our visit with descendants of Dodanim at Ithaca, I invited Prince Hercle to stay with me in the *Libri* cabin. During our voyage from Ithaca to Sicily, I mentored Prince Hercle and began to instruct him to read and write using Knossos Greek.

While sojourning on the island of Sicily, we learned from the Greek-speaking merchants there that the tribes living on the island were Achaean refugees who escaped to Tarshish after Ilion was destroyed in the days of King Ougomun. Captain King Alanus recollected stories that King Ougomun told him when he was a boy about the great battle at Ilion and its destruction. No doubt the Phoenician stories about the Achaean refugees finding the island inspired Captain Alanus to take a less-traveled northern detour instead of traveling west along the coast of Afri from Lpqy.

It was reported by the Phoenician oarsmen that the Aegean refugees helped develop the trade routes on the western extremities of the Great Sea referred to by many in Asia as Tarshish. The oarsmen explained to me that the Levantine Sea represents the eastern territories of the Great Seas while the Sea of Tarshish represents the western territories of the Great Sea.

I concurred with the oarsmen and explained to them that according to our ancient chronicles, we understood that Tarshish, the son of Javan, the father of all Ionians, was the first pioneer to explore the remote western coastal territories of the Great Sea. Like Captain King Alanus, Javan desired to lead his sons on expeditions beyond Tarshish, where it was recorded that Javan and his son, Tarshish, discovered the Great Isles.

I explained to the oarsmen that our tradition spoke about the western coastal territories and islands like Sicily amidst the Great Sea of Tarshish and the territories beyond Tarshish in Atlantis, where the Great Isles of Javan are located. Our Achaean friends marveled at our detailed knowledge about our kings, ancestors, and our well-preserved record-keeping disciplines.

From Sicily we traveled to Sardinia, where my father, Prince

Romanus, whose name means "strength," argued for us to end our journey and establish a settlement on the western coast of the peninsula of Italos. As the firstborn, my father emerged as a strong leader among our people. Under the advice of Prince Romanus, we moored our three vessels on a small, deserted island adjacent to the Etruscan settlement on the mainland Italos Peninsula. When my father discovered iron ore on the island, he argued that the mining of this ore would provide funding for building new colonies.

After building a furnace where the ore was smelted, Captain King Alanus named the island Aethalia because of the fumes emanating from the smelting iron ore in the fiery furnaces. After the lucrative discovery, we stayed on the island of Aethalia while my father and several of our scouts surveyed the western facing coast of Italos. My father brought me with him.

My father and I found the descendants of Japheth living to the south and to the north. Toward the south, Romanus and his sons discovered the legendary sons of Italos, the Oenotrian tribes. The Ionians tell the story of how Italos, the son of Telegonus, planted a vineyard there. The name Italos means "calf" in a primitive Greek dialect. His father, Telegonus, was a herdsman who bred strong bulls. The southern territory of Italos became known as "the land of cattle." Because of the ties to cattle, our ancestors believed that Telegonus was perhaps a child of King Iberus, the son of Patriarch Tubal, the Adventurer, who traveled with Javan and Tarshish according to our chronicles. In the north, Romanus and his sons discovered the descendants of Patriarch Tiras, the Etruscans. Both the Oenotrians in the south and the Etruscans in the north planted vineyards and exported their wines throughout the world.

Once Prince Romanus and our *familia* colonized along the coastal middle lands north of the Oenotrians and south of the Etruscans, the remaining kinsmen of Alanus boarded the three Europa sailing ships to continue their voyage westward toward the Iberian Peninsula and on to our final destiny on the Great

Isle of Javan on the Ocean Atlantis.

As I reminisced about those days, I recalled that my father was a disciplined man of duty who strictly adhered to the seven laws of Noah and established a judicial system according to the traditions of Noah. He was a wise governor who envisioned a literate culture as he had known on Crete. As long as he lived, my father encouraged literacy among all the sons of Captain King Alanus. My father spent much of his youth in the schools on the island of Crete in Knossos. He was literate in Knossos Greek, the written language of the Ionians, which borrowed the *alphabeta* from the Phoenician language of which Romanus was also literate. As a seasoned scribe, my father made a copy of *The Chronicle of the Kings of Iobaath* for his prodigy.

The familia of Prince Romanus and Prince Britto mined iron ore on the Island of Aethalia and negotiated trade with the Phoenicians. The tribal nation of Romanus prospered from their mining industry because of the well-established Phoenician trade routes. In the same year, the sons of Prince Romanus colonized the mainland in the midst of seven mountains south from their well-established Etruscan neighbors to the north.

While the familia of Britto remained on the island of Aethalia with Europa I, Francus and Albanus, the younger brothers of Romanus and Britto, boarded Europa III along with my grandfather, Hessitio, and my great-grandfather, Captain King Alanus. It was difficult for us to separate from our beloved cousins, but we understood the mission at hand. The tribal nations of Armenon boarded Europa II, and the tribal nation of Negue returned to Europa III and made room for the additional passengers.

Instead of traveling southwest to Carthage and along the southern coast of the Sea of Tarshish, they navigated their two ships northwest from Sardinia along the northern coastal territories of the Sea of Tarshish. It was reported to me many years later that Prince Burgundus was excited about the newfound coastal territory between Italos and Iberia, and the prince desired to explore the land. So they moored their two vessels on the coast.

After several days of scouting the territory, Burgundus returned with great news about the land and his belief that this territory was the final destiny for his colony.

So Burgundus and his tribal nation established a settlement on the mysterious southern coastal territory nestled between the two massive peninsulas. Prince Longobardus stayed on with Burgundus to assist with the development of the territory. In the tradition of Noah and Japheth, Prince Burgundus was delighted to find land suitable for making wine. So with roots purchased from his Etruscan and Oenotrian neighbors, Burgundus and his sons planted a vineyard. Burgundus worked in the vineyards of Fetebir and knew much about winemaking. In the course of time, the "burgundy" wines of Burgundus were exported all over the world. Trade negotiations were established with their Etruscan neighbors, the colonies of brothers Romanus and Britton, Ionian cousins in Sicily, and the Phoenician merchants.

In search of gold and wonder, Prince Longobardus scouted out the furthermost northern territories of the Italos peninsula, north of the Etruscans and east of the colony of Burgundus. He established a city there that I named Mediolanum. Like his older brother, Burgundus, Prince Longobardus was committed to the tradition of Captain King Alanus. Prince Longobardus established a sanctuary in the middle of his city, a sacred holy place where God-fearing people could congregate to worship the LORD God of Abraham and learn about God. Mediolanum was also a place to execute the laws and just practices of our great progenitor Noah, the Herald of Righteousness. In the course of time, sanctuaries like the original one in Mediolanum were established in several newly established colonies in Europa and became the favorite meeting place for the God-fearing chroniclers.

It was reported that Prince Longobardus also founded the River Bodincus, which meant "bottomless," and the River Rhodanus, which meant "to run," and bespoke of Rhodanim the Runner. To the south the River Bodincus flowed from the

Adriatic Sea, the body of water that lay northeast of the islands of Iobaath in the Ionian Sea. Prince Longobardus soon discovered that the River Rhodanus flowed from a glacier in the white mountains that he named the Glacier Rhodanus according to the Dodecanese tradition recorded in *The Book of the Chronicles of the Kings of Iobaath.*

Prince Longobardus established a great city in northern Italos known to us as Bona; however, I named it Bologna. The territory of Prince Longobardus was situated on the edge of the plains of the River Po at the foot of the Apennine Mountains, at the meeting of the Rhodanus and Savena river valleys. In the course of time, the tribal nation along the River Bodincus enlarged and became a prosperous kingdom in the midst of many wealth-generating waterways.

While Prince Britto and his colony sojourned on the Island of Aethalia, Prince Elishah and his colony made their home aboard Europa I while delivering wine and iron ore to the ancient cities of Syracuse, Carthage, Ithaca, Ellis, Crete, Rhodes, Panphylia, and on to Ilion as weather permitted. Dardanus and his son Trous followed in the footsteps of their father, Prince Elishah, and the patriarchs as merchant marines.

Anchises, the son of Trous, tired from a rugged seafaring existence and returned to the ancient merchant city of Ilion, where he was schooled in linguistics in Knossos, as was the custom of our *familia*. Like me, Anchises became the chronicler for the sons of Britto and Elishah sojourning in ancient Ilion.

I executed the desires of my father, Romanus, with excellence, and invested my life educating my offspring, the Latins, in the nurture and admonition of the LORD. In temperament and character, I was not at all like my king. Unlike my father, who was assertive and extroverted, I tended to be passive and introverted. King Romanus was driven by tasks that needed to be completed quickly with little patience; I was more thorough, enjoying the process, and desiring a perfect finish to all of my father's projects. I was not driven by the task at hand in a manner that it would be completed quickly and yet haphazardly and roughshod. In the end, we worked well together. I am a teachable man, a man under authority, and was pleased to submit to the desires of my noble king, his moral ethics, and the rules of his kingdom. I know that pleases the LORD.

Understanding that I was a knowledgeable and literate scribe, Captain King Alanus and Romanus encouraged me to continue to develop my new Latin language. In time, the tribal nations of Romanus and Britto began to speak and write in Latin. The Latin language distinguished the tribal nations of Captain King Alanus and became the root language for several other romantic languages among the emerging Catalonian colonies of Captain King Alanus in Europa. For a season the Latin words I developed on board Europa I were used as a secret script for the Catalonians throughout Europa.

The four princes, Romanus and Britto, the sons of Hessittio, and Burgundus and Longobardus, the sons of Armeno, assembled in conference on the Island of Aethalia with their tribal nations every other year for many decades. Aethalia became a commons for their tribal nations as in Ilion after the flood. On Aethalia their sons and daughters were given in marriage. All three tribal nations expanded and grew large in numbers. In those days I renamed the island of Aethalia as Elba.

From the Port of Burgundus, the remaining tribal nations of Captain King Alanus boarded one remaining ship. Burgundus was given Europa II as a gift for his winemaking enterprise. King Alanus boarded Europa III with Prince Hessittio and his two sons, Prince Francus and Prince Albanus. Prince Armenon boarded Europa III with Prince Gothus, Prince Walagothus, and Prince Gepidus. And Prince Negue boarded Europa III with his three sons: Wandalus, Saxo, and Boguarus.

It was later reported to me that Captain King Alanus navigated Europa III southwest from the Port of Burgundus around the Iberian Peninsula and north toward the Great Isles, where the ancient Ionians buried Patriarch Javan at the great stone henge on the island in the midst of the Ocean Atlantis.

As the various tribes chose their European territories, I made it a priority to understand where all the princes of King Alanus migrated. With the exception of Prince Hercle and, later, Prince Anchises, it was uncertain to me if any of my other cousins would advance their literacy and maintain ancestral records. Throughout my life I asked questions and investigated the whereabouts of the various tribal nations, their discoveries as well as their occupations.

It was reported to me that from the Great Isles of Javan, Prince Hessittio boarded Europa III along with Prince Francus and Prince Albanus. I later learned that Prince Francus and Prince Albanus made a short voyage across a narrow channel of water that coursed between the coastal territories of the Great Isles of Javan and what the Catalonians labeled as the European mainland. The Catalonians established colonies along the northern coast on the mainland going northeast from the peninsula of Iberus. Many decades later, the children of Francus became known as the Franks; the children of Albanus became known as the Alemanni.

From the Great Isle of Javan, Prince Armenon boarded Europa III with Prince Gothus, Prince Walagothus, and Prince Gepidus. I later learned that these tribal bands ventured northward on the same channel of water into the *Mare Germanicum* and settled on a large peninsula they discovered on the northern coast, where it was reported that they found the hospitable seed of Riphath, the Pfeifer.

From the Great Isle of Javan, Prince Negue boarded Europa III with his three sons, Wandalus, Saxo, and Boguarus. As Prince Hercle boarded Europa III, we made an oath to reunite again one day. We had become such great friends during the long voyage. On a brief visit by Prince Hercle many years later, I learned that these tribal nations discovered a river that they named Elba, which flowed into *Mare Germanicum* from the south. I was honored that they named the river after the island of Aethalia where we first landed many years ago and in time became known as Elba Island. The tribal nation of Prince Saxo settled on the western side of the River Albis and along the coast of *Mare Germanicum* where the sons of Gothus also colonized.

I learned from Prince Hercle that the tribal nation of Prince Wandalus settled on the eastern side of the River Albis and frontiers in the east, where it was reported that they too found the hospitable seed of Gomer. And the tribal nation of Boguarus traveled to the mouth of the River Albis and settled the eastern territories of Regen on the ancient River Danu of Riphath.

As long as he lived, Captain King Alanus made the trip to the Island of Elba to visit his sons, Romanus, Britto, Burgundus, and Longobardus. I interviewed him on each visit to gather information for our chronicles. Like Japheth of ancient times, King Alanus visited his tribal nations and encouraged trade and the development of their own distinct romantic tribal languages. His love for the oceans and seas of the world never abated. I was comforted to know that Captain King Alanus and his crew aboard Europa III returned to Island of Elba with few casualties.

Knowing that Captain King Alanus longed to revisit Lukka, Panphylia, and Kilikia before his death, Elisha and his crew organized and funded an excursion back to our homeland. God was with our king on his voyage back to Panphylia. They completed the first leg of the journey that our king had desired since he was a young sailor; soon it became time to complete the second leg of the journey and travel back to Fethiye and Alanya. So, desiring great adventure, I also boarded Europa III with Captain King Alanus, and we returned to the Great Isles of Javan.

King Negue, Prince Hercle, and I accompanied Captain King Alanus as we traveled south on the river named Rhodanus. After sojourning in the land of Hesse for a few days, we abandoned Europa III and traveled by foot to the mouth of River Danu where we built a riverboat to navigate the great river. When we completed the riverboat, we passed through ancient Regen to Morava. From Morava we sailed downstream toward the land of Dodanim to avoid inhospitable Cimmerian and Scythian warriors, the children of Gomer and Magog in the east. Then from Thessalonica we traveled east by caravan on well-trodden trade routes to our destination at Ilion.

While visiting the ruins at Troy, I was saddened to learn that the ancient aurochs were extinct and no longer grazed the ancient steppe lands of Asia; however, I was encouraged by news that the Aurochs of Asia were crossbred with bulls from Iberia, and that the Aurochs lived on in other breeds. We reunited with Anchises in Troy, where he shared his story with us.

From Troy we were in familiar waters and traveled south along the coast to Apasa, then to the Island of Rhodes, and finally moored our vessel at the cove in Fethiye, completing the epic voyage of Captain King Alanus. We visited the gravesite of King Fetebir, who died during our prolonged absence. The locals protected the property of Fetebir hoping that his son, Captain King Alanus, would one day return.

And by God's grace King Alanus did return and collect his father's ancient *libri*, which included a complete copy of the Pentateuch of Moses recorded in the Hebrew language of Eber. Many years later I was honored to receive the manuscript for my libri. I read the pages of the ancient text regularly and identified the stories that paralleled our own ancient genealogies and stories.

Captain King Alanus also returned with a rare copy of the psalms of Moses. I made copies of Moses' psalms for all who worshipped the LORD God of Japheth. With the help and encouragement from King Alanus and Prince Hercle, we instituted a priestly representative group of divines and judges to seek counsel from the LORD God and lead our Catalonian tribal nations.

Like the Levitical priesthood in Judea, the literate chroniclers among us attended to the wonders of God. Copies of the Pentateuch of Moses as well as the psalms of Moses were copied and distributed among the chroniclers. In those days we allied with the friendly, like-minded Skuthai chroniclers, and like the judges and prophets of Israel, our chroniclers united the tribes of Europa, seeking the LORD God for tribal discernment and guidance.

Captain King Alanus was blessed by God with long life and lived one hundred and ninety-eight years. The last days of Captain King Alanus were spent in Catalonia, where a young colony was forming.

The gathering of nations to lay Captain King Alanus to rest near the Great Stone Henge of Javan was the most significant experience in my life. Only highly esteemed descendants of Javan were granted lots for burial in the sacred fields surrounding the circular hedge of stone. I found the event a great opportunity to meet privately with my nephew, Trous, the son of Dardanus, and tell him about our ancestry. Dardanus, the son of Elishah, the son of Britto, had little interest in ancestry, but Prince Thous expressed a desire to learn the history of our well-documented Dodecanese heritage. So I told him the epic stories of the sons of Noah, and those of Tarshish, Iobaath, Fetebir, and Alanus.

The chroniclers officiated the interment at the Great Stone Henge. As was our custom, the chroniclers cremated the body of Captain King Alanus and gathered the ash remains into an urn. We buried the urn of King Alanus in a field next to what we believed to be the field of Tarshish, the son of Javan, who was buried next to the field of progenitor Javan, the son of Japheth, on the Great Isles. Most of the progeny of the king arrived to pay respect to their progenitor. If it were not for the faith and vision of Captain King Alanus and the generous funding provided by King Fetebir, I realized, our tribal nations would still be sojourning in war-torn Asia.

After many years of study and research and in the tradition of Japheth, the Great Voice of our people, I, Latinus, the privileged chronicler for the blessed sons of Iobaath sojourning in Roma, hereby preserve a record for future generations in *The Book of the*

Chronicles of the Kings of Iobaath:

Latinus was the son of Romanus. Romanus was the son of Hessittio. Hessittio was the son of Alanus. Alanus was the son of Fetebir. Fetebir was the son of Ougomun. Ougomun was the son of Thous. Thous was the son of Boib. Boib was the son of Simeon. Simeon was the son of Mair. Mair was the son of Ethach. Ethach was the son of Aurthach. Aurthach was the son of Ecthet. Ecthet was the son of Oth. Oth was the son of Abir. Abir was the son of Rea. Rea was the son of Ezra. Ezra was the son of Izrau. Izrau was the son of Baath. Baath was the son of Iobaath. Iobaath was the son of Rhodanim. Rhodanim was the son of Javan. Javan was the son of Japheth. Japheth was the son of Noah, Noah was the son of Lamech, Lamech was the son of Methuselah, Methuselah was the son of Enoch, Enoch was the son of Jared, Jared was the son of Mahalaleel, Mahalaleel was the son of Cainan, Cainan was the son of Enos, Enos was the son of Seth, Seth was the son of Adam, Adam was the son of God.

FIVE

THE CHRONICLES OF KING BOIUS
(900 BC)

THE CATALONIAN KINGDOMS OF Captain King Alanus expanded on the continent of Europa. Before his death, interment, and burial at the Great Stone Henge, King Alanus established a loose-knit confederation of blood-related, ethnic tribal nations extending from the coastal beaches of Panphylia, passing by several ports of call on ancient trade routes toward Tarshish, along the southern coast of Iberia, through the passage at Tingis, and onward to *Mare Germanicum* and *Mare Suebicum*.

In our day, the descendants of Captain King Alanus inhabited most of the European continent. We Catalonians established natural boundaries between our tribal kingdoms, trade routes, and tribal languages, maintaining many ancient Greek and Latin root words. We are a pioneering, agricultural, and industrious people who multiplied and prospered wherever we colonized, all the while expanding knowledge and maturing ancient occupations such as herdsmen, ironworkers, and musicians.

As I, Prince Boius, studied and contemplated our inspirational tribal history, I surmised that the legendary voyage of Captain King Alanus was perhaps one of the greatest seafaring adventures and migrations of tribal nations since the first migration of the former days when the seed of Patriarch Japheth ventured from the land of Kau. According to the traditions of our Catalonian ancestors from Panphylia, this second migration of nations occurred after the first migration, when God divided the people and gifted the nations with various tongues.

I learned that King Hercle, the first prince of King Boguarus, the first prince of King Negue, was just a lad when he left his former homeland in Alanya and his great-grandfather, Fetebir, on the cliffs of Fethiye. Prior to his death, it was said that King Hercle often reminisced about living on board Europa III on the Great Sea and on what was then the mysterious ocean waters of Atlantis.

King Hercle recalled that it was a very long journey from the Port of Alanya in Panphylia to Europa, taking more than seven years on water to reach their final destination. Europa III was his home for those seven wearisome years although the young prince did spend much time with Latinus, the son of Romanus, aboard Europa I in the *libri* cabin.

We understand from King Hercle that the crew found occasional mooring along the way where they restocked, replaced weary or sickened oarsmen, and repaired vessels, but they never forgot the salty, windy, seafaring adventure that was branded indelibly on their hearts and minds. While at sea they must have eaten every kind of saltwater fish and crustacean imaginable and marveled at the many oceanic species that God had created. When they were not deep sea fishing, Prince Hercle spent much time learning from his cousin, Prince Latinus, as they updated the ancient *Book of the Chronicles of the Kings of Iobaath*.

They learned that King Romanus encouraged Prince Hercle in classic literacy. On many of their expeditions, Prince Boguarus agreed with his cousin, Romanus, and granted permission to his young prince to bunk with Latinus to be schooled in the *libri* on Europa I. As a well-tutored chronicler, Prince Hercle also learned to read the ancient Hebrew chronicles of Moses. During their *libri* cabin experience, Latinus and Hercle grew in their knowledge of the world and one another.

I learned that it was aboard Europa III that King Boguarus received the nickname Boib, so named after the valiant warrior king who founded the village of Bottia near the city of Iopolis in Kilikia. Like Latinus, Prince Hercle enjoyed learning from the wise men aboard the ships, listening to their stories and traditions of our ancestry, and about the LORD God of Noah, the Herald of Righteousness, and of Japheth, the Great Voice. They had much time for storytelling while traveling. The heart of Prince Hercle was filled with such wonder as he listened attentively to the stories, studied the ancient scrolls, and worshipped the LORD God of Creation by reading the psalms of the renowned Hebrew, Moses, the Man of God, the son of Pharaoh's daughter.

It was reported that King Boguarus loved to pray the prayer of Moses that he learned from Captain King Alanus while sojourning in Catalonia before his death. It appeared to King Boguarus that the LORD God inspired Moses to author this prayer for all the tribal nations of the earth, not just the Hebrew tribal nation. The wise king helped his son, Hercle, memorize the prayer of Moses.

The Boib king and the young prince prayed Moses' prayer as if it was their own, specifically written for their tribal nation.

Lord, you have been our dwelling place
in all generations.
Before the mountains were brought forth,
or ever you had formed the earth and the world,
from everlasting to everlasting you are God.
You return man to dust
and say, "Return, O children of man!"
For a thousand years in your sight

are but as yesterday when it is past,
   or as a watch in the night.
You sweep them away as with a flood; they are like a dream,
   like grass that is renewed in the morning:
in the morning it flourishes and is renewed;
   in the evening it fades and withers.
For we are brought to an end by your anger;
   by your wrath we are dismayed.
You have set our iniquities before you,
   our secret sins in the light of your presence.
For all our days pass away under your wrath;
   we bring our years to an end like a sigh.
The years of our life are seventy,
   or even by reason of strength eighty;
yet their span is but toil and trouble;
   they are soon gone, and we fly away.
Who considers the power of your anger,
   and your wrath according to the fear of you?
So teach us to number our days
   that we may get a heart of wisdom.
Return, O Lord! How long?
   Have pity on your servants!
Satisfy us in the morning with your steadfast love,
   that we may rejoice and be glad all our days.
Make us glad for as many days as you have afflicted us,
   and for as many years as we have seen evil.
Let your work be shown to your servants,
   and your glorious power to their children.
Let the favor of the Lord our God be upon us,
   and establish the work of our hands upon us;
   yes, establish the work of our hands!

(This psalm would become part of the collection of the Book of Psalms, Psalm 90, ESV.)

When reading and studying *The Book of the Chronicles of the Kings of Iobaath*, Prince Hercle learned, as I am learning, and saw the steadfast love of the LORD God to all the sons of Adam. God indeed established the works of the nations; Prince Hercle knew this full well. From age to age, from kingdom to kingdom, time marches on, and we do well who "number our days" as Moses the Man of God prayed. Many kingdoms and chroniclers like me have come and gone, and many kingdoms and chroniclers will come and go in the future. But this I know: only God and His government will remain forever.

King Boguarus and Prince Hercle reasoned that life is short, between seventy and eighty years, just as Moses prayed. The titans of old lived for nearly a thousand years; however Moses the Man of God, lived for one hundred and twenty years. Today, often, men live less than eighty years! I have observed that it is just as our legendary Patriarch Japheth, the Great Voice, taught our people, saying, "We appear to be devolving, not evolving." It appears to me that like the beasts of the field, the germ of man has lost features in body, soul, and spirit. We are certainly not the men we used to be!

I observed that the chroniclers rarely depicted their ancestors in terms of weakness; on the contrary, they did so in terms of the strength as titans, even as demigods. Except for a few exceptional giants, gifted wise men and women who appeared among us from time to time, ordinary people are becoming progressively ignorant, without understanding, and in some cases, reprobate fools. I marvel that the ancient geniuses accomplished so much with so little prior knowledge to build on. I am thankful to God for the chronicles recorded by faithful and wise men.

Although many of the princes of Captain King Alanus were reported to be a literate, God-fearing generation, they were also said to be a festive band that enjoyed intoxicating beverages while on board their vessels. I imagine that on numerous special occasions the minstrels would perform jubilant songs for the European crew members after picking up their pfeife and stringed guitars. In the tradition of Jubal, the Father of the Sound of Music, all sang familiar folk songs and danced gaily. The sound of music probably filled their hearts with great comfort and happiness as they proceeded patiently, day by day, to their final destinations.

The treasured pfeife of Jubal in its leather case, made from the herds of Jabal, has been handed down from generation to generation, from king to king, since the days of Noah, along with the cast iron kettle of Tubal-Cain. King Fetebir loved Prince Negue and passed on those precious pieces of antiquity to the prince, who had been denied a mother; later, King Negue passed on the pfeife of Jubal along with the other pieces to Prince Boguarus. As the many kings who had gone before him, Boguarus, later king, guarded the precious pfeife of Jubal with his very life and instructed Hercle to do the same when he passed along the king's treasure.

According to our tradition, the pfeife, leather sheath, and kettle survived the flood of Noah on board the ark and during the adventurous voyage of Captain King Alanus. Today, I am keeper of these precious heirlooms as part of our cherished *familia capitale.*

And although the Catalonians of old experienced great tribulation, as some of our people and oarsmen died of various diseases on those three ships, all were glad to flee the unrest and warfare that seemed never-ending in our ancient homeland in Asia.

From the stories of King Boib, I learned that Captain King Alanus and his sons were not the first to homestead in European territories. I was instructed from our tradition that Riphath, the son of Gomer, the firstborn son of Japheth, sojourned on the Regen River and built quite an enterprise there along with his younger brother, Morava, the Pfeifer, who colonized on a neighboring tributary on the Danu. In those days, the Riphean seed of Riphath were allies and friends of the Dodecanese seed of Rhodanim.

After the days of Regen and Morava, some among the germ (or seed) of Riphath, the Gomerites, migrated southeast away from their remote homelands on the ancient River Danu to aid our ancestors in waging war against the kings in Mesopotamia. According to the tradition of King Boguarus, some Riphean bands fled away from the violence, like Captain King Alanus, the Peacemaker, and as the massive plates of glacial ice of Rhodanim receded after the flood, this band of Riphean men migrated into the great northwest territories beyond *Mare Germanicum* and *Mare Suebicum*. It was in these regions that they called themselves *Víkingr*.

Like the sons of Peirates, the *Víkingr* men of the north were skilled shipbuilders who moored their vessels in coves, inlets, and small bays. But unlike the sons of Peirates, I learned that the ancient *Víkingr* were a people of sound Riphean values and character.

Like the sons and grandsons of Japheth, the sons and grandsons of Captain King Alanus maintained their connection to one another and established land trade routes throughout ancient Europa and nautical trade routes around the world. Like the descendants of Japheth, the sons of King Alanus were highly educated, spoke in various tongues, and a few, mostly noble-blooded chroniclers, were literate and had an understanding mind about the Way of the LORD God of Japheth and Noah.

Also like Patriarch Japheth, Captain King Alanus believed God and had a great sense of destiny. He understood God's plans and purposes: God's key objective for men was and is and always will be to marry one wife, procreate, and spread the glory of God throughout the world to all tribal nations. And to this end, few kings in our chronicles had such deliberate intentions as Captain King Alanus, who was a wise man indeed, a seer among our people, a man of God who "numbered his days."

So with small colonies established in southern and northern Italos, the Iberian Peninsula, Franconia, and in Scandinavia, I learned that Captain King Alanus encouraged Prince Negue and his sons, Prince Wandalus, Prince Saxo, and Prince Boguarus to penetrate the ancient territories of Gomer and the Riphean tribal nations south of *Mare Germanicum* along the ancient River Danu.

So with a heart filled with great curiosity, enthusiasm, and determination, Captain King Alanus traveled southeast from the land of Francus on the *Mare Germanicum* on Europa III. Captain Alanus would have stayed on with Francus, but the king had not yet retired from adventure and questing. I learned that once the mobile king returned to Alanya in Panphylia, but he was persuaded by many kinsmen to forsake his quests and invest in his posterity among his expanding royal progeny in Europa. So the noble king returned to Catalonia.

I learned that King Boguarus desired to confirm that Patriarch Riphath and his twenty-eight sons penetrated the territory from the Blach See of the ancient Gomerites of Skythia, the Cimmerians, along the River Danu in the southeast. So King Boib and Prince Hercle explored that territory to see if there was evidence of our ancient cousin, Regen, the fourth son of Riphath, and Morava, the eighth son of Riphath, both comrades of Patriarch Iobaath.

It was reported that they rediscovered several rivers that provided access southward into the ancient Riphean territories. They rediscovered the River Rhodanus, the river that progenitor Rhodanim reported in our chronicles. They rediscovered that the River Rhodanim was in close proximity to the infamous River Danu. From the River Danu near the Schwarzwald, they were able to access the Blach See in the east as well as the Aegean Sea traveling south on the great River Morava to the Dacian territories of Patriarch Dodanim and the Thracian protégée of Patriarch Tiras. In the course of time, these ancient trade routes along the rivers proved profitable to Boguarus's kings just as they were profitable to Regen and Morava.

They discovered another river in the land, the River Albis. Giant mountains, like the mountains of Tiras and the mountains of Kau, fed the River Albis and its tributaries. They also discovered the River Suevos. The many freshwater rivers and tributaries provided hydration for their crops, cattle, and the tribal nation as in the fertile pastures of Kilikia in Anatolia.

The mountains and rivers that Captain King Alanus, Negue, Francus, Wandalus, Saxo, and Prince Boguarus discovered provided a peaceful and pleasant homeland for our expanding Catalonian nations into eastern Europa. The giant mountains provided recreation in the cold seasons as the peaks of the majestic mountains were covered with snow and could be seen for miles. Waterfalls and freshwater rivers provided recreation in the warm seasons. And the flooded plains, like Egypt, provided rich loamy soil for agricultural development as well as healthy grassland for their cattle.

I learned that Prince Wandalus, the Wanderer, lived up to his very name when he reached the great mountains. When he became King Wandalus, he and his nomadic tribal nation wandered about eastern Europa amidst the mountains and rivers surrounding the River Albis, the River Suevos, and the River Ouistoula. The River Suevos and the River Ouistoula flowed north from the mountain ranges emptying into the *Mare Suebicum*. We discovered that many of the great rivers in the fertile Pomeranian territories of Wandalus flowed north and emptied into either *Mare Germanicum* or *Mare Suebicum*, the bodies of water that Prince Latinus named for us.

King Wandalus and his wondering princes discovered that access to the River Danu was provided south of the Beskids mountain range. They discovered that there were several existing native tribal nations sojourning south of the Beskids; these were presumed to be descendants of the Ripheans. King Boguarus, Prince Hercle, and the others were intrigued by their simple and quiet way of life. The tribes there lived in primitive stacked boulder houses, just like Patriarch Gomer built in ancient days in Skythia according to our traditions: an ordinary people, gathering fish from the rivers and wild game from the forests.

Their tongue was mostly foreign to the curious pioneers, but because of the relationships they had with their relatives in Anatolia, they knew some vocabulary. They learned to communicate with the friendly and hospitable indigenous Riphean tribes. They incorporated their tongue into their developing languages. They lived in peace with the ancient tribes, intermarried with this people, and together expanded the population of eastern Europa. Like the ancient Ripheans and Dodecanese, they became tribal friends and relatives; over time they blended cultures and became one.

I marveled when it was reported that our legends about the Moravian pfeifers and the pfeife of Jubal were known among the Riphean tribes who survived there. After thousands of years, the pfeife of Jubal once again united the ancient seed of Riphath and the newly arriving Dodecanese. Had it not been for the Moravian pfeife, the situation might have been extremely grave for trespassing newcomers. Instead of a peaceful coexistence enjoying the sound of music and dancing, surely there would have been tribal warfare and much bloodshed among our tribal nations.

I learned that Prince Saxo and his seed were neighbors colonizing a central location in Europa along the lower Albis River Valley. The lower territories of River Rhodanim of Saxony provided a natural boundary in the west with coastal access on the *Mare Germanicum*, which provided a natural boundary in the north. There was evidence of a former people sojourning in the land who were assumed to be descendants of Riphath.

King Boguarus, his father Negue, his son Hercle, and all their colony ventured south, away from *Mare Germanicum,* toward the River Danu into the legendary territory of Riphath. And there they restored the ancient ruins at Regen on the Regen River and Morava on the River Morava. The homestead of the Riphean pfeifers was in ruins, so they totally demolished the ancient structures and built their own farmstead using materials salvaged from the treasured ruins. In the course of time, they settled on the River Regan in the midst of the broad Hercynian Forest.

On the banks of the River Morava, they found artifacts of merriment, instruments of the pfeifers who inhabited this territory: the lyre, pfeife, and tambourine. The discoveries of these primitive instruments of worship inspired them to celebrate our Creator, the Maker of everything that has been made, just as our ancestors had. So there they reproduced like instruments and resurrected worship in song and dance. They resurrected the supra festivals of their ancestors in Kau during the harvest and cheered many downtrodden souls with the sound of music and dancing.

King Iobaath the Chronicler recorded much about Regen and the merry pfeifers along the rapidly flowing Danu. Although we were born sons of Javan, Boguarus understood the deep, loving relationship that existed between Regen and Iobaath. Because of *The Book of the Chronicles of the Kings of Iobaath,* our forefathers understood their relationship to these ancient tribal nations and their connection to the Creator-God of Noah, the Herald of Righteousness.

Exactly as our ancient chronicles reported, they discovered the vineyards and breweries of Riphath. The son of Boguarus were amazed that the very roots of the vines were from the ancient vineyards of Noah in Armenia and the vineyards of Japheth in the land of Kau. As former marines and warriors, they understood little about the process of making beer, touted as "the beverage of angels," or of stowing and aging fine wines. But this discovery inspired them to learn more about making and marketing these popular and desired spirits.

I learned that King Negue took advantage of his great resources and reestablished trade routes by land and water. He reestablished trade with the ancient nations of the Blach See and with the ancient world of Dodanim the progenitor. King Negue explored and established settlements along the River Rhodanim flowing southwest from the Rhodanim Glacier to the River Rhodanim in Swabia flowing north. Our king explored and established colonies in the east as far as the River Morava in Moravia. Later Prince Boguarus established trade with the sons of Longobardus along the Po River Valley in the west.

According to the desires of King Negue, his tribe ventured south, from the River Regan on the River Danu into the ancient Riphean salt mines known in our chronicles as the Salt Castle on the River Salt, a right tributary of the River Inn, which flowed north and emptied into the Danu. They restored the ancient Riphean salt mines and built riverboats to export the coveted salt preservative to the emerging tribal nations in Europa and on the Great Sea. The wealth generated from their *capitale* provided sustenance and funded building projects for many years.

In Salzburg, at the Salt Castle, and in the nearby colony at Hallstatt, all the enterprises of the Riphean seed were found just as marketable in the days of King Boguarus and Prince Hercle as in the days of Noah. Europa provided an emerging market for the ancient industries of Gomer and his like-minded entrepreneurial sons. The natural resources of Salzburg and Hallstatt still yield much salt and provide prosperity to the Catalonian tribal nations.

It was reported that they discovered additional evidence of the sons of Riphath everywhere in the Riphean Mountains. They found corroded ironworks and celts that the pfeifers used to fell tannenbaum trees for making leather. They found well-crafted bows and arrows for hunting. They even discovered supporting evidence of our tradition when they discovered scallop shells from the quadrennial games at Ellis Island, where Regen and Iobaath had competed for the victor's wreath.

It was then that King Negue named the twenty-eight tributaries of the River Danu after the sons and respected seed of Riphath according to our chronicles.

As they ventured further west on horseback, they discovered evidence of ancient swine farms west of the Swabian Sea, where the River Rhodanim in Swabia is birthed. They discovered more abandoned and dilapidated stacked-stone cabins and lean-to huts, rotted leather boats, and wooden oars surrounding the mountain lake—all as documented in our ancient Catalonian chronicles.

Whenever Prince Hercle was able, he made the long journey from Hallstatt to visit Prince Latinus in Roma. He was pleased to find that Latinus had converted the chronicles from deteriorating Egyptian papyrus to the more durable calf-skin vellum from various ancient Asian and Hellenic languages to Latin, the emerging language of the literate and commercial enterprises among the Catalonians.

On one of his visits, Prince Hercle recorded our genealogy on Kilikian linen manuscripts for our people in Salzburg and Hallstatt with notations about our heritage, and with special emphasis given to the pfeifer nation and the loving friendship of Regen and Iobaath. He also wrote about the Moravian cave bone pfeife given to Iobaath as a wedding gift. But the best-kept secret among the Catalonian princes was that of the passage of the cherished and precious pfeife of Jubal, the iron kettle, and the knife of Tubal-Cain, along with its leather cover.

King Boguarus, the Boib warrior, and his Boius sons where mighty defenders and settled west of the River Morava and southern territories along the River Danu. Our Creator blessed their homeland and greatly multiplied their seed. In the course of time, and since all of their people, both men and women, developed into great warriors, they were called, locally, *Boi-warioz*. But the Latin sons of Romanus spoke of the Boius warriors as *Bio-hemum*, and their homeland where they sojourned as *Baiern*. Due to the knowledge and wisdom of Negue, the Catalonian colony in Hallstatt became the dominant kingdom during this expansion period into Europa.

According to the traditions among our ancient kinsmen—and like all the European tribes—our ancestors once lived in the land of Kau, the White Mountain territories of Japheth. Today the Boius sons of Boguarus occupy in the land of Albus, the white mountain territories in eastern Europa. The Albus Mountain range is birthed in the Great Sea of Tarshish in the land of Longobardus in the west and continues to our Boihaemum homeland in the east. Our tribal nation migrated into the northeast regions of the Albus Mountains and into the southeast regions of the Albus Mountains. The crescent-shaped Albus Mountains united the Catalonian tribal nations of Captain King Alanus in western, central, and eastern Europa, but sadly, separated us from the sons of Romanus and Latinus in Italos.

As Prince Hercle aged, he made time to enjoy God's creation. Prince Hercle reported that he discovered wild goats in the higher elevations of the mountain chain. The large males use their large, hard horns to buck and challenge opponents for their mate; therefore, the Albus Mountain folk refer to the lustful hard buck as Steinbock while the sons of Latinus refer to the goats as Capri. The brown male Capri have large curving horns, while the brown female goats have short horns.

Prince Hercle wondered how any creature survived the harsh Albus weather. However, as he hiked through the ancient mountains, he discovered a noble white flower that he named *Edelweiss* because the fragile plant survived the rocky elevations. Prince Hercle was inspired and told me, "The humble white flower speaks of purity in the midst of challenging circumstances and of God's common graces that are lavishly bestowed on all God-fearing sons who walk by faith and not by sight alone." Since the days of Prince Hercle, Edelweiss has been a symbol of Boib nobility and endurance among the Albus tribal nations.

We were very much aware that we were not the first sons of Japheth to arrive in the Albus Mountains. The sons of Riphath hiked, camped, and hunted on these same majestic hills. We found evidence that confirmed our traditions that Riphath roamed the Albus Mountains and that he was an ironworker and cobbler. Prince Hercle reported that they discovered a copper axe, leather shoes, and other evidences of former White Mountain tribes.

Our *germen* predecessors also discovered the white mountain mineral wealth. Salt, precious iron ore, copper, and gold have been mined for thousands of years since the days of Noah. Crystals such as the wine-colored amethyst, the crimson cinnabar, and thousands of other colorful varieties of quartz have been hunted and mined by stonecutters for jewelers since the days of Dodanim in Ilion. Quartz from the white mountains has adorned the bodies of royal ancestors since the days of King Iobaath.

Many among the Catalonian nations of Captain King Alanus became superstitious, believing that the wearing of amethyst quartz amulets helped prevent drunkenness and encouraged sober-mindedness for our warriors in battle. Amethyst thus became the symbol of sobriety and self-control. Hence the noble sons of King Alanus were buried with their amethyst torcs, or neck rings, and other pieces of jewelry. I am not given to superstition, but embrace the concept of wearing amethyst as a symbol of self-control and sobriety.

Intoxication was discouraged among the God-fearing and righteous sons of Captain King Alanus as it was in the days of Noah. For some, alcoholic beverages had to be forsaken altogether as these drunkards were said to be madmen when under its influence. For these men, alcohol was unmanageable and became their master.

It was reported that Hercle was such a madman at times that he had to be forced to stay sober and to entrust his disease and his unmanageable ways to God. Hercle came to believe that a power greater than himself could restore him to sanity. He surrendered his disease to the Catalonian God of Captain King Alanus. He discovered that the only permanent cure was faith in God, total honesty, and total surrender to his plans and purposes.

When I, Prince Boius, the firstborn son of Daedalus, was of age to procreate, I married and was blessed with four princes: Raetus, Eluveitu, Allobroges, and Latène.

My firstborn, Prince Raetus, was granted the central territory of our kingdom, which I named Suittes, because I had to burn the forests in order to build cities. For many years the burning of the forest created a black soot under our feet. The territories of Prince Raetus became synonymous with "mountain land" and his descendents as "mountain people." The young Prince Raetus developed trade negotiations with the Etruscans and the Latins.

The Soot-land of Prince Raetus was beautiful, bounded by the River Danu at the River Regen in the northeast; by the upper River Rhodanim in Swabia that flowed from the Swartz Sea in the northwest; and the upper River Rhodanim in Suittes flowed to the Great Seas of Tarshish. The southernmost territories of the Soot-land bordered the land of and tribes of Lombardo.

I named my second son Eluveitu, and he settled with this sons and daughters in the westernmost Soot-land territory between the Albus Mountains and the sub-alpine mountains called the Jura Mountains that separated the River Rhodanus in Suittes from the River Rhodanus in Swabia. This land given to Eluveitu was suitable for herding cattle and graced with multiple grasslands, dales, and pastures. The forests of Prince Eluveitu were given the name, by many nations, Eluveitie. In the course of time, Prince Eluveitu and Prince Latène established their claims with borders to the west of Raetia.

My third son was named Allobroges. The Soot-land of Allobroges lay between the River Rhodanus and the Genfer Sea.

My fourth son was named Latène. The Soot-land of Prince Latène was in the western Albus Mountain territory of the Neuenburger Sea, where the sons of Latène harvested deep water trout.

The other sons and daughters of Daedalus sojourned in Salzburg and Hallstatt in the eastern territories of the Albus Mountains. Some of the descendents of King Negue occupied the region to the north of Radasbona, where they became known as Thuringians.

According to our chronicles, the Soot-land was originally

the ancient southern territories inhabited by the sons of Regan, the son of Riphath. The vineyards of Riphath at Regan were restored there. The wines of Raetus became renowned, the preference of kings throughout the world. The swine farms of the sons of Riphath also were restored.

The fresh waters that flow from the Albus Mountains were the main source of hydration for the tribal nations of Alanus, their herds, and their farmsteads for many generations. The major rivers of Europa flow from the White Mountain territory, such as the two Rhodanus rivers, and the River Inn, the River Ticino, and the River Po, all of which have headwaters in the Albus Mountains and flow into neighboring territories. Like the Great River Euphrates, these life-giving community waters empty into the *Mare Germanicum,* the *Mare Suebicum,* the Great Sea of Tarshish, the Adriatic Sea, and the Blach See—all the places where the genetic descendants of Captain King Alanus colonized and expanded.

Ancient rivers such as the River Danu of Riphath have major tributaries flowing into them that originate in the Albus Mountains. The glacial-sourced River Rhodanus shared with the sons of Francus in the west is second to the River Nile of Patriarch Egypt as a freshwater source to the Great Sea of Tarshish. The River Rhodanus flows into the Genfer Sea.

The tribal nations of Negue, Boguarus, Boius, Raetus, Eluveitu, Allobroges, and Latène formed a close-knit league of nations and began to wage war to defend their God-given territory from foreign invaders from all points on the compass. Although many of their neighbors also were descendants of Captain King Alanus, in the course of time ignorance concerning our geological roots abounded and the strong relationships and alliances among the Catalonian tribes gradually broke down.

Sadly, within a few generations most of the descendants of Captain King Alanus became ignorant of their ancient roots and *The Book of the Chronicles of the Kings of Iobaath.* Only the learned Latini chroniclers understood the secrets of our success in Europa. On the whole, Catalonians became as lost coins in the sand, unaware of their ancient heritage, their identity, and their Creator.

Ignorant of their ancient past and their genetic connection to the LORD God of Noah, the tribal nations of King Alanus and central Europa began to build alliances and wage war with each other and neighboring tribal nations.

History was repeating itself as in the peaceful days of Noah before the dispersion of the tribal nations at Babylon.

The Grecian sons of Javan called the early Riphean tribes and the later Catalonian sons of Captain King Alanus *Keltoi*, so named after the arrowhead celt that Riphath invented to fell trees; at the same time, the Latin sons of Romanus called the Catalonians *Galatae*. The other sons of Captain King Alanus developed and spoke with a Keltoi tongue. The original homeland for the Keltoi-speaking Catalonians was generally located south of the River Danu along the Albus White Mountains range, with Moravia in the east and the Salt Castle and Hallstatt in the west.

After many years of research, I, Boius, the Latini chronicler for the pedigree of Boguarus, the son of Negue, sojourning in Salzburg, hereby preserve a record for future generations in *The Book of the Chronicles of the Bohemian Kings*:

Ewald was the son of Raetus. Raetus was the son of Boius. Boius was the son of Daedalus. Daedalus was the son of Telmun. Telmun was the son of Amphare. Amphare was the son of Hercle. Hercle was the son of Boguarus. Boguarus was the son of Negue. Negue was the son of Alanus. Alanus was the son of Fetebir. Fetebir was the son of Ougomun. Ougomun was the son of Thous. Thous was the son of Boib. Boib was the son of Simeon. Simeon was the son of Mair. Mair was the son of Ethach. Ethach was the son of Aurthach. Aurthach was the son of Ecthet. Ecthet was the son of Oth. Oth was the son of Abir. Abir was the son of Rea. Rea was the son of Ezra. Ezra was the son of Izrau. Izrau was the son of Baath. Baath was the son of Iobaath. Iobaath was the son of Rhodanim. Rhodanim was the son of Javan. Javan was the son of Japheth. Japheth was the son of Noah. Noah was the son of Lamech, Lamech was the son of Methuselah, Methuselah was the son of Enoch, Enoch was the son of Jared, Jared was the son of Mahalaleel, Mahalaleel was the son of Cainan, Cainan was the son of Enos, Enos was the son of Seth, Seth was the son of Adam, Adam was the son of God.

SIX

THE CHRONICLES OF KING HAGANO

(750 BC)

THE ALBUS MOUNTAIN SONS of Captain King Alanus grew stronger in numbers and wealth as trade among the related Catalonian tribes of Europa expanded in accordance with the blessings of Noah, the Herald of Righteousness. The descendents of Captain King Alanus from Panphylia inhabited all of Europa and established trade routes by land, river, and sea; they emerged as twelve tribal nations of great significance and influence.

When I, Prince Hagano, the son of Prince Ewald, the son of King Raetus, was mature and literate, I was introduced to *The Book of the Chronicles of the Bohemian Kings*. As I read the Latin manuscript, I was amazed that so many ancient chroniclers were so wise and desired for us to know who they were and from where we came. It was then that I determined that I would do the same as these great kings. So, in the spirit Captain King Alanus, a friend of Homeros, I set forth to catalogue the Catalonian tribal nations of Europa for future generations.

King Raetus, the son of Boius, was still alive and told me about his fortunate relationship with the Etruscans by marriage to a Rhaetian princess sojourning in the Po River Valley. King Raetus often spoke and wrote in the tongue of the Tyrsenoi, so his dialect was often difficult to interpret. But I pressed on through the language difficulties and learned that King Raetus married among the daughters of Tiras, the youngest son of Japheth, among a people who migrated from Thuras in the northern territory of the Peninsula of Haemus to Tyrsenoi in the territory north of the seven mountains of Romanus on the coast of *Mare Tyrrhēnum*. The Etruscans called themselves Rasenna. The Tyrsenoi-speaking Rasenna planted vineyards there.

King Raetus told me that my father, King Ewald, was intrigued by the Tyrsenoi and their ancestral connection to Tiras, the Red Bull, the uncle and friend of Rhodanim and Ashkenaz, who together built the ancient city of Ilion in Asia, the city that is now remembered as Troy. The mining and commerce of metal, especially copper and iron, led to the prosperity of the Etruscans and their expansion in the region and the western coastal territories on what was once known by the ancients as the Great Sea of Tarshish.

The territory of Raetia was very large, bounded on the west by the country of the Helvetii, on the east by Noricum, the north by Vindelicia, the west by Cisalpine Gaul, and on the south by Venetia et Histria in eastern and central Suittes-Land (containing the Upper River Rhodanus and Lake Constance), and also by Bohemia to the east, and Upper Swabia, Vorarlberg, the greater part of Tirol, and part of Lombardy along the Po River Valley.

Raetia was very mountainous. So in those days, we chiefly supported ourselves by breeding cattle and cutting timber as our ancestors once did in Panphylia. We gave little attention to agriculture, although some of our dales were quite rich and fertile. We produced wine, which was considered equal to any in Italos and Catalonia. We traded pitch, honey, wax, and cheese throughout the world.

I was fascinated by the tradition of our people and of our many kings who dated back to the days of Patriarch Noah. It appeared to me that, as detailed in the Catalonian chronicles, our people were at times a mountain people and at other times a people of the seas. This all made sense to me since Noah was the first shipbuilder sojourning in the mountains of Ararat in the land of Kau on the eastern coastal territories of the Blach See. And later, our people in Kilikia, Panphylia, and Lukka settled in territories where the majestic purple mountains of Tiras rose high above the fertile plains of Tarzu in the north and the Great Sea bound our coastal territories in the south.

I learned much about the methods used for collecting our ancient stories, those passed down from generation to generation, and the ancient chroniclers, how they interviewed the kings and princes of their day, and how they frequently traveled to ancient destinations where our kings formerly sojourned. It occurred to me, in retrospect, that our Albus tribal nation had lived in Suittes-Land for a very short period. It was my understanding that for thousands of years our ancient ancestors lived in the territory of the ancient cities of Tarzu and Iopolis, in Kilikia north by northwest from the ancient Phoenician cities of Byblos, Sidon, and Tyre.

Although I had a strong desire to visit the ancient coastal lands of King Fetebir in Lukka and King Alanus in Panphylia, my father persuaded me to center my studies on learning more about the local Catalonian tribes of Europa and building a catalogue. I heeded my father's counsel.

Our tribes found no delight in predatory booty expeditions, so as our kings taught us, we maintained a strong defense. My project was mostly academic, not initiated with military ambitions. But it was important to our kings that we understood the locations and movements of potential enemies.

King Boius, the son of Daedalus, the son of Telmun, the son of Amphare, died when I was an infant. Fortunately, I learned much about our people from King Raetus, the son of King Boius, who was advanced in years but eager to share stories about our tribal history and traditions.

As the chronicler for our tribe, it was my charge to learn about our ancient history and understand the relationship between our tribal nations and our trade partners around the world. It was also my duty to be studied in the art of war and the geography of Europa. This required me to draw maps for our warriors as in the ancient days in Çatalhöyük.

Early on, it was my observation that the Albus tribesmen preferred conference to chronicle. The few literate ones among us, mostly chroniclers, understood the importance of literacy, documenting our ancestry, and making connections to the LORD God of Noah. So I made it my quest to visit as many of the Catalonian tribes as possible, conference with their tribal chronicler, and record their circumstances.

I learned from our chroniclers that the wisdom of Captain King Alanus was insightful and prophetic in nature. King Alanus encouraged the European tribes to speak with new tongues, build strong defensive citadels in high places (as in Ilion), and construct farmstead communities in strategic territories on defendable plateaus, near rivers for hydration and commerce and in fertile valleys for all our agricultural activities.

It was then that the sons of Captain King Alanus united and built a fortress of refuge, an *oppidum*, with a place of worship for our chroniclers in the Blach Forest of Hesse. It was evident to me that God's favor was on the God-fearing and righteous sons of King Alanus, and that this favor was on all God-fearing Kaucasian tribal nations.

I learned that there were twelve God-fearing tribal colonies in Europa with ancestral ties to Captain King Alanus. The chroniclers compared the migration of King Alanus and his sons in Europa to the migration of the twelve tribes of Israel into Canaan. The chroniclers recorded that God, the Sovereign Ruler of the Universe, apportioned specific territories to the tribes of Alanus as he did in the days of Joshua to the sons of Abraham.

I observed similar apportioning of land to the twelve tribes of King Alanus. Territories were apportioned to King Hessittio and his four sons: Francus (the Franks), Romanus (the Latins), Albanus (the Albans of Swabia who call themselves Germans), and Britto (the British). The Kaucasian brothers and sons of King Hessittio, the son of King Alanus, mapped their territories and early on established trade among themselves by land and water.

And although the tribal nations of Alanus shared common characteristics, they also had their distinctions in industry, art, language, fashion, and science. All the tribal nations supported their chieftain, usually their ancestral king. All cremated their common dead, but they honored their chieftains with ancient tumulus burials. The once peace-seeking Catalonians grew militant and formed armies of warriors to defend their territories from unwelcomed predators.

As the son of Prince Ewald, the son of King Raetus, I learned much about their tribal history, tradition, and rules from my father, whose very name, Ewald, means "rule of law." Even before I became literate, my father instructed me in the Way of our Creator and made me memorize and recite stories from our tradition. I was educated by my father and learned to speak and write in Greek, the ancient phonetic language of all Catalonians, including our Latin cousins, the sons of Latinus, the son of Romanus, who settled on the Italos Peninsula.

My father understood much about our Creator and received instruction in the Way of Righteousness from his father, King Raetus, who led our tribal nation honorably. I learned from King Raetus that King Ewald established a strong alliance with the Rasenna tribes sojourning on the northern-west coast of Italos.

Per our Ionian tradition, the Rasenna were known as Tyrsenoi, and these sojourned by the Sea of Tyrsenoi where Romanus, the firstborn of King Alanus, the son of King Fetebir, first landed. Because of King Raetus, their people also learned to speak in the tongue of the Tyrsenoi, and these became our trade partners on the Great Sea from the Levantine Sea in the east to the Sea of

Tarshish in the west.

After the death of Captain King Alanus, it was reported that the Tyrsenoi became hostile and invaded the territories of Longobardus and Burgundus, the sons of Armenon, and Romanus, the son of Hessittio. It was then that Longobardus and Burgundus abandoned their original settlements and vineyards in the balmy south and migrated north, vowing to return to their homeland in Catalanya one day. But the sons of Romanus grew strong in numbers and defended their territories. The sons of Romanus successfully resisted the aggression of the Tyrsenoi, and that has lasted to this day.

Disconnected from our ancient chronicles, sadly, I discovered that most of the Catalonian tribes in Europa forsook the righteous Way of Noah and Japheth to form tribal unions with nations who did not know the Lord God of Japheth. Myths about the ancient cultures and idolatry of the Canaanites and Egyptians infiltrated and bewitched our Catalonian people. These descendents of the God-fearing Fetebir and Alanus became misguided, greedy, militant, and vulgar.

Although most believe in an intelligent and sovereign Creator who by His Word spoke everything into existence, today some misguided Catalonians have contrived myths of their imagination; they are not living within the Catalonian philosophy per the chronicles of Alanya. So many Catalonians lost understanding about their seed and sadly became unaware of their spiritual genesis, ignorant of the Way of Righteousness handed down to us by King Iobaath and our great kings. Sadly, they grew ignorant and did not refer to themselves as the Catalonian sons of Captain King Alanus.

The one exception to this trend in philosophy was due to the noble works of King Hercle and King Latinus, schooled in the finest schools of Crete. It is my understanding that they all continued in the tradition of our forefathers and recorded the chronicles of kings and kingdoms. They were intentional and understood the conservative values represented in the recordings of Fetebir and Alanus. I was extremely fortunate to be a descendant of King Hercle, one who honored the record and tradition of our Catalonian ancestors.

I learned from King Raetus, the son of King Boius, the son of King Negue, that the peaceful centuries that existed during the expansion under Captain King Alanus were short-lived. The violence and greed that many of my people fled from in Panphylia resides deeply buried within the heart of every man, along with the desire to defend, the desire to aggress, the desire to protect, the desire to seize, the desire to love, and the desire to hate. All these desires issue from the unstable and restless hearts of all men and women. These evil desires that proceed from the heart need to be restrained and harnessed like wild horses.

Full of selfish ambition, the Catalonian tribes began feuds, quarreling, and fighting among themselves. On some occasions, the sons of Captain King Alanus became mercenaries and allied themselves with the emerging Latins of Italos or the ancient Aegean tribes against their own European cousins. As their ancient Aegean ancestors, tribal warfare became the dominant culture among European tribes.

I reasoned that the motives for their many skirmishes have been lodged in the hearts of men since the beginning of the first tribal nation expansion after Noah's death. It seems as if a warrior lives in the brave heart of every man. Our tradition taught them that King Nimrod of Babylon was the Father of War, and just like King Nimrod, the kings and all the king's men seek economic, political, and territorial advantage.

I reasoned that because the hearts of men are desperately wicked and beyond cure, history will forever repeat itself. Men will seek lasting peace in this world, but instead of finding peace, they will only find tribulation. For a season righteousness elevates the souls of a nation, but in the heart of man is great evil, foolishness, and a haunt for selfish ambition that gives birth to every evil practice under Heaven; eventually, the peacekeeping soul loses heart. I concluded that wars and rumors of wars will continue until the end of days. There is no such thing as lasting peace apart from the righteous Way of the coming Peacemaker foretold in our chronicles.

I learned that our Albus ancestors have been miners and iron-workers since our early days dwelling in the Kaucasus Mountains of Japheth. The Hebrew chronicles and our chronicles record stories about Tubal-Cain, the Father of Ironworks. Patriarch Japheth made sure that his sons were skilled in smelting metals, herding cattle, and the sounds of music. The Albus people, the descendents of Rhodanim and Iobaath, have preserved these arts and sciences since our genesis. I observed that this tradition lives on among European Catalonians.

As the sons of Alanus in Europa expanded, they manufac-tured bronze swords and leather scabbards for hunting and tribal warfare. Per *The Book of the Chronicles of the Bohemian Kings,* tanning and leather production has remained the industry of the Albus people since the days of Riphath and Patriarch Tiras. I was informed that the foul-smelling tannenbaum process that Riphath invented originated in the very forests where he hunted and gathered game.

I live in a time in which all men—and some women—are fit with sword and scabbard; all men are trained as men of war, ready to fight, ready to defend, ready to aggress. All men and women have a God-given right to bare arms to protect them-selves from the evil warrior in the heart of other men. We give great priority to defending our inalienable rights and freedoms. Elite warriors emerged amid our tribal nations and led our prepared and armed warriors into battle.

Four-wheeled chariots and charioteers emerged in Europa as on the plains of Kadesh when the Hethite kings and charioteers waged war with the inferior two-wheeled chariots of Egyptian pharaohs. So we buried our charioteers with their chariots as our forefathers did in the ancient world in Anatolia to honor them.

However, the sons of Elishah, the son of Britto, the son of

Hessitio, who eventually colonized on the Great Isles of Javan, did not manufacture chariots as most continental tribal nations. Instead, they continued in the tradition of Noah and of Japheth, Javan, and Tarshish: building merchant ships. Like their forefathers from Panphylia, the British sons of Britto remained shipbuilders, sailors, merchants, and explorers.

It has also been my observation that the Albus Catalonian nations cherished their jewelry as they did in the land of Kau. Our tribes adorned their bodies with bronze, silver, and gold rings, bracelets, anklets, twisted bronze neck ring torcs, and amber and amethyst necklaces and chokers. We harvested golden amber for the necklaces from the *Mare Germanicum* and the *Mare Suebicum*. We gathered amethyst from our European white mountains.

We also established trade with our ancestors in Asia and the tribal nations of the Blach See. The advantaged among our people purchased ivory, pottery, red dye, and the finest of wines of Europa from their southern neighbors and allies, the Dardani, who sojourned southeast of the River Danu. These were believed to be our cousins, descendants of the Patriarch Dodanim.

In the tradition of our people, the sons of Alanus understood the necessity of pan-tribal commerce and established trade routes through many of our tribal territories for exporting amber to emerging nations in the port of Marseille established by Burgundus, the son of Armenon, to ports of call in Italos, in the Balkans, in Asia, in Iopolis, in Carthage, and in Egypt. Our amber gemstones even made their way to the Far East on the ancient silk roads of Haran and by sea.

Like our ancestors, Dodanim and Iobaath on Marmara Island, the Albus sons of Alanya became stonecutters and grew proficient in creating sandstone stelae. We were familiar with stonecutting, having made stelae since the days of Noah. The Hebrew Moses, the Man of God, created stelae for inscribing God's Ten Commandments. Significant edicts through history have been inscribed or painted on stelae to preserve the historic record. It is my understanding that stelae bust of god-like Egyptian pharaohs survive in our day.

*****

While visiting a like-minded Skuthai chronicler sojourning on the isle north of Briton, I sought to learn more about the affairs of Israel. Our tradition taught us that Captain King Alanus was inspired by a Skuthai chronicler from the land of Patriarch Magog. The Skuthai chroniclers kept a chronicle of their kings going back to Noah, as was the custom among our people. I was curious to meet with chroniclers from the Skuthai tribal nation who claimed to be descendants of the Patriarch Magog. I was not certain that their people continued in the tradition of record keeping.

After many days of searching on the island for the Skuthai chronicle of kings, I was pleased to find their records with their chronicler, a God-fearing Skoth, a sailor named Simon.

Will the help of translators, Simon told me the story of a man named Jonah, a prophet of God who resisted God's charge and boarded one of their vessels returning from a merchant trip from Tyre to Tarshish. The story went this way.

> "Now the word of the Lord came to Jonah the son of Amittai, saying, 'Arise, go to Nineveh, that great city, and call out against it, for their evil has come up before me.' But Jonah rose to flee to Tarshish from the presence of the Lord. He went down to Joppa and found a ship going to Tarshish. So he paid the fare and went down into it, to go with them to Tarshish, away from the presence of the Lord.
>
> "But the Lord hurled a great wind upon the sea, and there was a mighty tempest on the sea, so that the ship threatened to break up. Then the mariners were afraid, and each cried out to his god. And they hurled the cargo that was in the ship into the sea to lighten it for them. But Jonah had gone down into the inner part of the ship and had lain down and was

fast asleep. So the captain came and said to him, 'What do you mean, you sleeper? Arise, call out to your god! Perhaps the god will give a thought to us, that we may not perish.'

"And they said to one another, 'Come, let us cast lots, that we may know on whose account this evil has come upon us.' So they cast lots, and the lot fell on Jonah. Then they said to him, 'Tell us on whose account this evil has come upon us. What is your occupation? And where do you come from? What is your country? And of what people are you?' And he said to them, 'I am a Hebrew, and I fear the Lord, the God of heaven, who made the sea and the dry land.' Then the men were exceedingly afraid and said to him, 'What is this that you have done!' For the men knew that he was fleeing from the presence of the Lord, because he had told them.

"Then they said to him, 'What shall we do to you, that the sea may quiet down for us?' For the sea grew more and more tempestuous. He said to them, 'Pick me up and hurl me into the sea; then the sea will quiet down for you, for I know it is because of me that this great tempest has come upon you.' Nevertheless, the men rowed hard to get back to dry land, but they could not, for the sea grew more and more tempestuous against them. Therefore they called out to the Lord, 'O Lord, let us not perish for this man's life, and lay not on us innocent blood, for you, O Lord, have done as it pleased you.' So they picked up Jonah and hurled him into the sea, and the sea ceased from its raging. Then the men feared the Lord exceedingly, and they offered a sacrifice to the Lord and made vows."

(This passage would become part of the Hebrew Bible, book of Jonah, 1:1-2:16.)

Simon ended the tragic story about Jonah and the mariners aboard the ship who tried to spare Jonah from death. Though they tried desperately to save this God-fearing man who was running away from God's mission, sadly, Jonah perished in the deep waters of Tarshish. I said to Simon, "Those God-fearing British mariners were so aware of their sinfulness in throwing

151

Jonah overboard to his death that they offered up a sacrifice to atone for their sins."

Like the British mariners returning from Joppa, Simon and I were sobered by the story of Jonah's tribulation and considered the message that God was speaking, admonishing us to fear God and obey his commandments.

Simon and I were of kindred spirit, sons of righteousness, and we could conference for days about our common interest in God and his Way. We both sought after the ultimate in wisdom, the LORD God of Noah, our Creator. Together we prayed for understanding minds so we could grasp the length and width and depth of God's love for all men that He created. We encouraged one another daily to obey the LORD God and to honor Him by keeping His precepts. I perceived that the bond between us was a special gift from our Creator in these desperate times.

While I extended my visit on the lovely, green Skuthai isle, Simon called for a special conference. He invited all the tribal chroniclers on the British Isles. As was the tradition of our people, we congregated at the Great Stone Henge and, in turn, shared our tribal traditions.

It was interesting to me that some of the chroniclers who attended the conference recorded the Hebrew name, Japheth, as Sceaf. I reasoned that the British and Bohemian chroniclers preserved the Hebrew name, Japheth, because of our close relationship with Eber, and later Abraham, while sojourning in Haran. The Skuthai tribes had little or no relationship with the sons of Eber. So, I presumed that Sceaf was the name given for Japheth at the tower of Babylon, where the nations received their root tongues.

Also during my visit, which was most enlightening, Simon spoke well of one man, Xenophanes, a philosopher, a lover of wisdom who also exulted our Creator, as did the philosopher Hesiod, who spoke of a "void" that existed before the earth was created. As a seasoned mariner, Simon had this insight: "The creation tradition is universally understood throughout the earth by every tribe and nation. Hesiod spoke of our Creator who formed the earth out of the void. Then out of the void came darkness, and out of the darkness came light and day as in our tradition."

Simon memorized and shared with me, precisely and word for word, the very words of Xenophanes, who spoke of fellow philosophers Homeros, an academic friend of Captain King Alanus, and Hesiod. Xenophanes had said:

"Homeros and Hesiod attributed to the gods all the things which among men are shameful and blameworthy—theft and adultery and mutual deception. But there is one God, greatest among gods and men, similar to mortals neither in shape nor in thought. He sees as a whole. He thinks as a whole. He hears as a whole. Always he remains in the same state, changing not at all. But far from toil he governs everything with His mind."

I learned from Simon that Xenophanes was from Ionia. He was an adventurer who traveled throughout the world influencing the lives of mariners, like those who tried to save Jonah. Like me, Xenophanes was a poet and a student of philosophy, history, and theology. He was reported as one who often criticized social practices and organized religions of men.

Simon said that when Xenophanes was visiting the Skuthai, he was critical of the mythology of Homeros. Like me, the Ionian poet thought the Greeks where obsessed with athleticism, and he was often heard satirizing the ridiculous pantheon of anthropomorphic gods.

Xenophanes was a man who knew the Way of God and was concerned about future generations of Ionians. Whenever he had the chance, he called them back to the God of Noah, Japheth, and Javan. In a world of misguided idolatries and philosophies of men, it was refreshing to learn of another God-fearing soul, one from the pedigree of our Ionian brothers. Simon reported that Xenophanes retuned to Syrakousai after visiting our British neighbors to the south.

I was informed by Simon and the other chroniclers that they maintained communications with Israel through the British mariners. Simon was told about a scribe from Judea named Baruch, the son of Neriah. Baruch was the trusted Hebrew scribe and chronicler for a prophet of the Most High named Jeremiah, a great man who wept out loud prophesying the destruction of Jerusalem and prophesying a world at war. Baruch wanted the whole world to be warned about the impending doom, so he made copies for the Phoenician mariners for distribution among the coastal nations of Japheth.

I learned from Simon that Baruch gave express orders to the Phoenician merchants to convey this message to Xenophanes and to the Catalonian chroniclers on the British Isles beyond the seas of Tarshish. Baruch believed that if God-fearing tribal nations in the world exercised faith in their Creator—like the Hebrew Abraham—humbled themselves, repented of their idolatry, and prayed to their Creator, God would hear their prayers, forgive their sins, and heal their land.

Hearing these words, I desired to know the LORD, and appealed to Simon to read me the Word of the LORD. I did not know the Hebrew language, so Simon translated the scroll and read aloud:

> "In the fourth year of Jehoiakim the son of Josiah, king of Judah, this word came to Jeremiah from the Lord: 'Take a scroll and write on it all the words that I have spoken to you against Israel and Judah and all the nations, from the day I spoke to you, from the days of Josiah until today. It may be that the house of Judah will hear all the disaster that I intend to do to them, so that every one may turn from his evil way, and that I may forgive their iniquity and their sin.'
>
> "Then Jeremiah called Baruch the son of Neriah, and Baruch wrote on a scroll at the dictation of Jeremiah all the words of the Lord that he had spoken to him. And Jeremiah

ordered Baruch, saying, 'I am banned from going to the house of the Lord, so you are to go, and on a day of fasting in the hearing of all the people in the Lord's house you shall read the words of the Lord from the scroll that you have written at my dictation. You shall read them also in the hearing of all the men of Judah who come out of their cities. It may be that their plea for mercy will come before the Lord, and that every one will turn from his evil way, for great is the anger and wrath that the Lord has pronounced against this people.' And Baruch the son of Neriah did all that Jeremiah the prophet ordered him about reading from the scroll the words of the Lord in the Lord's house.

"In the fifth year of Jehoiakim the son of Josiah, king of Judah, in the ninth month, all the people in Jerusalem and all the people who came from the cities of Judah to Jerusalem proclaimed a fast before the Lord. Then, in the hearing of all the people, Baruch read the words of Jeremiah from the scroll, in the house of the Lord, in the chamber of Gemariah the son of Shaphan the secretary, which was in the upper court, at the entry of the New Gate of the Lord's house.

"When Micaiah the son of Gemariah, son of Shaphan, heard all the words of the Lord from the scroll, he went down to the king's house, into the secretary's chamber, and all the officials were sitting there: Elishama the secretary, Delaiah the son of Shemaiah, Elnathan the son of Achbor, Gemariah the son of Shaphan, Zedekiah the son of Hananiah, and all the officials. And Micaiah told them all the words that he had heard when Baruch read the scroll in the hearing of the people. Then all the officials sent Jehudi the son of Nethaniah, son of Shelemiah, son of Cushi, to say to Baruch, 'Take in your hand the scroll that you read in the hearing of the people, and come.' So Baruch the son of Neriah took the scroll in his hand and came to them. And they said to him, 'Sit down and read it.' So Baruch read it to them. When they heard all the words, they turned one to another in fear. And they said to Baruch, 'We must report all these words to the king.' Then they asked Baruch, 'Tell us, please, how did you write all these words? Was it at his dictation?' Baruch answered them, 'He dictated all these words to me, while I wrote them with ink on the scroll.' Then the officials said to Baruch, 'Go and hide, you and Jeremiah, and let no one know where you are.'

"So they went into the court to the king, having put the scroll in the chamber of Elishama the secretary, and they reported all the words to the king. Then the king sent Jehudi to get the scroll, and he took it from the chamber of Elishama the secretary. And Jehudi read it to the king and all the officials who stood beside the king. It was the ninth month, and the king was sitting in the winter house, and there was a fire burning in the fire pot before him. As Jehudi read three or four columns, the king would cut them off with a knife and throw them into the fire in the fire pot, until the entire scroll was consumed in the fire that was in the fire pot. Yet neither the king nor any of his servants who heard all these words was afraid, nor did they tear their garments. Even when Elnathan and Delaiah and Gemariah urged the king not to burn the scroll, he would not listen to them. And the king commanded Jerahmeel the king's son and Seraiah the son of Azriel and Shelemiah the son of Abdeel to seize Baruch the secretary and Jeremiah the prophet, but the Lord hid them.

"Now after the king had burned the scroll with the words that Baruch wrote at Jeremiah's dictation, the word of the Lord came to Jeremiah: 'Take another scroll and write on it all the former words that were in the first scroll, which Jehoiakim the king of Judah has burned. And concerning Jehoiakim king of Judah you shall say, "Thus says the Lord, 'You have burned this scroll, saying, "Why have you written in it that the king of Babylon will certainly come and destroy this land, and will cut off from it man and beast?" Therefore thus says the Lord concerning Jehoiakim king of Judah: He shall have none to sit on the throne of David, and his dead body shall be cast out to the heat by day and the frost by night. And I will punish him and his offspring and his servants for their iniquity. I will bring upon them and upon the inhabitants of Jerusalem and upon the people of Judah all the disaster that I have pronounced against them, *but they would not hear.'*

"Then Jeremiah took another scroll and gave it to Baruch the scribe, the son of Neriah, who wrote on it at the dictation of Jeremiah all the words of the scroll that Jehoiakim king of Judah had burned in the fire. And many similar words were added to them."

(This passage would become part of the Hebrew Bible, book of Jeremiah, 36:1-32.)

Simon paused, then continued, this time reciting from memory the words of the prophet Jeremiah.

"Let not the wise man boast in his wisdom, let not the mighty man boast in his might, let not the rich man boast in his riches, but let him who boasts boast in this, that he understands and knows me, that I am the Lord who practices steadfast love, justice, and righteousness in the earth. For in these things I delight, declares the Lord."

(This passage would become part of the Hebrew Bible, book of Jeremiah 9:23, 24.)

Simon spoke of the great knowledge and wisdom of the prophet Jeremiah. I discerned that these prophetic words of knowledge were truths and wisdom from God for all nations. I understood that the prophet Jeremiah was an ambassador of the LORD God reasoning with the wayward sons of Israel with great hope that the sons of Israel and King David, reported as a man after God's heart, would repent and turn back to their Creator-God. I learned from their ancient chronicles that these practices are the things that delight the LORD God of Noah. Man's conscience also speaks loudly of our Creator's Way. Baruch went on to report the words of the prophet Jeremiah to Simon, saying,

"And many nations will pass by this city, and every man will say to his neighbor, 'Why has the Lord dealt thus with this great city?' And they will answer, 'Because they have

forsaken the covenant of the Lord their God and worshiped other gods and served them.'"
(This passage would become part of the Hebrew Bible, book of Jeremiah 22:7-9.)

Simon told me that Jeremiah spoke of a coming Redeemer, a righteous Branch who would execute justice and righteousness. Simon continued with Jeremiah's words.

"'Behold, the days are coming,' declares the Lord, 'when I will raise up for David a righteous Branch, and he shall reign as king and deal wisely, and shall execute justice and righteousness in the land. In his days Judah will be saved, and Israel will dwell securely. And this is the name by which he will be called: "The Lord is our righteousness."'"
(This passage would become part of the Hebrew Bible, book of Jeremiah, 23:5, 6.)

As Simon spoke about the Branch who is to come, I understood from our chronicles that the Branch was the same as the Seed of Abraham who would bring righteousness by faith to Israel and all the tribal nations of Ham and Japheth. This was wonderful news to my soul. I spontaneously began worshiping the blessed name of God, saying, "The LORD is our righteousness." Simon responded in faith also, repeating, "The Lord is our righteousness."

Concerning all the nations of the earth and with great soberness of spirit, Simon reported to me that our Maker was not going to let the earth and all the kingdoms of the earth go unpunished for worshiping idols. God's justice prevails in all the earth. Simon continued and read from the chronicles of Baruch and the prophet of God.

Thus the Lord, the God of Israel, said to me: "Take from my hand this cup of the wine of wrath, and make all the nations to whom I send you drink it. They shall drink and stagger and be crazed because of the sword that I am sending among them."

So I took the cup from the Lord's hand, and made all the nations to whom the Lord sent me drink it: Jerusalem and the cities of Judah, its kings and officials, to make them a desolation and a waste, a hissing and a curse, as at this day; Pharaoh king of Egypt, his servants, his officials, all his people, and all the mixed tribes among them; all the kings of the land of Uz, the homeland of Job, and all the kings of the land of the Philistines (Ashkelon, Gaza, Ekron, and the remnant of Ashdod); Edom, Moab, and the sons of Ammon; all the kings of Tyre, all the kings of Sidon, and the kings of the coastland across the sea; Dedan, in Arabia, the sons of Raamah, the fourth son of Cush, the son of Ham; Tema, on the Atlantis coast of Africa where calabash gourds are grown and exported all over the world; Buz, the younger brother of Uz, the second son of Nahor, the son of Terah, Abraham's brother, and all who cut the corners of their hair; all the kings of Arabia and all the kings of the mixed tribes who dwell in the desert; all the kings of Zimri, all the kings of Elam, and all the kings of Media; all the kings of the north, far and near, one after another, and all the kingdoms of the world that are on the face of the earth. And after them the king of Babylon shall drink.

Then you shall say to them, "Thus says the LORD of hosts, the God of Israel: 'Drink, be drunk and vomit, fall and rise no more, because of the sword that I am sending among you.'"

And if they refuse to accept the cup from your hand to drink, then you shall say to them, "Thus says the Lord of hosts: 'You must drink! For behold, I begin to work disaster at the city that is called by my name, and shall you go unpunished? You shall not go unpunished, for I am summoning a sword against all the inhabitants of the earth,' declares the Lord of hosts."

(This passage would become part of the Hebrew Bible, book of Jeremiah, 25:15-29.)

The words of the prophet—"I am summoning a sword against all the inhabitants of the earth" —was branded on my soul. Like Simon, my heart was sobered. My flesh was quiet and still. Peace filled my soul, but also terror. In the stillness of the moment, and humbly lying prostrate with the ground beneath me and before the Holy One, I worshiped, crying out, "I am a man of unclean lips amid a people of unclean lips. Save us, Oh God, or we perish like Jonah!"

My time with Simon the Skoth was well spent. Simon was a man of great faith and character. From deep within, I thought of Baruch, and what a great privilege it must have been to record the words of Jeremiah, such a great prophet and spokesman for God. Baruch was so concerned for the plight of the nations that he wanted to proclaim the Word of the LORD to all the tribal nations of this world.

Although I knew in my heart that our Maker chose the bloodline of Israel to bring redemption for all the nations of the earth, it was after speaking to Simon that I understood the great love and care that the LORD God has for all the world. It was not God's desire that any should perish, but that all would come to their senses and repent of their many idolatries. As a good father disciplines his son, so our Creator-God disciplines all His sons who call upon His name. God is just and executes righteous judgments with a purpose—to turn our hearts toward Him.

I was sobered when I understood from the prophecies of Jeremiah that all the kingdoms of the earth were about to be thrust into tribal warfare. The LORD God of Noah was using the sword of one king to discipline another, the sword of one tribal nation to discipline the next. I perceived that unless the nations of the world repented from their lawless deeds and cried out for mercy, soon the Albus tribal nations of Alanus, along with all the other nations of the world, would enter a time of great tribulation and judgment. Our Creator was about to discipline the Kaucasus sons of Japheth as he disciplined the sons of Eber when they turned from the Way of the LORD.

Unlike the flood of Noah, which resulted in a new earth, creating seven divided continents while destroying all the inhabitants of the earth (save eight men and women), I understood that this coming judgment was a corrective measure designed to prepare the hearts of men for the coming righteous Branch of David. This time God was going to spare plants and animals from judgment. God's loving purpose in discipline is always to turn the wayward hearts of His sons and daughters back to Himself.

When it was reported that the city of King David was destroyed and the people of Judea were taken into captivity to Babylon, this was a sign for all nations that the sword was set against all of mankind. I reasoned that if God did not spare the sons of Eber and Abraham, who would endure the Day of God's judgments? It is a fearful thing indeed to fall into the hands of our living God.

Once again, history repeated itself. As in the days of Patriarch Noah, the LORD God was not pleased with covetous and greedy men and was orchestrating chaos in the world to bring the nations to their senses, to bring all the nations of Shem, Ham, and Japheth to repentance.

Most tribal nations of the world had forsaken their records and were ignorant of their genesis, which was rooted in the LORD God of Noah, the Creator of the heavens and the earth. I acknowledged that most of the tribal nations of the world had forgotten that we are all from one source, and all sons of Noah and sons of Shem, Ham, and Japheth. As Japheth, the Great Voice, said, "We are eighty shades of brown."

Knowing that our Creator exists from everlasting to everlasting and demands our worship, the nations stubbornly and willfully spurned God's love and turned to idols of man's imagination and coveted the prosperity of their neighbors.

So, encouraged by the report of my dear friend, Simon, and with great hope, I vowed to call upon the LORD God of Noah most earnestly, as long as I have breath and life, praying, "Come, thou Branch of the Most High. Come, redeem us from the curse of Adam's sin. Come, 'The Lord Is Our Righteousness,' and bring lasting peace, joy, and love to our fallen and depraved world. Rescue us! Come, thy kingdom! Be done, thy will!"

Like Baruch, I vowed to spread the word of this prophesy to the tribal nations of Captain King Alanus in Europa. Everywhere I traveled I purposed to sound an alarm that the wayward kingdoms of this world were about to experience the judgments of God. I purposed to make appeals to my kinsmen and, like Xenophanes, to urge them to renounce their foolish myths and seek mercy from the LORD God of Noah, the Herald of Righteousness, and Japheth, the Great Voice of our people. I prayed for an understanding mind into the spiritual mysteries of God and for listening ears among the tribal nations of Japheth.

After spending several weeks with Simon the Skoth, I returned to my libri and scrolls where I continued to catalogue the destinations, accomplishments, and circumstances of the prodigy of Captain King Alanus. I routinely investigated and catalogued the twelve tribes of Alanus and their territories.

First, I researched the territories of Francus, Romanus, Britto, and Albanus. Second, I researched the territories of Gothus, Walagothus, Gepidus, Burgundus, and Longobardus. Last, I researched the territories of Wandalus, Saxo, and their own tribal nation, the descendents of Boguarus.

THE COLONIES OF FRANCUS KINGS

I learned from King Raetus and the other chroniclers that the territory of King Francus, the firstborn son of Hessittio, the firstborn son of Captain King Alanus, was bound by the River Seine in the west and the middle River Rhodanus in the east, with access to both the channel of the Britons and the *Mare Germanicum*. In the early days of expansion, the Catalonian tribes of King Francus settled in the wetland territory where the River Rhodanus empties into *Mare Germanicum*.

The River Meuse with all its tributaries was the homeland to various tribal nations. I discovered no chroniclers among the sons of King Francus, so it was difficult to determine which tribal nations had Catalonian roots and which did not.

I am not certain, but it appeared to me that there were at least six bands who might be descendents of King Francus: the Sicambri sons of Francus, the Salii sons of Francus, the Bructeri sons of Francus, the Ampsivarii sons of Francus, the Chattuarii sons of Francus, and the Chamavi sons of Francus. A league of these six Catalonian tribes made up the kingdom of Francia.

The Sicambri Franks colonized the low country, the delta swampland of the upper, right bank of the River Rhodanus and River Meuse, which often flooded like the plains of Egypt. I learned that the Sicambri warriors tied their hair in knots and were men of war given to frequent raids.

The Salian Franks colonized the upper River Meuse basin with the shallow River Scheldt as their northwestern boundary. The Salian Franks were reported and characterized as a mischievous bunch, reminiscent of the wicked spawn of Peirates, the son of Tiras, who terrorized our ancestors along the southern shores in Panphylia.

The Bructeri Franks colonized the swampy Emsland territory between the River Ems and the Lippe tributary of the River Rhodanus, both birthed in the uplands of the Teutoburg Forest. The River Ems has its source at the western base of the southernmost portion of the Teutoburg Forest.

The Ampsivarii Franks are known as the "men of the Ems" and sojourn around the middle of the River Ems, which flows into the *Mare Germanicum.* The Ampsivarii tribal nation made their homeland north from their neighboring Bructeri cousins.

The Chattuarii Franks colonized a territory east of the northern River Rhodanus. Their land was south of their Bructeri cousins.

And I learned that the Chamavi Franks were settlers who colonized a territory along the north bank of the Lower River Rhodanus.

As I continued my investigation, I discovered that seven other tribes emerged from the sons of Francus in the central and western territories of Europa: the Seduni, the Sequani, the Allobroges, the Segusiavi, the Eluveitie, the Vocontii, and the Volcae.

The Seduni tribe settled the territory in the valley of the Upper River Rhodanus. Their people lived to the east of the Veragri, in the region of Valais. Their chief town was Sedunum in Suittes-Land.

I learned that the Sequani tribe colonized a territory in the upper river basin of the River Saône, the valley of the Doubs and the Jura Mountains, their territory corresponding to a section of the land of Burgundy.

The Jura Mountain range divided the Sequani from the Helvetii in the east. The Jura Mountains belonged to the Sequani. A narrow passage ran between the River Rhodanus and Lake Geneva, which also belonged to the Sequanians. The Sequani tribe did not occupy the confluence of the Saône into the Rhodanus, as their neighbors, the Helvetii tribe, plundered that territory and its occupants.

Toward the west from the Jura Mountains was the Aedui tribe on southern border at Mâcon. The River Saône separated the Sequani from the Aedui tribe. The Sequani occupied the eastern bank of the River Saône. The northeast corner of their territory touched on the River Rhodanus.

I learned that the Allobroges tribe settled the territory between the River Rhodanus and Lake Geneva in Suittes-Land in the Vienne River Valley. The Allobroges herded goats there.

The Segusiavi tribe settled the territory of Lugdunum. I learned that their name means "victorious ones."

The Eluveitie tribe occupied the grassy Suittes-Land plateau. The people of Eluveitie were numerous and prospered from the terrain. The Eluveitie were divided into three descendant tribes: the Verbigeni, the Tigurini, and the Töygenoi. All of them where known to have close trade relations with the Etruscan sons of Tiras.

I learned that the Vocontii tribe occupied the east bank of the River Rhodanus and were reported as those who controlled the trade routes between the River Rhodanus and River Durance.

And the Volcae tribe settled the territory of Mittelgebirge in Moravia, east of the Boii tribe. The land was suited for agriculture, but the Volcae tribe excelled in smelting metals. The quality of their weaponry was reported as unsurpassed in all the world. Early on, the Volcae tribe established a close relationship with the Boii tribe to the east in the upper basin of the River Albis.

THE COLONIES OF ROMAN KINGS

I learned from King Raetus and the chroniclers that the descendents of Latinus, the firstborn son of Romanus, the son of Hessittio, along with Longobardus, the son of Armenon, inhabited the Peninsula of Italos to the south and to the north respectively. As the tribes of Romanus and Longobardus enlarged and prospered, they established their own tongues. In time, the Latins distinguished themselves from the Ionians, who spoke Greek.

Understanding the purposes of God, Captain King Alanus encouraged the development of tribal tongues. It appeared to me that the LORD God of King Alanus continued to provision glossolalia and promoted greater diversity among the dispersed Catalonian tribes. According to God's plans and purposes, several romantic languages emerged from the Latin tongue of Latinus, the Father of all European languages. In our day, as it was in the beginning of the expansion, the sons of Latinus were distinguished as the most informed and literate band among the tribes of Captain King Alanus.

THE COLONIES OF BRITISH KINGS

After a few years of record keeping, I revisited Simon and the other chroniclers on the British Isle. It was during this second visit that I learned about several royal houses that chronicled back to Noah. I was introduced to Ferrex, the first prince of King Gorboduc, a descendant of Elishah, who reported that the tribes on the British Isle were on the verge of civil war. I also discovered that the chronicles of Prince Ferrex agreed with our chronicles, but Elishah added all the sons and grandsons of Captain King Alanus. *The Book of the Chronicles of British Kings* rightly recorded our people as Bavarians, descendents of Negue. The British Chronicles also referred to Japheth and used Hebrew names. Later I amended our chronicle of kings, adding the sons and grandsons of Captain King Alanus.

Prince Ferrex informed Simon and me that the royal houses of Hessittio intermarried. He reported that then Prince Aeneas from Ilion married the Latin Princess Lavinia, a descendent of King Hessittio. And the niece of Princess Lavinia married the grandson of King Aeneas, Prince Silvius. Then Prince Brutus, the son of Silvius, married Ignoge, daughter of Grecian King Pandrasus. It was no surprise to me that the descendents of Elishah and Latinus would intermarry being that they were such good fellows onboard Europa I. Later Queen Cordelia, the daughter of British King Leir, married Aganippus, King of the Franks, also a descendent of King Hessittio.

Prince Ferrex informed Simon and me about other chroniclers, the eight sons of King Woden, the son of Frithuwald. Like the sons of Captain King Alanus, the sons of Woden became the chieftains of several royal houses and all of King Woden's sons chronicled their lineage back to Bedwig, the son of *Sceaf*, the son of *Noe*. Prince Ferrex and I know *Bedwig* as Magog, *Sceaf* as Japheth, and *Noe* as the great Noah, the Herald of Righteousness. Per these ancient chronicles, the royal houses of King Woden descended from his sons: Prince Baeldaeg, Prince Winta, Prince Witta, Prince Wihtlaeg, Prince Waegdaeg, Prince Caser,

Norwegian Prince Niodr, and Danish Prince Skjoldr. These royal houses trace their lineage to King Woden and all the way back to *Noe*.

Again, I realized that many of the chroniclers that I met on my second journey to the Great Isles mentioned that they had no connection with the sons of Eber, the Hebrew nation of Shem. They spoke exclusively of *Sceaf* the great progenitor and the righteous instructions given to him by *Noe*.

I learned from Prince Ferrex that the descendants of Elishah, the son of Britto, the son of Captain King Alanus, inhabited the Great Isles where Dodanim and Iobaath built the Great Stone Henge. I was so intrigued by our chronicles, and I felt I was part of something extremely significant, the fulfillment of God's plan to expand Japheth according to the prayer of Noah.

I learned from Prince Ferrex that much of our understanding of British pedigree was due to the brilliant work of King Brutus, the youngest son of King Silvius, who colonized the Great Isle of Javan and became the first of British kings. I discovered that King Brutus wrote extensively and with great detail about the migration of the sons of King Aeneas from Ilion to the early British colony. I understood from our chronicles that then Prince Aeneas returned to Ilion, but I did not know the rest of the story, one that King Brutus so well described in the tradition that accompanied *The Book of the Chronicles of British Kings*.

I was pleased to learned that other distant Kaucasian cousins sojourning in Europa also were literate and maintained ancestral chronicles dating back to the days of Noah. In fact, I discovered that there were many chroniclers in Europa. The Skuthai tribes sojourning to the north of Briton maintained a record of their past kings, as did several other tribal nations on the British Isles. This discovery proved fascinating to me. When I was ignorant, I falsely presumed that all our historical records were maintained in verbal tradition only and thus subject to exaggeration and myth. That there were so many chroniclers like me who would be charged and disciplined to record their connection to the LORD

God of Creation was sobering and provoked a deep worship of the LORD that arose from the depths of my soul. I realized that the LORD God of Noah inspired Kaucasian chroniclers to record their ancestry; this was not exclusively the province of Hebrew chroniclers.

I was inspired by the chronicles and had a strong desire to worship the LORD God of Noah, and I was inspired to learn the sounds of music like Jubal. So shortly after I returned home, I became a pfeiffer like the sons of Riphath and learned to dance before the LORD like Madai.

During my second visit, I also learned from Prince Ferrex that six other tribal nations emerged on the British Isles: Parisii, Siturii, Dumnonii, Belgae, Atrebates, and Iceni. These six tribes were related to the Veneti tribe that sojourned on the western coast of Europa north of the Iberian Peninsula. Several of the tribes also established settlements northeast of the Veneti tribe.

The Parisii tribe and the Siturii tribe occupied the northern half of the Great Isles. Much is known about the Parisii tribe since half of this tribe sojourned on the Great Isles; the other half lived on the banks of the River Sequana, which provided a water trade route from the Great Isles to the land of Burgundus. However, little is known about the Siturii tribes, which settled to the southeast of the Parisii tribe on the Great Isles. I speculate that the Siturii probably practiced a quiet and simple lifestyle.

The Dumnonii tribe colonized the southeast regions of the Great Isles, the territory of Dumnonia on the banks of the River Exe.

Although the Dumnonii people supported both agricultural and fishing communities, the primary industry of the Dumnonii tribe is tin mining. Per our tradition, Captain King Alanus helped to establish trade with the Phoenicians in Gadir from the Port of Ictis. From the Phoenician city of Gadir on the Iberian Peninsula toward the south, Dumnonian tin was exported to many Great Sea nations.

When I turned my attention to the mainland of Europa, I

learned that the Belgae tribesmen are a militant band, quick-tempered, and often incite conflict with their industrious neighbors. The Belgae joined a league of warrior nations that settled along the River Rhodanus. Like the Parisii tribe, half of their people dwell along the River Rhodanus and half on the Great Isles.

The Atrebas tribes tolerated their militant Belgae relatives on their southern border and were reported as an inland people living in placid farmstead communities. Like the Parisii and the Belgae people, the Atrebates also settled in the territory of Francus.

The Iceni inhabited a small peninsula on the west coast of the British Isles. The Iceni tribesman wore torcs of silver and gold around their necks and shoulders and are said to be an equestrian people with a great love for horses, just like the great progenitor Magog.

THE COLONIES OF SWABIAN KINGS

After my extended second visit with Prince Ferrex and the Britons, I returned to my prolonged home in Glauberg in Raetia. In periods between my interviews with King Raetus, I learned from King Ewald that Albanus, the son of Hessittio, shortened the name of his father, Hessittio, to his nickname: Hesse. Albanus and Hesse left the British Isles and traveled south on the River Rhodanus, the river that our tribes distinguished from the portion of the River Rhodanus in the south, which flows into the Great Sea of Tarshish. Both words derive from the same root—"to run"—and bespeak of our ancient ancestors who were Olympic runners, King Rhodanim and King Iobaath.

King Albanus and King Hesse inhabited and settled the southwestern territories of the River Rhodanus, southeast from the territory of King Francus. Foreigners called the territory of Hesse and Albanus *Alemanni*. The descendant tribes of Hesse and Albanus sojourn in the upper Rhodanus River Valley to this day. The territory that they occupied also became known as Swabia.

They expanded south and occupied territories surrounding the Swabian Forest and the Swabian Sea at the confluence of River Rhodanus.

In the beginning as the Alemanni expanded and developed, the sons of Hesse and Albanus maintained a strong connection with their immediate kinsmen, Francus and Britto. They maintained a strong brotherhood with their cousins, the sons of Armenon, to the north and in western territories. They also maintained relationships with their cousins in south central Europa, the sons of Negue, from Hesse toward the east and southeast at Hallstatt, at Saltsburg, and at Radasbona on the River Regen, one of the twenty-eight tributaries of the River Danu of Patriarch Riphath.

The Catalonian sons of Albanus also developed their own Alemannic tongue to set them apart from other tribes. Their language derived from a root word meaning "all men." The Alemannic language united the sons of Albanus as several Alemannic dialects emerged from the root language. The Hessian dialect named after Hessittio is spoken to this day.

It was quite interesting to me that the continent of Europa and the ancient tribal nations that sojourn there—the sons of Romanus, the Latini in their Latin language, the Grecian sons of Javan in their ancient Greek language, the sons of Eber in their ancient Hebrew language, and the sons of Armenon in their ancient Armenian language—referred to our people and language as *Germania*. I discovered that the word *Germania* was derived from the Ionian word for *germ*, which spoke clearly of the procreative philosophy of the men of Germania and their great progenitor, Riphath, the Germ Man. I was reminded of the charge of Noah to Japheth: "Be fruitful and multiply and inhabit the earth." I was reminded of the blessing of Noah over Japheth and his sons, encouraging them to enlarge.

However, I discovered that the Catalonian sons of Captain King Alanus and many coastal nations of the world call the descendents of Hesse *Allemagne*, so named after Albanus, the son of Hessittio. But I, along with the tribal nations on the

Mare Germanicum, the germ of Riphath, the son of Gomer, refer to these ancient lands in the ancient tongue of Riphath as *Deutschland*.

The Hessian sons of Albanus distinguished themselves physically from other tribes in Europa, especially the sons of Francus to the northwest. The Suebian warriors combed their hair to the side and twisted their hair in a knot. The more sophisticated the knot, the more noble and wealthy the warrior.

I learned from King Raetus about the Catalonian sons of King Armenon and their settlements: the territories of Gothus, Walagothus, Gepidus, Burgundus, and Longobardus. From what I already knew about the sons of King Armenon, I was certain that no written records were maintained and the tribes of Armenon have lost sight of the expansion plans and purposes of the LORD God of Noah. It appeared to me that these tribes did not appoint and educate chroniclers, and sadly, they were largely barbarian.

I learned from King Raetus that the sons of Gothus, the firstborn son of Armenon, was the father of the nomadic Goths. King Armenon loved his vineyards and his wines. It was reported that King Armenon loved his wines so much that he named his firstborn son to "pour"! Among the Catalonians it is rumored that King Armenon was drinking wine when Prince Gothus was born in Alanya on the coast of Panphylia.

However, as an adult, Prince Gothus despised fine wines in favor of mead and beer. Unlike his younger brothers, Burgundus and Longobardus, who followed in their father's footsteps as settlers, planting vineyards in their newfound territories, Prince Gothus, as well as Prince Walagothus and Prince Gepidus, were unsettled adventurers who had little time to care for vineyards and stow wine.

From their homeland on the small Island of Gotland amid *Mare Suebicum*, east of Scandza, the aggressive, compulsive sons of King Gothus were unsatisfied with their territorial lot. So these Catalonian tribes became men of war and pursued a course of plundering and pillaging. At first, the sons of Gothus avoided confrontation with their Catalonian cousins. Instead they conquered various ancient Germanic tribal nations sojourning between *Mare Suebicum* and the inhospitable Blach See, Cimbrian tribal nations north and northeast of the great River Danu of Riphath and into the Scythian territories of Patriarchs Magog, Meshech, and Tubal. Per the chronicles of Alanus and the legions of Homeros, the Asian Poet, the Goths took the wives of the warriors they had conquered.

It was reported to King Raetus that Prince Berig, the son of King Gothus, the son of Armenon, sailed from Scandza on one of the three ships of Captain King Alanus to the small, uninhabited island. For this reason, we refer to the island of Gothus as Scandza of the Goths. In time, the insatiable sons of King Gothus invaded southern Scandza, and they have headquartered there to this day.

King Walagothus was the second son of King Armenon, the son of Captain King Alanus. At first King Walagothus and his Catalonian sons colonized the southern territories of the Iberian Peninsula. Walagothus was a wise leader who feared the LORD God of Noah and established the seven laws of Noah among his tribal nation. The sons of King Walagothus expanded and inhabited the land between the River Rhodanus in the east and the River Ebro in the west along the Great Sea of Tarshish.

I learned from the oral tradition of the Catalonians that King Walagothus and King Gothus, oldest sons of King Armenon, were distinctly different. King Walagothus was a dweller, while his older brother Gothus was restless and always on a quest. Like Noah and Patriarch Japheth, King Walagothus planted a vineyard, was a homesteader, and drank wine. King Gothus preferred beer, was unsociable, and had no time for homesteading. King Walagothus was an astute follower of Captain King Alanus.

The reputation of King Walagothus spread throughout Europa, and the wine-yielding territory his tribal nation occupied became known in all tongues as *Catalanya*, which I learned means "according to, or from, Alanya." Alanya in Panphylia was founded by Captain King Alanus, the son of Fetebir, and the birthplace of King Walagothus. King Gothus was born in Kilikia and idolized his cousin Lukka, a well-known chieftain warrior among the Sea People on the Levantine Sea.

In the tradition of the ancient patriarchs, King Walagothus established trade with the Phoenicians, the Egyptians, and the Punic city of Tarshish also known as Carthage. The wines of Catalanya were stowed in amphora vessels, fastened with twine, and exported throughout Great Sea nations. The wines of Catalanya are exported to this day.

The Catalonian sons and daughters of Walagothus inter-married with the native Iberians who sojourned there, and they migrated throughout the Iberian Peninsula. King Walagothus was familiar with ancestral tradition and the stories of Iberus, the son of Patriarch Tubal, who ventured to the peninsula that has carried his name since the days of Noah.

Unlike his older brother, Walagothus, Prince Gepidus, the third son of Armenon, embraced the adventurous spirit of the firstborn and oldest brother, Gothus. Prince Gepidus ventured into the *Mare Germanicum* and the *Mare Suebicum* with Gothus. The tribal nations of Gothus and Gepidus have been allies until this day.

In time, the Catalonian sons of King Gepidus settled in the fertile land of the Gepids, the sons of Gepidus, known as Pannonia. The ancient Danu River of Riphath runs through the heart of the Gepids territory. The loamy soil of Pannonia was excellent for food production. It was said that all of Europa could be fed from this soil. I understood that the soil of Pannonia was comparable to the legendary soil of Kilikia.

King Armenon learned details about these twelve trib-al nations from King Raetus, who spent much time with the Etruscans of northern Italos, and he found that the descendants of King Burgundus, the son of King Armenon, the fourth son of Captain King Alanus, established communities on the confluence of the River Seine at Vix in the territory settled by the Burgundians.

Like Walagothus, the Catalonian sons of Burgundus built a strong defensive community, a citadel. They planted vineyards and exported their fine wines throughout Europa, allowing them to prosper. The Burgundians are one of our trading partners. And by way of the River Seine, they also regularly traded with the British sons of Brutus. Their fine "burgundies" are exported throughout the world until this day. I learned from King Raetus that the descendants of Burgundus, the son of Armenon, inhabited the central territories of western Europa west of the River Rhodanus and south of the Great British Isles.

The other River Rhodanus rose from Suittes-Land and emptied into *Mare Tyrrhēnum,* named by Latinus after the Etruscan sons of Tiras. It took three weeks to navigate the well-traveled, brisk-flowing river by barge from its source, the Rhodanus Glacier, in the Suittes-Land Alps. It was reported by the Catalonian tribes who sojourned on the river that progenitor Rhodium accompanied Regan, the son of Riphath, when they discovered the ancient glacier, which has remained since the global flood of Japheth, the Great Voice. Had they known that the mysterious glacial river flowed south to Tarshish, the territory might have been inhabited much earlier.

During my exploration of the glacial river, I observed a healthy flow of cargo to and from the Great Sea markets. The River Rhodanus in Suittes-Land provided transportation to and from the Salt Castle in the eastern Alps as well as La Tène in the western Alps. Several Catalonian tribes settled the lucrative Rhodanus lands. The Seduni, Sequani, Segobriges, Allobroges, Segusiavi, Helvetii, Vocontii, and Volcae Arecomici tribes settled there. The River Rhodanus in Suittes-Land served the sons of Captain King Alanus well through the centuries, uniting the Dodecanese sons of Rhodes.

I learned that Longobardus, the youngest son of King Armenon, the son of Alanus, matured into a strong man, like

Patriarch Tiras, the Red Bull. In the days of Captain King Alanus, Longobardus scouted the Po River Valley of northern Italos with his older brother Burgundus. Longobardus traveled on with Captain Alanus and the three legendary ships. The Catalonian descendents of Longobardus, like the Etruscan descendents of Tiras, elevated his legacy to godlike status. It was understood by some that one of the many mythical gods, Wôdan, is the persona of King Longobardus, who was a man of faith and known to be somewhat of a seer. It was reported to me during one of my visits to the British Isles that the Scandinavian King Woden was named after Longobardus; Wôdan was the nickname of Longobardus.

While aboard the three European ships of Captain King Alanus, I learned that Longobardus spent much time studying the myths of Homeros. King Longobardus, Wôdan, established his own myths. Prominent among the deities of Longobardus were Donar and Wôdan. Many among the germ of Riphath and the seed of Captain King Alanus adopted the myths of Longobardus. Having begun in this spirit, many Catalonian chroniclers also were bewitched by Wôdan's fantastic tales.

Longobardus held the view that every tribe in every tongue attributes their own names to their ancestral gods. He reasoned that since no man has ever personally known or seen God since the days of Noah, he could challenge ancient tradition, asking questions such as, "What difference does it make to call God whatever we wish?" He reasoned that the Ionians also ascribed names to their deities. He argued still more, citing our very own legends and traditions about Patriarch Manu, the son of Patriarch Madai, who believed that everything was created by God and was an extension of God himself. Like the sons of Javan and the sons of Manu, Longobardus departed from the teachings of Noah, the Herald of Righteousness, and invented titans of his own idolatrous imagination.

Longobardus invented Donar, the angry god of war, the son of Wôdan. His Donar the Warrior was mean-spirited. Reasoning that since God created all things, both visible and invisible, he envisioned and crafted Donar as a mean-spirited sovereign, an invisible warrior fighting and bringing great advantage or disadvantage to the tribal nation of his choosing. I perceived that this aversion to tradition was due to his observation of the warfare in Kilikia among the tribal nations of Noah and the chosen nation of Israel under the leadership of Joshua, who systematically cleared Canaanites tribes. The sons of Longobardus followed in his misguided faith, inventing Wôdan.

I perceived that the idolatry that arose among the Catalonian sons of Captain King Alanus was about to be reckoned with by the LORD God of Noah. God is a jealous God and will not allow men, made in His image and after His likeness, to worship created things. He will not permit the sons of God to be exulted. The prophet Jeremiah said that a time of judgment was coming to all the earth because of idolatry. I understood that God is far from being a mean-spirited Donar, as Longobardus envisioned. As long as I live, like Noah, the Herald of Righteousness, I will not be silent, and I will demand that the Catalonian sons of Captain King Alanus renounce mythology and return to the faith of our fathers and to the LORD God of Japheth, the Great Voice of all Kaucasian peoples of the earth.

The Winnili sons of Longobardus united with our Suebian people. We welcomed them, as they were fierce fighters and expanded as encouraged by the blessings of Noah and Japheth. Like Abraham, they sought a land they could call their homeland.

I learned that distinct territories were apportioned to King Negue and his three sons: Wandalus (the Vandals), Saxo (the Saxons), and our people, Boguarus (the Boii). It was my understanding that King Negue had other sons and daughters who were known as Thuringians. The sons of King Negue, the third son of Captain King Alanus, settled their territories and, early on, established trade routes among themselves. The Catalonian descendents of Wandalus, Saxo, and Boguarus inhabited the eastern territories of Europa east of the River Reno and along the

River Danu of Riphath. The Bogari tribe, the Vandali tribe, the Saxoni tribe, the Tarincgi tribe, the Volcae, and the Boii tribe all descended from Negue, the son of Alanus.

The descendents of Armenon, son of Alanus, inhabited the Iberian Peninsula facing the ocean of Atlantis. At first the tribal nations of Armenon inhabited the southern coastal territories of *Mare Tyrrhēnum*. It is my understanding that the Gothi tribe, the Valagothi tribe, the Cibidi tribe, the Burgiundi tribe, and the Longobardi tribes all descended from Armenon. The tribal nations of Armenon found a more peaceful existence inland and toward the ocean of Atlantis. Traveling north along the shores were the Lusitani tribe. Traveling farther north along the shore, the Gallaeci tribe sojourned. The Galli tribe along the coast to the east were their neighbors. The Celtiberi tribe were not a nautical people, but they lived inland. They inhabited the land where Iberus, the son of Patriarch Tubal, the son of Japheth the progenitor, had ventured several millennia earlier along the River Ebro.

Prince Wandalus was the firstborn son of King Negue. The many rivers of the Pomeranian territories of Wandalus flowed north and emptied in the *Mare Suebicum*. The territory of the sons of Wandalus is bounded by the Rocky Mountains in the south. The Catalonian descendents of King Wandalus built a fortified farmstead in the midst of a lake there. Fearful of extermination from hostile intruders, King Wandalus reasoned that the waters surrounding the island would provide added protection to his people. They cultivated the fertile land around the lake and prospered there.

Prince Saxo was the secondborn son of King Negue. I learned that the Catalonian princes of King Saxo sojourned in the area north of the lower River Albis and River Saale. The territory of the Saxons extended westward toward the River Rhodanus. In the west, the Saxons had direct access to *Mare Germanicum*.

✳ ✳ ✳ ✳ ✳

After mapping out the Catalonian tribes in Europa, I completed my project. Some were beginning to say I was obsessed with ethnology and linguistics. So, pressured by my peers, I agreed it was time to turn to some merriment.

Like all men, I desired to love and rescue my Eve from the snare of Beelzebub. I enjoyed frequent visits to fine wineries of Europa. I stowed and exhibited a fine stock of the vintage wines of Burgundus to the west of Raetia and Longobardus to the east of Raetia.

One evening a like-minded, God-fearing married couple, Dardan and Felicitas, invited me to share a meal with them. Playing the matchmaker, they told me about Julia, who they believed would be a healthy distraction from my academic pursuits. They informed me that Julia was well-bred in the nurture and admonition of the Lord and that she was a woman of proven character and enterprise. Then they told me they had also invited Julia to our meal.

Julia's good reputation preceded her, and she was everything that had been told about her. It was rare when my expectations found satisfaction. Julia was a kind and gentle spirit, soft-spoken, and bred with good character and much grace, which was a rare virtue among our Albus kinsmen. Albus Mountain Catalonians tended to be very industrious, a works-oriented kind of people. They were given to obeying rules and regulations to achieve social status and favor with God. In our common tradition, commandments like "God helps those who help themselves" were enforced like the laws of Noah by all men in our day. We all knew that God blessed industry in all its forms and shunned laziness in all its forms.

From my initial visit with Julia at the farmstead of Dardan and Felicitas, I perceived that she was no stranger to difficulty and, like Job, had learned to trust the LORD God in difficult and challenging circumstances. At first I was unaware of her specific circumstances, but I was curious to learn more about how Julia became such a loving, caring, and gracious woman.

On a subsequent visit with Julia, I learned more about her challenging circumstances. As we shared a hot pot of cheese and a gourd of sweet Hessian apple wine, I studied this young woman. Julia was fearful and timid, a sure sign of previous abuse. When Julia was comfortable and relaxed in my company, she told me her story. It was as if God had granted me the compassion and boldness to study her spirit and care for her heart. I grew in my affections for Julia and cherished her, just as Darden and Felicitas had hoped I would.

I learned that Julia was orphaned when both her parents were slaughtered by a renegade and wandering warrior tribe that was attempting to sack Mont Lassois in the land of Burgundy. Julia, a young virgin at the time and a direct descendant of King Burgundus, grieved the loss of both parents, but somehow found an instinct to survive.

For a short season, she fell victim to the lustful, wandering eyes of the savage warriors who had invaded Mont Lassois. Julia was captured and taken against her will to their tents, enslaved, and forced to provide sexual services for the savage, lust-filled warriors. With great emotion and tears, Julia confessed her dark secret with me, saying, "One evening, in total desperation, I made the decision to escape. So I stole and stowed a bronze dagger within my straw bed. When the opportunity was right, I drove the dagger through the heart of one of the young warriors. I escaped my captors quietly in the night."

Julia was completely honest with me and confessed that in those cruel days of enslavement, she had been the subject of much sexual abuse. During a prolonged season of abuse, Julia felt ruined, experiencing great darkness and despair in her soul. During those evil days of mistreatment, Dardan and Felicitas approached Julia with a hospitable proposition. With much mercy, the God-fearing couple offered Julia a place of refuge, a safe harbor from the savage warriors, and ample provision; in short, a place of respite from her abusers.

Being of strong character, Julia refused to board without

payment. So she offered to serve Dardan and Felicitas for room and board, working as an indentured servant for the gracious couple as needed around the farmstead. Their Albus Mountain farmstead was massive, so the indentured services were warmly welcomed. Their primary industry was swine farming, but they also raised cattle. They produced many products from the cattle and marketed them to local Albanian kinsmen. They planted a profitable vineyard and exported all their wine to emerging European and Great Sea nations. The LORD God prospered them in all their agricultural enterprises.

When I heard about Julia's tragedy and the story of how she escaped her abusers, my heart grew in appreciation and admiration for her honesty, but also for her courage in enduring such extreme abuse.

I loved Julia even more, and I married her during the harvesting of the grapes. Dardan and Felicitas offered their farmstead for the marriage celebration and provided an abundance of wine for the traditional Catalonian wedding celebration. They invited kinsmen from all the surrounding territories and a few select foreign trade partners. The tables and goblets were filled in abundance. Catalonians speak about the event to this day.

The historical connection between the Etruscan wine country and the Burgundy wine country was well established. Since being drunk with wine was discouraged among Catalonians, *ákratos* was served. *Akratos* was a mixture of water and wine. A large quantity of *ákratos* was mixed in a *krater*, a large vase. The krater was often decorated and became valuable chattel. Serving undiluted wine was considered a *faux pas*, a social blunder. Although our people believed that a little wine was good for the belly, those who drank undiluted wine were characterized as drunkards. The wedding supra mixed the *ákratos* in a ratio of one part wine to two parts water in a bronze krater that stood as tall as my beloved Julia!

After the royal wedding supra that united the eastern and western Albus kinsmen, Julia left the steep, flat-topped, fortified oppidum at Mont Lassois in Burgundy and joined me at our palatial manor in Glauberg, the governing seat of our expanding Catalonian league of nations. But we often returned to Mont Lassois, where I was building a palace for Julia. She was hospitable and enjoyed entertaining many guests. Mont Lassois became our western retreat.

We desired to have many children, but were uncertain of the vaginal damage that had been inflicted on her from repetitive sexual abuse. So we believed in, and for, God's blessings, called upon the name of the LORD, and trusted that the God of Noah would heal her womb and shine His favor upon us. God heard our desperate cries and answered us through His plans and purposes. Julia became great with child.

When the Mont Lassois palace was completed, we decided to celebrate. So my very pregnant Lady Julia invited guests from all the fortified settlements and trade partners in Europa. Guests arrived from Grächwil, west of Lake Geneva. They arrived from the salt mines of Dürrnberg and Hallstatt in the east and from as far as Kleinklein in the southeast, a territory rich in iron ore. Guests arrived from Hohenasperg to the north and from Hohmichele to the west of Heuneburg. They also arrived from the northern territories of King Saxo from Eigenbilzen, Basse-Yutz, and Waldalgesheim. And still more guests arrived from the land of Franco, from Schwarzenbach. Most of the chroniclers made their way to Mont Lassois. Everyone brought gifts for Lady Julia as a token of appreciation for uniting the Catalonian tribes.

Pottery and urns were imported from around the Great Sea for the event, as were the very best in wines. I served as the supra for the event and sampled all the wines; I selected the finest to be served. Julia and I cherished this special time with our kinsmen.

But after the birth of our Aalen, tragically, Julia died an untimely death when she was only thirty-five, a death from causes that remain a mystery to this day. I was brokenhearted and mourned her passing for decades.

In the custom of our people, Julia was buried within a small chariot that had its wheels removed. I buried my Lady along with a large bronze wine krater from our wedding celebration and the jewelry I had purchased to grace her natural beauty. A tumulus of rock was piled high over Julia's gravesite.

* * * * *

After the death of Lady Julia of Mont Lassois, the genetic offspring of noble kings was exulted in society as royalty. The advantaged royal house lived in manors and enjoyed delicacies that their pioneering and often austere forefathers did not. The demand for iron and Catalonian gold increased and provided an abundant economy. The Albus sons of Captain King Alanus prospered from the trade of salt, tin, copper, amber, wool, leather, furs, and gold with the Etruscan and other Great Sea countries.

In the course of time, the Albus Keltoi Galatae culture spread throughout Europa. The Catalonians spoke a similar language and shared many of the same traditions, religious beliefs, and appreciation for art and artistic techniques.

Although the Catalonian tribes spoke a common trade language, we often inscribed our tongue phonetically by using Greek or Latin characters. The Catalonians did not have their own writing system, as did the Greeks or Latins, so they were falsely assumed by many to be illiterate savages. Throughout our history we have preferred the classical Knossos Greek alphabet of our forefathers and the more modern Latin alphabet of Latinus for formal communications and inscriptions. I have observed that many historians often misinterpreted this because there are so many details that are missing from verbal and written tradition. Had it not been for literate chroniclers, mankind would know little about his past.

And although our Catalonian people forsook the LORD God of our ancestors and created idols of their own imaginations, our priesthood of chroniclers maintained a strong belief in procreation, the notion of "be fruitful and multiply and inhabit the earth." This was reflected in the horned god of nature and fertility who was often surrounded by animals, as Japheth the progenitor (Jupiter), the son of Noah. We understood the exulted nature of the genes, or germ, of men and woman as Cernunnos, like the Indian, Pashupati, the Lord of the Animals, who often held a coiled snake in his right hand representing the semen of man and torcs in his left hand representing the egg of woman. Horns represented leadership. And like the Greeks and the Etruscans, the people exulted ancestors, like Longobardus, to godlike status.

Our Catalonian ancestors built roads across Europa connecting their tribes and trade industries. We traded tools and weapons made from iron for Great Sea wines and pottery. In several of our cities, high walls were erected, forming citadels, where the village people were protected from attack. We were advanced in some scientific, political, and economic disciplines. Because of our history in stargazing, our calendars were very accurate compared to other tribal nations of the earth.

There were some domestic differences among Catalonians in architecture. I observed that the sons of Brutus on the Great British Isles built round houses like the dwelling places in Asia, while the tribes occupying Gaul built rectangular houses patterned after the sons of Gomer.

Each Catalonian tribe was organized in clans termed *septs*. The septs where ruled by a tetrarch chief or king. They appointed judges, as Japheth the progenitor had instructed. They appointed a general and deputy general. Each sept sent twenty-five senators to a central shrine called Drunemeton.

Our Catalonian ancestors were blessed by God and prospered wherever they sojourned. I learned from our miners that there are more than four hundred gold mines located in the land of Gaul alone. The great expectation, risk, and quest for gold that Captain King Alanus and his sons envisioned led them all to great prosperity in Europa. The reports of the Etruscan sons of Patriarch Tiras proved true.

The Catalonian nobles were clean-shaven. The Albus sons of

Alanus followed in the footsteps of Japheth and honored their women. Virtuous Keltoi women like my beloved Lady Julia lived as equals among men. They proved to be powerful barterers and often fearlessly fought alongside the male warriors.

Influenced by the Etruscans, the Catalonians developed mail armor for our warriors. Our brave warriors were suited from head to toe with an iron chain-link mail to protect them in conflict. A mail coif hood protected the warrior's head. A mail collar hanging from the warrior's metal helmet was called an *aventail*. The warrior's mail shirt was a *hauberk* if it went to the knees but a *haubergeon* if it was longer, down to the middle of the warrior's thighs. One or more layers of mail sandwiched between layers of fabric was called a *jazerant*. A mail *chausses* covered the warrior's legs. And the warrior's hands were protected by mail mittens. The mail armor covered the warrior's venerable body parts and reduced the number of stab wounds and casualties among our Catalonian warriors.

The mail-suited Albanus warriors were equipped with decorated iron weaponry. The iron mail and weaponry of our warriors gave them a great advantage over their foes. Their highly engineered mail and weaponry provided confidence to the warriors and influenced the expansion of the Albus Keltoi Galatae into lucrative neighboring territories.

After King Ewald died, I found love again. My second wife, Dierdre, and I were blessed with several children and grandchildren. However, Prince Aalen was my firstling and the only son of Julia, and he was cherished and educated in all my ways.

Prince Aalen married and had one son and many daughters. His firstborn and only son, Arbor Felix—which means "happy tree"—also married and had many sons and daughters. The firstborn son of Prince Arbor Felix was Rheticus, who also married and had many sons and daughters. And Wilton was the firstborn son of Prince Rheticus.

After many years of research, I, Hagano, the chronicler of

the seed of Boguarus, sojourning in Glauberg of Raetia, hereby preserve a record for future generations in *The Book of the Chronicles of the Bohemian Kings:*

Wilton was the son of Rheticus. Rheticus was the son of Arbor Felix. Arbor Felix was the son of Aalen. Aalen was the son of Hagano. Hagano was the son of Ewald. Ewald was the son of Raetus. Raetus was the son of Boius. Boius was the son of Daedalus. Daedalus was the son of Telmun. Telmun was the son of Amphare. Amphare was the son of Hercle. Hercle was the son of Boguarus. Boguarus was the son of Negue. Negue was the son of Alanus. Alanus was the son of Fetebir. Fetebir was the son of Ougomun. Ougomun was the son of Thous. Thous was the son of Boib. Boib was the son of Simeon. Simeon was the son of Mair. Mair was the son of Ethach. Ethach was the son of Aurthach. Aurthach was the son of Ecthet. Ecthet was the son of Oth. Oth was the son of Abir. Abir was the son of Rea. Rea was the son of Ezra. Ezra was the son of Izrau. Izrau was the son of Baath, Baath was the son of Iobaath. Iobaath was the son of Rhodanim. Rhodanim was the son of Javan. Javan was the son of Japheth. Japheth was the son of Noah. Noah was the son of Lamech, Lamech was the son of Methuselah, Methuselah was the son of Enoch, Enoch was the son of Jared, Jared was the son of Mahalaleel, Mahalaleel was the son of Cainan, Cainan was the son of Enos, Enos was the son of Seth, Seth was the son of Adam, Adam was the son of God.

SEVEN

THE CHRONICLES OF KING BIATEC

(BEGINNING WITH 450 BC, AND THE RECORD OF WARS)

THE KELTOI GALATAE CATALONIANS occupied an area that stretched from the Iberian Peninsula in the west to the Peninsula of Haemus in the east. For several centuries the strength of our confederation was concentrated and led by the sons of King Boius, who sojourned in the Albus Mountains toward the east at the Salt Castle beside the River Salt, a tributary of the River Inn that led to the River Danu, the river that is the mother of many nations.

The princes of King Boius emerged as kings and established a military connection with all the Catalonian sons of Captain King Alanus. As the Keltoi-speaking confederation expanded and enlarged across Europa, the tribal nation of Prince Latène—the son of King Boius, the grandson of King Boius in Suittes-Land, in the central and western territories of the Albus Mountains—became the headquarters for their confederation of tribal nations.

The city-state of Prince Latène, on the north side of Lake

Neuchâtel in Suittes-Land, emerged as the cultural commons for the Galatian tribes of Captain King Alanus. The Latène culture in central Europa developed and flourished as a great Albus Mountain league of tribal nations.

Meanwhile, to the south across the Albus Mountains, the descendants of Romanus, the Roman Kingdom, had been replaced in leadership by a newly formed Roman Republic. Under the rule of this new republic, the Romans enlarged and inhabited many territories in Italos. The city-state of Roma, situated in the midst of seven mountains, maintained well-established armies, and the republic grew in strength and numbers. A conflict between the Roman Republic and the Albus tribal nations seemed inevitable.

As the Roman Republic expanded in southern Europa, the sons of King Saxo enlarged in northern Europa. The sons of Saxo emerged with a great military presence among the tribal nations of Captain King Alanus on the southern coast of *Mare Germanicum* and *Mare Suebicum*. The city-state of Jastorf in Lower Saxony became their cultural center.

In the course of time, the ancient Riphean sons of Gomer migrated south from their isolated northern territories beyond *Mare Germanicum* and *Mare Suebicum,* which was also called *Mare Balticum.* They returned to their original homeland along the River Rhodanim. The sons of Riphath discovered that, in their absence, foreigners inhabited their former homeland. Without a major conflict, the ancient tribes of Riphath established trade and commingled with the new tribes of Saxo, the son of Negue, the son of Captain King Alanus.

The tribes of King Saxo in the village of Jastorf in Lower Saxony learned the ancient tongue of Riphath and Regen and spoke in a dialect of their original ancient tongue provisioned by God Almighty at the tower of Babel. Because of this commingling with the sons of Saxon, their Jastorf culture became one. The Jastorf culture of Lower Saxony distinguished themselves from the sons of Boguarus in the south and the sons of Wandalus in the east. Like a sausage made from a variety of ground meats, the blended diction of Jastorf was culturally infused by the seed of Riphath as many began to speak in an ancient Diutisc tongue.

The Iberian Peninsula nations of Iberus in the west also expanded, adapted to the culture of the Catalonians, and spoke a dialect of the Keltoi tongue, the language that united the tribal confederation across Europa. The Iberian Catalonians were concerned with the growing Punic-speaking Carthaginian Empire that emerged on the northern coast of Africa on the southern shores of the Great Sea of Tarshish. However, their concern about the Roman Republic coveting their gold was of greater concern.

So the son of Captain King Alanus formed alliances with the ancient Baltic tribes of Japheth, who sojourned along the east banks of *Mare Balticum*. The Balts also expanded and emerged as a powerful league of tribal nations. At first their Baltic tongue was foreign to the Catalonians, but in time the amber trade negotiators commanded the Baltic language.

The seed of the Baltic tribes and their language has been debated for centuries. Some report them as being the sons of Gomer, others the sons of Dodanim, others the sons of Magog, and yet others the sons of Tiras. But most believe that their Baltic tongue evolved from one of the original languages issued from God at the Tower of Babel. I understood from the tradition of our forefathers that the spoken and written language of every tribal nation was rooted in approximately one hundred original tongues! It was the LORD God of Noah who authorized and maintained this diversity among the nations as part of His original plans and purposes to divide the tribal nations. One day we may understand the mystery related to the development of all the many spoken languages in our world.

To the south of the Baltic tribes, the Dacian sons of Dodanim, the northern descendants of Rhodanim, sojourned in the territory on the western shores of the Blach See and along the River Danu toward the east. They also expanded and emerged as a powerful tribal nation. The Dacian tribes also spoke their own language, one believed to have evolved from an original Indo-European tongue of Patriarch Dodanim. Most believe that the Dacian tongue was the original tongue that Dodanim, the son of Javan, received at the tower of Babel. Our forefathers understood that the sons of Dodanim sojourned to the north of the Balkans and there spoke their original language, while the sons of Rhodanim sojourned to the southeast of the Balkans on the Islands of Rhodanim, where they abandoned the tongue of Dodanim, preferring to speak and write in the more universal Ionian tongue of Patriarch Javan.

In those days the Media-Persian Empire, descendants of Madai and Caspian, enlarged and prospered. Their men of war invaded and captured our ancient homelands in Asia, the land of the descendants of Ashkenaz, Riphath, and Togarmah, the sons of Gomer, the firstborn son of Japheth. They invaded and captured the land of the descendants of Javan, Tiras, Meshech, and Tubal, the younger brothers of Gomer, all sons of Japheth.

After several aggressive military campaigns of Aléxandros ho Mégas—this was translated by many as, simply, Alexander the Great—the king of Macedonia, the centers of Hellenism shifted away from the great city-states of the Peninsula of Haemus to Alexandria in Egypt and Antioch of Syria, which to our people was the great ancient city of Iopolis. Many sons of Javan migrated away from the Peninsula of Haemus, leaving Roman and Galatian imperialism into the eastern lands of the Seleucids. The city-states that remained formed two leagues: the Aegean League, which included the city-states of Thebes, Corinth, and Argos; and the Aetolian League that included the city-states of Sparta and Athens. The Hellenists fought against the Roman Republic on the side of the Seleucids.

In time, the Alban Mountains people, once friends of southern and northern cousins, began to separate themselves both culturally and militarily from other powerful coastal nations of Japheth. Once again languages, cultures, and geographic territories separated the Kaucasian sons of Japheth. They all continued to drift away and became ignorant of their common root.

Since the days of Noah, the sons of Japheth remained a people of industry, trade, and commerce. The tribal nation of Latène prospered with the city-states of Marne and Moselle in the west. The tribal nation of Boius prospered from their trade connections in Bohemia and from commerce with the people of Golasecca. And our Albus Catalonian ancestors continued to export ambers purchased from the Balts, along with metals like copper. We traded furs and wool. And we traded gold, leather, and salt from the Salt Castle. All these products were exported to the Mediterranean nations and found passage into all the world.

Prince Glauberg arose among our Albus Catalonian nations as a mighty military leader. He built a fort in the Hessian oppidum at Glauberg, which was named for the prince. Glauberg is north from Suittes-Land and accessible by the River Rhodanus. Hesse emerged as the principle seat for all trade negotiations in the north. The Hessians also provided military protection from migrating, hostile tribal invasions from the north.

I learned from *The Book of the Chronicles of the Bohemian Kings* that the Riphean tribes established this ancient territory after the glacial ice receded, approximately five hundred years after the worldwide flood of Noah. From our excavations there, we discovered that the territory had once been a permanent settlement during those ancient times. It was obvious that the people who sojourned there were a highly cultured tribal nation because of their elaborate burials, monumental architecture, and sculptures influenced by Riphath, the inventive and industrious son of Patriarch Gomer.

Prince Hirschlanden also emerged as a mighty warrior in Wurttemberg, the land of Prince Glauberg on the River Rhodanus in Hesse. The river flows through the heart of the ancient, enchanting Schwarzwald. Access was also available to the furthermost eastern tributaries of the River Danu from Wurttemberg.

The River Danu and the River Rhodanus were separated by a small mass of *terra firma*. Many Hessian merchants desired to build a canal through the *terra firma* to connect these two well-traveled rivers. They envisioned that one day they would be able to export the ambers of the *Mare Suebicum* to the Blach See by water. But in their day, as in the days of Ox-ford in Anatolia, they had to transport cargo by land from the River Danu to the River Rhodanus and, likewise, from the River Rhodanus to the River Danu. This was extremely inconvenient for the enterprising merchants.

I suppose the canal would have been built sooner if it had not been for the many battles our Catalonian ancestors had been fighting. It appears from all accounts that most of their resources and young men twenty years of age and older had been trained as warriors, not merchants. *Militant* might be the correct term that best defines the way we were in the days of Prince Hirschlanden.

The LORD God was not going to let the earth and all the kingdoms of the earth go unpunished for worshiping idols. The appointed time arrived according to the Word of the LORD spoken through the Hebrew prophet Jeremiah. This was when he spoke on behalf of God a few centuries earlier: "Thus says the Lord of Hosts, 'I am summoning a sword against all the inhabitants of the earth.'" Europa became a large battlefield, just as the LORD God of Noah summoned.

I, Prince Biatec, a God-fearing chronicler for the sons of Boguarus sojourning in Istropolis, in the days of Julius Caesar, invested my life in a quest to provide a Bohemian perspective on the punishment that the Lord of Hosts authorized in all the earth upon the idolatrous sons of Noah the progenitor. Being of noble birth, educated in the *libri* of my father, King Brianan, I am a perpetual student of wisdom in the tradition of our ancestral kings, literate in both Greek and Latin. My father graciously funded my many excursions to foreign lands so I could study and gain insight into our shared history.

For a season, I studied at the academy near Athens, where

I met Philo, a Greek philosopher from Larissa, a key city in Thessalonica. By invitation and due to our Rhodanus roots and association with Homeros, I spent many years at the academy under his tutelage. Philo was the successor of Plato and a disciple of Clitomachus. Philo was invited to lecture in Rome in the presence of Cicero.

Not understanding that our ancestors from Panphylia maintained written tradition dating back to the days of Noah, a few chroniclers portrayed European Celts as bands of savage infidels. But since the beginning our kings have stressed literacy among our tribal nations.

So, to right the records of the ignorant, I dedicate the following summary of the Catalonian wars and of the return of our people back to the land of our forefathers in Galatia to future sons and daughters of Captain King Alanus and the Boii warriors of King Boguarus, the son of King Negue.

THE BATTLE OF ALLIA (390–387 BC)

I begin this correction of the records with the battle of Allia, when the British sons of Brutus lead a confederacy of Catalonian tribes and sacked the city of Rome. Before I describe the battle, I want to describe the culture of British Catalonians prior to the conflict.

The Britons were a people of simple law, and their simplified lifestyle influenced many Catalonian cultures throughout Europe. The Britons were an astute society that exemplified the God-fearing tradition of Captain King Alanus and Japheth the progenitor. The Britons maintained the traditions of Jubal, the Father of the Sound of Music, by deeming the harp as critical to life as the sheepskin clothing of Jabal and the iron cooking kettles of Tubal-Cain.

The British King Dunvallo instituted democratic laws of order and appointed judges (as directed centuries earlier by Noah) among the Britons who encouraged art, craft, and literacy. And like Job, King Dunvallo was compassionate to foreigners and the disadvantaged. The laws of King Dunvallo awarded education and hard work. Literate men were rewarded for their diligence and received an extra allotment of land.

Like Japheth, the Great Voice, King Dunvallo promoted hospitality and respected the rights of women, granting voting privileges to married women. The Great Voice would have been encouraged by the British bards and chroniclers who were held in high esteem as heralds of sound instruction in righteousness, virtue, wisdom, and hospitality. Kinsmen to the sons of Romanus, these Britons, and the other Catalonian tribes, were far from being barbarians as the pontificating Roman Republic propaganda ignorantly boasts.

I am disturbed that so much of our Catalonian history has been supplanted by biased historians who only report partial truths. This ignorance is astonishing. For instance, a Greek historian, Polybius, recorded that the Senones from Gaul crossed over the Alban Mountains and invaded the Umbrian tribal nation that occupied the eastern coastal territories in Italos. The Senones are reported to have inhabited the Umbrian territory to establish the city of Sena Gallica along the coast at the mouth of the River Misa, which became their capitol. But Polybius had no knowledge that the Senones of Italos were kin to Prince Latinus.

We understand from our British and Skuthai bards that Prince Brennius, the son of King Dunvallo, who is also recorded by Skuthai chroniclers as Bran, invaded Italos and sacked the city of Rome. Prince Brennius was the brother of British First Prince Belinus, who is also known by Skuthai chroniclers as Prince Beli. We understand that the Catalonian tribe from Sena Gallica was headed by none other than the British Prince Brennius. According to our ancestors, Prince Bran migrated with other Catalonians into eastern Italos, where they settled.

Another historian by the name of Titus Livius Patavinus, although a somewhat biased literate of the sons of Romanus, recalls the days of the battle of the Allia River, when our Catalonian ancestors, also known as the Gauls, the Gallic confederation of Albus tribal nations, first sacked the sons of Romanus. The Allia is a stream flowing into the River Tiber located about eleven miles from the city of Rome. Titus mentions one named Brennus, the chieftain of the Senones from Sena Gallica. Again, the Roman historian was unaware that Brennus was in fact a British prince.

It was documented by the Roman historian that the Senones led by Chieftain Brennus captured the entire city of Rome except for Capitoline Hill, which the Romans were able to defend. The Roman Republic agreed to pay one thousand pounds' weight in gold to the Senones, using Gallic scales to weigh the payment. Brennus, the king of the Galatian Senones, was reported to have boasted, proclaiming, "Woe to the vanquished!"

However, the British historians and chroniclers record the British invasion of Rome under the leadership of Bran as uniting Catalonians against their cousins, sons of Latinus, and that this was only the prelude to centuries of bloodshed that would follow.

THE CATALONIAN INVASION OF THE BALKANS (4TH CENTURY BC)

The world was at war. From their headquarters in La Tène near Lake Geneva, and through several migrations, our Catalonian ancestors became aggressive, waged war with their neighbors, and expanded into Hispania, the Po River Valley, the Balkans, and Anatolia. Our Catalonian warriors took advantage of the weaknesses they perceived among the various regions, and exploited them.

In those days the amber trade routes from the land of the *Mare Balticum* to *Mare Adriaticum* were well established. In the days of King Mair, it was reported that Pharaoh Tutankhamen of Egypt wore a breast ornament that contained several large Baltic amber beads. In our chronicles, King Fetebir reported observing amber gold in Mycenae. The amber road begins along the Baltic coastline in the north and meanders south through the Moravian Gate crossing the River Danu near the iron city that the Romans named Noricum. In the days prior to the invasion, a federation of twelve Catalonian tribes occupied the territory. The River Danu was the northern boundary of the Noricum territory with Raetia toward the east and Pannonia to the west.

As a Catalonian common for ironworks, cattle herds, and the sound of music, Noricum was blessed with gold and salt mines that furthered the use of the amber road. Due to the rich deposits of iron ore, Nordic weaponry has supplied our Catalonian warriors since our early occupancy of the land in the days of King Negue. Plants that produced Galatian nard grew in abundance and have perfumed our royal nobles for many generations. So these well-trodden amber roads provided an entrance into the Balkans for our Catalonian warriors.

The northern Balkans experienced constant leadership changes as neighbors plundered the territories. The Illyrians, who sojourned west of the ancient Haemus Mons and in the land of the Messapian tribesmen along the southeast coastal heel of the Italos peninsula, had been at war with the Greeks. This exposed the Illyrians to unfortified attacks from northern invasions.

The Macedonians who sojourned in the northeastern territories of the Peninsula of Haemus and settled in the land that surrounded the lengthy River Haliacmon and the black waters of Bardários waged war with the Thracians. But the Thracians were surrounded by warfare as they waged battle with the Scythian sons of Patriarch Magog to the north, the Galatian sons of Captain King Alanus to the northwest, the Illyrian sons of Patriarch Dodanim to the west, the Ancient Greeks to the south, and the Blach See bands of Gomer to the east.

While the Macedonians waged war against the Thracians, and in an effort to inspect the strength of the Macedonian military, the Catalonians sent representatives to pay homage to the renowned king Alexander the Great. They had little motivation to launch an attack on such a great leader. So our warriors patiently waited for opportunity.

As we studied *The Book of the Chronicles of the Bohemian Kings*, we realized that our Catalonian ancestors understood that they were descendants of the Ionians who first laid territorial claims on the Ionian peninsula, the land of Dodanim and Iobaath, and sojourned in many of the ancient territories east of Asia. We reasoned that as the descendants of Dodanim and Iobaath, we would find just cause to seize the ancient territories and recapture our former homeland.

Several military leaders emerged among the Catalonian forces in Europa. Chief among them was one, Cambaules. Cambaules and other leaders converged in Pannonia. Among them was one, Bolgios, believed to be of noble heritage, who emerged as a strong military leader among the Belgae warriors. Bolgios and his troops settled in Pannonia with the troops of Cambaules. The Catalonians launched an attack on the Balkans under the confederate leadership of Cambaules. The Galatian King Cerethrius and his warriors joined Cambaules and Bolgios in Pannonia along with the chieftain of the Senones, Brennus, the son of Dunvallo, the son of Cloten, according to *The Book of the Chronicles of British Kings*.

After what seemed a long wait, the opportunity to invade the Balkans arrived. All Catalonians were encouraged by the death of the mighty Alexander and by our victory over the Illyrian and Pannonian armies. With our base firmly established in Pannonia, our fearless warriors penetrated our ancient homelands with our eyes set on recapturing ancient Asia. Led by Molistomos, our Catalonian armies advanced on the southern regions of Macedonia and the rest of Greece. Our united warriors attacked deep into Illyrian territory, subduing the Dardanians, the Paeonians, and the Triballi tribes who settled there.

After the death of Alexander, the new Macedonian king,

Cassander, felt compelled to take the Illyrian enemies under his protection. The Catalonians attempted to penetrate deeper into Thrace and Macedon but suffered heavy losses and defeat near Haemus Mons. For a season this defeat at the hands of King Cassander discouraged the Catalonian armies from advancing into Asia.

THE BATTLE AT THERMOPYLAE (279 BC)

As a young prince endowed by the LORD God with under-standing in the art of war, Bolgios emerged among our Catalonian warriors and was granted the great privilege of leading our armies into a pitched battle at Thermopylae against the allied armies of Greek Aetolians, Boeotians, Athenians, and Phoenicians. In those days, our united Catalonian armies numbered 90,000 armed warriors.

Lead by Prince Bolgios, Catalonian warriors were divided into three divisions. Under the excellent leadership of Prince Cerethrius, a quarter of those warriors advanced against the Thracian and Triballi armies. Prince Cerethrius became the King of Thrace.

Prince Bolgios advanced against the Macedonians and Illyrians and marshaled a third division against the Paeonians, an historically strong ally of Ilion. The Macedonian king, Ptolemy Keraunos, had little concern about the Galatian-led Catalonian confederacy and refused aid from neighbors. Ironically, and igno-rant of our common ancestry, the sons of progenitor Dardanus, the son of Javan and the father of Iobaath according to *The Book,* he offered to send 20,000 soldiers to assist the Macedonians against our Catalonian warriors.

It was reported that Prince Bolgios sent ambassadors to King Keraunos demanding payment to call off the Galatian attack, but Keraunos was angered by this demand and refused to make such a payment. The king countered by demanding that the Catalonians return hostages and hand over their weapons.

The ferocious and violent Prince Bolgios of the Belgae nation attacked and was successful in defeating King Keraunos and the Macedonian armies. The proud Belgian prince returned with much loot from the invasion. Prince Bolgios captured and decapitated the Macedonian king, returning to our people with the head of Keraunos on a spear, a token of Bolgios's great success.

However, after his victory over the Macedonian king, Prince Bolgios met great resistance from troops led by a nobleman named Sosthenes. Bolgios's contingents were forced to retreat. Upon hearing of the strength of Sosthenes, Brennus led a division including the Tolistobogii warriors along with a division of Prince Bolgios. Together the Catalonian warriors defeated Sosthenes and his armies. At that point the Catalonian armies were free to ravage the country at will.

With the two victories on the battlefields, our Catalonian warriors, led by Prince Acichorius, pressed into the heart of the Peninsula of Haemus. It was reported that our allied Catalonian warriors were looting and collecting tribute from the defeated cities for several decades without any serious opposition.

It was also reported that while our Galatian-led campaigns were successful on the Grecian heartland, Prince Attalos of Pergamon defeated our Albus Mountain warriors in Asia. Pergamon was a city in Aeolis, an ancient district on the western coast of Asia, the land of Patriarch Tiras. Our ancestors in Panphylia and Kilikia were allies with the sons of Tiras who sojourned in Aeolis. It was reported that the young Grecian Prince Attalos had a strong allegiance to the descendants of Romanus in Italos. Attalos received a victor's welcome from the people of Pergamon after the battle. Prince Attalos, surnamed Soter by his people, was so popular that they erected stelae to honor their so-called "savior," and the death of the Gauls, who in great ignorance considered all our people barbarians. During his reign King Attalos strengthened the arm of Romanus in Asia, the land of the Hatti, and assisted Rome in the Macedonian wars during his reign.

THE COLOSSUS OF RHODANIM (280 BC)

It was reported among our people that during the Catalonian invasion from the north into the Balkans, the Dodecanese sons of Rhodanim under the leadership of the renowned sculptor, Chares of Lindos, erected a gigantic bronze colossus of Helios, the sun god. The enormous colossus was built as a monument eulogizing the resounding victory over the invading navies of Antigonus I Monophthalmus, the ruler over the island of Cyprus. I learned that the people of Rhodes allied with the Egyptians to defeat the invaders who emerged from the Kilikia Sea in the east. The sons of Rhodanim sold the abandoned siege equipment for 300 talents. The profits were used to purchase materials to construct the colossus statue of liberty that greeted visitors overlooking the entrance to the Mandraki harbor in Rhodes.

When the magnificent titanic bronze sculpture was completed, it was dedicated with these words.

> "To you, o Sun, the people of Dorian Rhodes set up this bronze statue reaching to Olympus, when they had pacified the waves of war and crowned their city with the spoils taken from the enemy. Not only over the seas but also on land did they kindle the lovely torch of freedom and independence. For to the descendants of Herakles belong dominion over sea and land."

This dedication text to Helios bespeaks of a former time when Nephilim giants like Herakles ruled the earth. We know from our tradition that the people of Dorian Rhodes were not the sons of the evil Herakles, who perished in the floods of Noah, but were sons of Dodanim, who was also called Rhodanim, the son of Javan. It was apparent to us that the Dorian Rhodes had succumbed to Ionian mythology and had forsaken the Lord God of Noah, the Herald of Righteousness. This made me extremely sad.

After fifty years, the statue of freedom and independence on the Island of Rhodanim was destroyed by an earthquake, an act of God that humbled the boastful edifice to Helios and the Dodecanese who were possessed by the evil spirits that once possessed Nephilim titans. The LORD God of Noah is a jealous God and will not share his glory with another. It took an act of God to tear down the bronze colossus of Helios erected at Rhodes.

THE PUNIC WARS

Warfare was not isolated to the Balkans nor to the Dorian Rhodes and Egyptians who triumphed over Antigonus. As the prophet Jeremiah predicted, violent judgments broke out throughout the earth. War emerged on the Italos peninsula. It broke out on the island of Silica. And it also began to rage among the Punic-speaking territories of northern Africa.

I learned that the name *Punic* is a Latin word derived from *Phoenici* and refers to the Carthaginians' Phoenician ancestry. This was the name that the Roman Republic attributed to the ancient peoples on the Great Sea of Tarshish who settled there. In time, the Punic Carthaginians who aided our forefathers in the establishment of trade throughout the world emerged as a great empire on the western coasts of the Great Sea of Tarshish.

For more than a thousand years the Phoenicians were the dominant naval power in Tarshish, securing the northern coast of Afri as well as the islands of Sicily and Corsica where the Catalonians established trade. They also maintained colonies in Iberia and lucrative trade relationships with our Catalonian ancestors throughout Europa.

But trouble was brewing in the ancient Sea of Tarshish. It was no secret that great wealth was flowing from the western waters of the Mediterranean that connects the southern coastal territories of Iberia and Europa, the islands of Sicily, Corsica, and Sardinia, and Italos with the African continent. The merchandise of Tarshish was heralded and coveted by kings throughout the earth.

But it was also known to us that the aggressive sons of Romulus were not going to let the wealthy sons of Sidon continue to dominate trade in their backyard in the shared western waters. First the Romans had to complete their aggressive campaign in seizing Italos, including the ancient Grecian-controlled territories to the south, where our Ionian ancestors colonized and controlled the coastal southern shores of the peninsula since the days of Javan.

One of the many greedy Roman ambitions was to seize control of the Osci nation. The Osci, believed by some to be tribal sons of Latinus, the son of Romanus, developed their own Latin-based tongue written with both Greek and Latin alphabetic characters representing both their northern Latin neighbors and their southern Grecian neighbors. Over time the Osci tribe colonized the fertile southern coastal plains of Campania in Italos. I learned that the Osci people developed out of three tribes: the Aurunci, the Sidicini, and the Ausones, and were called Mamertines, or "the sons of Mars," by their sophisticated, knowledge-seeking Ionian neighbors. The Mamertines were stargazers full of debauchery and known throughout Italos as a people of lascivious festivals, games, and plays. As mercenaries for the Latin sons of Romanus, their bad company corrupted and influenced the character of all Italians.

Also, the powerful and ancient Grecian city-state of Syrakousai, which was colonized by the Ionians on the southern coast of Silica, had to be reckoned with by the Roman Republic. As a strong ally of Sparta and Corinth on Ellis Island, Syrakousai was situated on a gulf by the same name and shared waters with the Ionian Sea. It was commonly reported by many Catalonian tribes that Syrakousai was the greatest of Ionian cities as well as the most beautiful of them all.

THE BATTLE OF HIMERA (311 BC)

In the days prior to the Punic Wars, it was reported that one named Agathocles hired Mamertine mercenaries who killed tens of thousands of native Sicilians and declared himself to be king of Syrakousai and the whole of Sicily. After the massacre, the self-proclaimed king established a democratic constitution. I found this news most disturbing and have no respect for Agathocles and his form of democracy. This was no democracy at all!

The Romans were not the only ones who desired to capture Syrakousai and control the wealth-generating trade routes of Tarshish. Punic-speaking Carthaginians also were interested in taking the coveted Greek island from Agathocles. In the Battle of Himera, the Carthaginians, under the leadership of Hamilcar, aided by 40,000 foot soldiers, 1,000 slingers, and 5,000 cavalry defeated King Agathocles's mercenary armies. It was reported that 7,000 warriors were killed, but only 500 Carthaginian warriors died in the conflict. The Greeks lost their beautiful Syrakousai and all of Sicily to the Carthaginians, who proved to be superior warriors. The Punic-speaking tribes of Carthage secured a strategic Sicilian base camp on the doorstep of the Roman Republic. This news gladdened the hearts of Catalonians throughout Europe.

THE FIRST PUNIC WARS (264–241 BC)

Meanwhile, for more than half a century, the Latin Roman Republic grew in strength and power, securing the greater portion of the Italos peninsula. Well established on the great boot-shaped arm of land, the Romans began to engage the Phoenician Carthaginians in battle on the island of Sicily. During the Roman campaign against our Punic allies in Sicily, our Catalonian warriors continued to maintain the Po River Valley in northern Italos. The sons of Romanus were sandwiched between the Carthaginians and the Catalonians. They were extremely vulnerable to attack from all directions.

THE BATTLE OF TELAMON (225 BC)

I learned about the Battle at Telamon, where it was reported that 40,000 Catalonian warriors lost their lives. Another 10,000 warriors were captured in the battle against the consuls and armies of the Roman Republic of Romanus at Telamon in the land of their Etruscan allies.

Long before the battle at Telamon, our Catalonian ancestors heard reports that the Romans had colonized the Gallic region of Picenum. The Roman aggression outraged our Boii warriors and the Insubres chieftains. The Insubres are known among our people as being early descendants of Longobardus, the Catalonian son of Armenon, who settled in Milan. Aneroëstes and Concolitanus emerged as powerful Gaesatae warriors, Gaulish tribesmen sojourning in the Alps near the River Rhodanus. These two mercenaries were hired by our Boii warriors and our ancient Insubres allies. Our allied Catalonian forces were led by Aneroëstes and Concolitanus into battle against the Roman Republic.

In the beginning our armed forces succeeded in campaigns in Etruria. The Catalonians lead by Aneroëstes overran Etruria and began to march on Rome. But when confronted by the army of Consul Lucius Aemilius Papus, Aneroëstes persuaded our warriors to withdraw. After a period of waiting, our patient troops overran our former allies, the Etruscan sons of Tiras, and there set our gaze on capturing Rome. Our warriors came up against the Romans who were stationed in Clusium, about a three-day march from Rome. It was in Clusium that the allied Galatian warriors camped and prepared for war.

I learned that in the night our warriors left their camp in Clusium as a decoy and built defenses in the town of Faesulae. Our Catalonian warriors had a more advantageous position at Faesulae and were able to view the positions of the Roman armies from their own elevated location. With such a great military advantage, the Catalonian warriors waged war with the sons of Romanus and killed 8,000 troops. The Romans were not annihilated, however, as some of their soldiers escaped to a defensible hilltop retreat.

Fearful of being slaughtered when the armies of Papus arrived, Aneroëstes convinced our Catalonian warriors to withdraw along the Etruscan coastline with their booty from the victorious campaign at Faesulae. Papus arrived late and followed closely behind our Catalonian warriors, aggravating their rear, but he did not desire to engage our army in a pitched battle. Unfortunately, our warriors were cut off by Papus and hindered from their advance at Telamon in Etruria.

Meanwhile, the other consul, Gaius Atilius Regulus, led his armies from Sardinia to Pisa on his way to Rome. Roman scouts ran into the Catalonian warriors head-on near the town of Telamon. Our nearly naked Galatian ancestors battled the Romans there, but the Roman javelins and short swords proved a better weapon than our Noricum long swords. Also, our smaller Noricum shields provided little protection for our unprotected, exposed bodies.

Our league of Catalonian warriors was engaged in battle with the forces of Regulus at our front and the forces of Papus at our rear. Our Catalonian and Insubres warriors fought at the rear against Papus while, with their wings protected by chariots, our Boii warriors and Taurisci allies confronted Regulus in the front. It was reported to me and many others that our Boii warriors fought tenaciously against the Roman armies. Boii warriors captured and killed Regulus. And like Bolgios, they mounted the head of Regulus, this time on a sword, and proudly delivered this symbol of victory to our Catalonian leaders.

But eventually the Roman cavalry secured the hill. Colcolitanus was captured. Aneroëstes escaped with a small band of proud warriors who fell on their Noricum swords rather than being captured, humiliated, and enslaved by the sons of Romanus.

Our Catalonian confederacy with its allied cavalry outnumbered the Roman cavalry four to one, but the Roman foot soldiers were 70,000 men strong. We went into a pitched battle with 50,000 warriors on foot. But two of their Roman consuls,

Regulus and Papus, and their comparatively larger foot soldiers (though smaller cavalry), surrounded our warriors. Although our men fought gallantly to their deaths and successfully killed one of the two consuls, Rome pushed our surviving Boii warriors and Insubres back into the Albus Mountains.

THE BATTLE OF CLASTIDIUM (222 BC)

I learned about the battle at Clastidium. The Insubres, who fought so fiercely alongside our Boii warriors and the Taurisci warriors, established an Insubrian in the land of Lombardo. Three years after our Catalonian warriors were defeated at Telamon, Viridomarus emerged to lead the Insubres into battle against the Roman Republic armies, which were led by Consul Marcus Claudius Marcellus. It was reported that Viridomarus fought Marcus in one-on-one, hand-to-hand combat. The Roman consul was victorious and killed Viridomarus. The Insubres were defeated by the Romans. It was later reported that in Rome Marcellus received the highest of honors for killing Viridomarus. This defeat in battle at Clastidium was extremely discouraging to our league of Catalonian nations.

THE SECOND PUNIC WAR (218–201 BC)

For thousands of years, our ancient Catalonian ancestors from Panphylia and Kilikia traded with a remnant of the sons of Tarshish, the son of Javan, who settled on the northern coast of west Afri. Later the Phoenicians established trade routes along the coast of the Great Sea from the Levantine Sea in the east to Sea of Tarshish in the west. Tarshish was known by some historians as Carthage and reported as a colony of the sons of Patriarch Sidon.

However, it is understood by our people that the trade relationships among the Carthaginian sons of Javan, the Carthaginian sons of Sidon, and the sons of Captain King Alanus comprised a long history of tribal interaction and commerce. So it was no surprise to me to learn that Hannibal, the Carthaginian leader of the Punic warriors, called upon his ancient trade partners for help and reestablished trade relationships to aid efforts in the overthrow of the aggressive conquests of the Roman Republic. Having experienced great loss at the hands of the Romans, our people welcomed and accepted this invitation.

The Punic language that Hannibal and his warriors spoke had linguistic roots in the Phoenician language that was spoken throughout the Mediterranean. Historians named the battles between the Romans and our Albanus warriors after the Punic language of Hannibal from North Africa; Hannibal led and consolidated various tribal nations. Numerous battles with the Roman Republic became known as the Punic War.

It was interesting to me that in the long-ago days of Abraham, the man of faith and son of Patriarch Shem, our ancestors sojourned in Ebla and most likely spoke in the Eblaite tongue. My understanding is that the Eblaite tongue is kin to the Akkadian tongue, and over time evolved into the Punic tongue of the Phoenician sons of Patriarch Sidon, who settled in north Afri.

In those days, any literate nobleman among the Catalonian nations perceived that it was simply a matter of time before the Punic-speaking sons of Javan and Sidon would resurrect their ancient alliance with the sons of Iobaath to defend their God-given territories in Europa. For centuries, the heroic stories of the chariot-heavy Battle of Kadesh between the Egyptians and the Hittite Empire resonated among our people, as many sons of Sidon and Iobaath under Hittite rule died in the same battlefields in Kadesh.

Like the aggressive Egyptian armies at Kadesh, the ambitious Roman Republic had to be stopped. So with a Carthaginian base camp secured in Sicily and with Catalonian allies eager to defend our Alpine treasures from aggressive Roman oppression, our league of Carthaginian-Catalonian warriors united and prepared for a long war.

THE BATTLE OF THE TREBBIA (218 BC)

Approximately four years after the defeat of the Insubres in Clastidium, the Catalonians joined with Hannibal's warriors near the River Trebbia, a southern, right tributary of the River Po in northern Italos. Although the battle was in winter, the confederate warriors of Hannibal were warm and well fed. Hannibal was as wise as a fox and enticed the Roman armies, commanded by Consul Tiberius Sempronius Longus, to tread through nearly frozen waters. Wisely taking advantage of their weakness, Hannibal planned an ambush.

Catalonian scouts kept Hannibal informed as to the whereabouts of the Roman legions. When advised that the Romans were prepared for battle, and in the middle of night, Hannibal dispatched 1,000 foot soldiers and the same number of cavalry under the command of his younger brother, Mago. These prepared for ambush by hiding in the thorny underbrush along the River Trebbia.

While Mago and his troops were hidden, Hannibal sent Numidian cavalry beyond the Trebbia to evoke a response from the Romans there. They discharged missiles on the night watchmen. Anxious to battle Hannibal and his Galatian allies, the impatient and headstrong Sempronius did not hesitate to respond to the provocation and sent out Roman cavalry to drive them off. Then shortly afterward, Sempronius sent 6,000 javelin throwers, 12,000 heavily armed infantry, and 20,000 Italic allies across the nearly frozen river, where they were caught off guard and ambushed by Mago's camouflaged warriors.

It is written that the temperatures were frigid; snow was falling heavily. We learned later that the Roman troops had not been cared for and had not eaten their morning meal. While the men were hungry and cold, Sempronius ordered his troops to wade across the ice-cold, chest-high waters of the Trebbia. The Roman soldiers were so cold when they reached the other side of the river that they were challenged to grip their weapons. Hannibal's combat strategy had been brilliant!

Meanwhile, Hannibal's warriors were well cared for, well prepared, and ready to engage the weakened enemy. The allied troops of Hannibal were armed with weapons and warm bodies. His men prudently anointed themselves with oil beside camp-fires. Hannibal patiently waited for the Roman armies to cross the Trebbia River and then launched his attack.

Hannibal fronted his battle lines with 8,000 light foot soldiers, javelin throwers, and Gymnesiae slingers. Known to many as the sons of Walagothus, the son of Armenon, the Gymnesiae tribes-men spoke Catalan, the language of Catalina. These ancestors of Captain King Alanus colonized the Gymnesic Islands under the coast of Iberia.

The inhabitants of the island were reported to be as naked as Adam and Eve in the garden! Thus the Gymnesiae slingers came to this battle nearly naked. It seemed reasonable to me that the tradition of the great King David slaying Goliath with a single stone influenced the Gymnesic slingers from Catalina. David also danced naked before the treasured arc of the covenant. I found that these two tribal features were a fixture among the Gymnesiae to be no coincidence, as they were still Catalonian tribes living according to Alanya after more than seven hundred years.

Behind the lightly armored Davidic Gymnesiae slingers, Hannibal formed the main battle lines with 20,000 foot soldiers of Africans, Iberians, and Catalonians. Flanking the battle lines, he assembled another 10,000 cavalry troops with a significant number of war elephants on both flanks.

Suddenly the Numidian cavalry behind the slingers attacked and pursued the Roman cavalry. It was reported that Sempronius withdrew his cavalry to the flanks. So the Numidian caval-ry harassed the light foot soldiers, causing them to discharge all their projectiles. Short on ammunition and weakened by hypothermia, the Roman light foot soldiers were forced to fall back and merge into the heavy foot soldiers. As the Catalonian Balearic slingers approached the heavy Roman army, they moved to the outside wings.

The heavy Carthaginian foot soldiers were now in full conflict with the heavy Roman foot soldiers while the Carthaginian wings attacked the Roman wings. After the Roman rear advanced, Mago's hidden forces emerged from the underbrush and attacked the Roman foot soldiers from behind. Hard-pressed, the less disciplined among the Roman soldiers broke rank and escaped to the river. The Roman cavalry escaped on horseback.

As the heavy infantry and cavalry on both sides were engaged in battle, the indifferent elephants had become wild, attacking both sides of the conflict. Hannibal ordered his highly skilled cavalry to drive the monstrous herds toward the Cenomani tribesmen who had defected and allied with the Romans. It was reported that most of the Cenomani warriors perished, trampled to their deaths, crushed by a herd of frantic elephants.

In the end the Carthaginian armies under Hannibal's astute leadership slaughtered the Roman armies at Trebbia. Longus escaped death with a few survivors. This was a great victory for the united Carthaginian-Catalonian warriors and their cause.

THE BATTLE OF LAKE TRASIMENO (JUNE 21, 217 BC)

I learned about the battle at Lake Trasimeno, which occurred the year after the battle at Trebbia. When Hannibal arrived at the lake, he reasoned that the land surrounding the lake was suitable for an ambush. So Hannibal prepared for another battle with the Roman Republic, this time led by Gaius Flaminius Nepos, who was in pursuit. On the north side of the lake, the Malpasso Road meandered along several densely populated wooded areas that were forested by the Etruscan people who sojourned there. Hannibal prudently set up camp above the lake on cliffs, where he had a full view of all enemy intruders.

Hannibal spent the night preparing his troops for battle with the Roman Republic. Below the citadel on a slightly elevated territory, he stationed foot soldiers comprised of Africans, Iberians, and Catalonians. Concealed deep within the heavily wooded forest, the location of the cavalry was strategic as the horses and riders were advantaged with the ability to race downhill in an ambush as the Romans entered the forest. Troops were also stationed at various locations in high places. To deceive Flaminius into thinking that their camp was much farther away, Hannibal brilliantly ordered that campfires be lit behind the warriors on the distant hills of Tuoro.

When the Romans were positioned on the road, the confederated warriors of Hannibal, like a disturbed nest of honey bees, swooped down the hill, charging the Roman lines from three different directions. Without preparation time to dress for battle, Hannibal's warriors blocked the road. Hannibal outmaneuvered their opponents and forced the Romans into hand-to-hand combat. Strategically divided into three parts, and in three hours of heavy combat, the Carthaginian, Iberian, and Catalonian warriors under the command of Hannibal cut down half the 30,000 Romans and annihilated 15,000 Roman Republic soldiers. Many defeated Romans drowned in the lake trying to escape the Noricum sword.

I learned that a Galatian by the name of Ducarius killed Flaminius. It was reported that 6,000 Romans attempted to escape in the fog; however, the fleeing warriors were apprehended by one, Maharbal, who was said to offer them safe passage in exchange for their weapons and armor. But when Hannibal arrived, he would have nothing to do with this treaty and sold the Romans into slavery. After enslaving 6,000 Roman soldiers, Hannibal and his warriors went on to destroy a Roman army of 4,000 reinforcements led by the propraetor Gaius Centennius. This also was a great victory for the Carthaginians and the Catalonians.

THE BATTLE OF CANNAE (AUGUST 2, 216 BC)

I also learned about our great victory at the battle at Cannae, one pitched on the plains of Apulia in southeast Italos. Recovering from their losses at Trebbia and Lake Trasimeno, the Roman Republic recruited 86,000 Roman warriors and allied troops under command of two consuls, Lucius Aemilius Paullus and Gaius Terentius Varro, who strongly desired to wage battle in Cannae.

Our chronicles indicate that our Carthaginian warriors under the command of Hannibal were about half in number: 8,000 Libyans, 8,000 Iberians, 16,000 Catalonians, and about 5,500 Gaetulian foot soldiers, a people from Getulia, a desert region south of the Atlas Mountains in northern Afri. The Carthaginian cavalry was comprised of 4,000 Numidians, 2,000 Iberians, 4,000 Catalonians, and 450 Liby-Phoenicans. Hannibal had about 8,000 skirmishers made up of Balearic slingers and spearmen. Our records report that the numbers totaled 50,000 allied warriors.

The Roman armies were deployed in a conventional manner with foot soldiers in the middle and cavalry on the wings. Understanding the strengths of his warriors as well as the advantages and disadvantages of their specific battle skills, and utilizing the terrain of his battlefield, Hannibal successfully killed about 80,000 Roman soldiers and captured another 10,000; our records indicate that approximately 2,000 escaped. The outnumbered Carthaginian warriors slaughtered the Roman Republic and their allies in southeastern Italos.

After heavy casualties at Trebbia, Lake Trasimeno, and now Cannae, the Roman armies were all but annihilated. For many years, the Roman Republic was in a state of complete disarray.

At that point, with successful campaigns on the Italian peninsula, the Galatian armies redirected their ambitions toward Asia. While studying, I thought to myself that this retreat was probably premature, if not unwise, and that Rome should have been annihilated and her people relocated to foreign territories so they would never resurrect and cause harm or disrupt the peaceful coexistence among Catalonians in the future.

THE CATALONIAN WARS IN ASIA

I learned about battles in Asia with warriors of Pergamum who were allies of the Roman Republic. Having defeated King Antiochus and the Seleucids who ruled Asia for nearly two hundred years since the Battle at Thermopylae, Consul Gnaeus Manlius Vulso set his gaze on various Catalonian tribes who had migrated back to Asia over the past century.

The Roman consul was disturbed that our Catalonian ancestors had aided their ancient neighbors, the Seleucids, and this became his excuse to wage war with our people. Without authorization from the Roman Senate, the consul, along with his Pergamum allies, set a military precedent by marching inland with plans to attack Galatian settlements in Asia.

THE BATTLE OF MOUNT OLYMPUS (189 BC)

After nearly a thousand years in Europa, some Catalonian tribes migrated back to our original homeland in Asia along the Aegean Sea. The Catalonians who migrated back to Asia were primarily comprised of three tribes: the Tolostobogii, the Tectosagi, and the Trocmi. They attempted to take back the land of our ancient forefathers. This desire to return to Alanya grew strong in their hearts, and eventually they put their desires to foot.

The Trocmi Catalonians settled near the ancient coast in Kilikia, the land of former kings Alanya and Fetebir. The Tectosagi Catalonians sojourned once again in the inland territories, the ancient lands occupied by the sons of King Iobaath in the days of Abraham, Isaac, and Jacob.

The Tolostobogii Catalonians migrated to Ionia, the ancient territories of Dodanim, the son of Javan, and Iobaath, the son of Dodanim. The Tolostobogii Catalonians also inhabited the ancient land of Aeolis, south of the Dardanelles of Dodanim, the coastal region of Tiras, the son of Japheth, the son of Noah.

Nearly three decades after their defeat at Cannae, the Romans and the Pergamese arrived at Gordium and found the city deserted. While the Romans camped in Gordium, the Catalonians prepared for battle high above in the ancient mountains of Olympus.

Preparing for battle with the Roman Republic led by Manlius, the Tolostobogii warriors occupied Mount Olympus, the highest mountain in Ionia, located in the Olympus Range on the border between Thessaly and Macedonia. There they built defenses and prepared for contact with Roman troops.

The Roman Republic advanced with the Pergamese against the Tolostobogii Catalonians occupying Olympus. The Tolostobogii constructed bulwarks aboveground and dug deep ditches underground to defend themselves against the aggressive, highly regimented Roman Republic legions.

The Tectosagi and Trocmi tribes were said to have occupied other mountains.

The Catalonians could fend off the Roman Republic armies from their positions on Mount Olympus, but the superior weapons and armor of the Romans soon gave them the advantage in battle. The Romans eventually massacred the Galatian warriors on Olympus when they were finally able to storm their camp. It was recorded that 10,000 Catalonians were killed and 40,000 captured.

After the Roman victory at Olympus, and buying time to regroup, our Catalonian ancestors pleaded with the Romans to not attack them a second time. In a strategy meant to delay the Romans while their women and children crossed the River Halys, the Catalonians requested a conference halfway between their demolished camp and Ancyra. The Romans agreed to meet the Catalonians halfway.

It was recorded that the Catalonians aspired to assassinate Manlius on their way to the conference. Our Catalonian warriors charged the Romans en route to the conference while attempting to capture and kill the Roman leader. The Catalonians could overpower the bodyguards, but they were unsuccessful in their attempt to kill Manlius when a band of Roman foragers arrived and pushed back the Catalonians. Our Catalonian warriors were forced to retreat.

Perceiving that the Catalonians were not giving up the fight, the Romans spent a few days scouting the area. On the third day, the Roman army met 50,000 Catalonian warriors and engaged them in battle. The Romans defeated the Catalonians and plundered their camp. The Catalonian warriors that survived retreated across the river and met up with their women and children, who were under the protection of the Trocmi tribesmen.

In those days Consul Gnaeus Manlius Vulso negotiated a peace treaty with the Seleucid Empire and divided Asia in two regions. Antiochus III, ruler of the Seleucid Empire, regretfully abandoned all the territories north beyond the Taurus Mountains; the Tolostobogii and the Tectosagi Galatians were ruled by King Eumenes II of Pergamum, and the Trocmi Galatians who returned to their southern homeland in Panphylia and Kilikia were ruled by Antiochus.

After two years Vulso, a lawless one, returned to Rome, where he was reprimanded for attacking the Galatians without consent of the Senate. Vulso believed that he made the best decision for the Roman Republic and successfully pleaded his case before the Senate. Eventually, after persuading the Roman senators, Vulso was awarded a triumph by those same senators.

And after nearly a millennium in Europa, a tribal remnant of the once God-fearing Catalonian tribes settled in our ancient homeland east of Asia in a column of *terra firma* between the Blach See and the Kilikian Sea in the midst of the dispersed sons of Abraham, who also had sojourned into what the Romans began to call, in the territory surrounding Ancyra, *Galatia*.

THE SELEUCID EMPIRE (312–63 BC)

Approximately a decade after the Roman Republic and the Pergamese defeated the Galatians in Ancyra, Mithradates, the youngest son of Antiochus III, with the help of King Eumenes of Pergamum, became ruler of the Seleucid Empire and assumed the name Antiochus IV Epiphanes. In an unusual set of circumstances, Mithradates became coregent alongside his older brother's infant son. A few years later, Antiochus IV brutally murdered his nephew and became the sole regent of the Seleucid Empire.

When the guardians of King Ptolemy VI of Egypt demanded the return of Coele-Syria, Antiochus IV Epiphanes was outraged and attacked the Egyptians. Antiochus captured King Ptolemy and conquered all of Egypt except the great Grecian city of Alexandria, which was under Roman rule. Not desiring to arouse Rome, Antiochus permitted King Ptolemy to rule Egypt. To avoid civil war in Egypt, King Ptolemy's brother, Ptolemy VIII Euergetes, coruled in Alexandria.

Then Antiochus IV attacked Egypt and simultaneously sent a fleet of ships to capture the island of Cyprus off the coast of Kilikia. But when the Seleucid king approached Alexandria, he was met by Gaius Popillius Laenas, an ambassador from the Roman Senate who delivered a stern message to Antiochus to withdraw his armies from Egypt and his navy from Cyprus. If the Seleucid king did not withdraw his men, he was told, the Seleucid Empire would be declared as in a state of war with the Roman Republic.

Antiochus appealed to the ambassador for time to discuss the matter with his council. Upon hearing the recalcitrant request, the impatient Roman ambassador drew a line in the sand around the feet of Antiochus and demanded that he give affirmation to the Roman Senate to leave Egypt before he stepped outside the circle. Antiochus agreed to withdraw from Egypt and so avoided war with Rome.

I learned from our records that while Antiochus was delayed in Egypt, a rumor spread among the retreating Seleucid armies that their king had been murdered. While en route back to Syria, a deposed Jewish high priest named Jason, the brother of Onius III the high priest, assembled a thousand-man army and attacked Jerusalem by surprise. Menelaus, the high priest appointed by Antiochus, was forced to flee Jerusalem during the invasion.

When the living Seleucid king returned from Egypt, he falsely assumed that Judea was in a state of revolt. Angered by the Roman ultimatum to withdraw from Egypt and misinformed about the situation in Judea, Antiochus rushed to judgment and vented his anger like a wild beast on the city of David. Without a confrontation, the angry and violent king executed thousands of Hebrews living in Jerusalem.

It was recorded that 80,000 Hebrews lost their lives, 40,000 by violent death; 40,000 Hebrews were sold into slavery. This record saddened the hearts of many Jews throughout Galatia, along with many Catalonians who had been friends of Israel since the days of Noah.

After slaughtering and enslaving tens of thousands of Jews, Antiochus consolidated his empire, strengthened his grip over the region, and reinstalled Menelaus as high priest. Seeking political advantages, Antiochus sided with the Hellenized Jews and outlawed Jewish religious practices and traditions. Then the Seleucid king ordered the worship of Zeus as the supreme god in place of the LORD God of Abraham.

This report that the government had suppressed the freedom to practice our ancient faith in the LORD God of Japheth also angered my heart. The Catalonian ancestors of Captain King Alanus understood Zeus as Japheth, who was immortalized by the Greeks, and later the Romans, as Jupiter.

Although some wealthy, urban families—notably the Tobiad family—embraced Hellenization, the fundamental transformation of Jewish society was considered an abomination and outraged traditional Hebrews. Understanding that there was great risk and possible death for disobeying Antiochus, the Jews protested and refused to worship the Olympian Zeus as their supreme god. I was gladdened to learn that our ancestors also refused to worship Zeus.

When the news of the Jews' refusal to obey his orders arrived, Antiochus sent an army to enforce his decrees. One of the Athenian senators forced Jews to abandon the customs and traditions of their ancestors and no longer practice the laws of Moses. They dedicated the Second Temple, the temple built to replace the First Temple of King Solomon, to Zeus and desecrated the holy temple of God by fastening an idol of Zeus on the holy altar, a practice strictly forbidden by Jewish law. The Hebrews were commanded to renounce their faith, forced to abandon their sacred Sabbath Day—a day of rest that was instituted by the God of Creation in the beginning—and forced to cease from celebrating holy feasts like Passover. Antiochus made possession of the Torah a capital offense and burned all the copies of the Torah he could find. The sacrifices of animals to God, a tradition that our very own people had observed since the days of Noah, was forbidden.

This abomination of desolation outraged lawkeeping Jews and God-fearing Gentiles, especially among the Catalonians, everywhere in the Mediterranean world. The sons of Abraham who had escaped the Babylonian captivity settled in territories throughout the earth, like the ones who lived among the Asians and Galatians. Some God-fearing Catalonians replaced their Mediolanum synagogues with Jewish synagogues and practiced similar law and justice along with the sons of Abraham.

It was reported that two women who had their sons circumcised were arrested and were made a spectacle of; they were forced to walk through town with their infants on their breast. Then the circumcised infants were separated from their mothers and thrown from the top of the city wall to their deaths. Subsequently, entire families caught circumcising their males were executed. It was also reported that a remnant who met in a secluded cave to observe the Sabbath were betrayed by a man named Philip. All were burned to death for their insubordination to the lawless, demon-hearted Seleucid king.

Again, thousands who refused to worship Zeus were slaughtered. Jerusalem was desolated. A Greek military citadel, the fortress of Acra, was erected. The vain despot renamed the ancient Ionian city of Iopolis as Antioch of Syroi; several cities were renamed or named Antioch. This too angered my heart, since I calculated that, over time, these great ancient cities would be forgotten as having been named for unknown soldiers, the voice of their ancestors, and these voices would be silenced.

It was in a moment of clarity that I understood why our forefathers were such avid chroniclers of our kings and traditions. Understanding that the tongues of men are fickle and unruly, our ancients engraved and scribed truths about our origins in stone, papyrus, and linen. They understood that lawlessness would rule the earth and that self-serving despots like Antiochus would emerge and propagate popular philosophies and hypotheses about the genesis of mankind. Rulers would rewrite history to serve their own subjective quests to be worshipped and served. After this epiphany with truth, my desires to chronicle increased, growing with an even greater passion. I perceived that writing was and is the medium of communication that God preferred for documenting the chronicles of kings.

THE MACCABEAN REVOLT (167-160 BC)

After the tyrannical Antiochus forced the Hebrews into Hellenist practices and outlawed the Jewish religion, a rural, ultra-orthodox Jewish priest by the name of Mattathias the Hasmonean, from the village of Modiin, situated south of Hebron, an extremely brave leader, refused to worship Zeus as the supreme god. This refusal sparked a revolt against the Seleucid Empire.

Mattathias was outraged by the godless political circumstances in his day and was reported to have killed a Hellenized Jew who asserted himself and sacrificed to a Greek idol in the place of the priest, Mattathias. After the Hasmonean priest murdered the Hellenized Jew, Mattathias, like Moses, fled to the wilderness with his five sons. About a year later, Mattathias died in the wilderness.

It was then that Judas, the son of Mattathias the priest, led a successful guerilla-style campaign against the repressive Seleucid Dynasty. These initial campaigns were targeted against multitudes of Hellenized Jews who forsook their religion. The Maccabees destroyed pagan altars, forced the circumcision of all Jewish males, and established an outlaw state.

After a series of well-executed guerilla campaigns against the Seleucid armies, the Maccabees reestablished the worship of the LORD God of Noah, ritually cleansed the temple, reestablished tradition, and installed Jonathan Maccabee as high priest. The Maccabean victory over the Seleucid Empire has been celebrated by the Jews and God-fearing people to this day and is known as the festival of Hanukkah. It is the story of how men of great conviction and courage can be used by God to break the chains of government oppression and tyranny.

As news spread on the Great Sea about the Maccabees, many of the Diaspora synagogues stood with Judas in protest of Seleucid rule. Meanwhile, support grew for what seemed to be a more civil Roman Republic. The God-fearing people of Iopolis in Syroi, Tarsus in Kilikia, Alanya in Panphylia, Festive in Lukka, and Roman Galatia stood with Israel in opposition to the Seleucid Empire. Many believed that the time was coming when the promised Seed of Abraham would appear to redeem mankind from Adam's sin and bring the righteous kingdom of God to earth. We longed for this blessed hope and the coming of this Messiah.

THE HASMONEAN DYNASTY (164–63 BC)

The Hasmonean Dynasty in Judea lasted about one hundred years and came to fruition after Judas the Maccabee, sometimes called "the Hammer," led a rebel army that defeated and ended the Seleucid Empire. Two decades later, the younger brother of Judas the Maccabee, Simon Maccabaeus, established this Hasmonean Dynasty. Inspired by Mattathias, the Maccabees took advantage of a vulnerable Seleucid Empire that was weakened by the rising power of the Roman Republic in the west and the Parthian Empire in the east. The Maccabees reestablished the Jewish religious practices and traditions that Antiochus had outlawed.

The Roman Senate recognized, but also exploited, the Jewish state. Simon Maccabaeus had two grandsons, Hyrcanus II and Aristobulus II, who became pawns of the Roman Republic in a proxy war between Julius Caesar and Pompey the Great.

THE JUGURTHINE WAR (112–106 BC)

I read still more records, these about our trade partners in the Great Sea. The reports in those days were predominantly news about wars, just as the great prophet Jeremiah had predicted, of God's desire to punish Gentiles for their idolatry and for exulting men as God. While the Maccabees were reestablishing their tribal nation, I learned from the merchant marines about King Jugurtha's war with the Roman Republic.

The Jugurthine War was fought in Numidia in northern Afri, not too distant from the Carthaginians, the Punic-speaking archrivals of the Latin-speaking Romans. The king of Numidia exposed moral and character weaknesses within the ranks of the Roman Republic.

This war took its name from the Berber king Jugurtha, at first the nephew, and later the adopted son of, Micipsa, king of Numidia. It was recorded that King Jugurtha had great success bribing Roman civil and military leaders, but in the end, the Roman Republic defeated the Berber king.

THE CIMBRIAN WAR (113–101 BC)

It was also recorded in our chronicles that the sons of

Romanus had strengthened and annexed territories once held by the Catalonians. I learned that the northern Gothic sons of Gothus in Jutland migrated south and took advantage of their opportunities in a weakened Europa. The motivation behind the Gothic migration south remains a mystery among Catalonians to this day. I reasoned and understood from our own tribal experience that many ancient Catalonians and Germanic tribal nations were discontent, moving about from territory to territory in search of better circumstances.

I had special insight into origins from our sacred *Book of the Chronicles of the Bohemian Kings*. I understood that since the days of Noah, our God-fearing forefathers were habitually and by command a migrating people, a people instructed to go into all the world and proclaim the glory of the LORD God. This great commandment was spoken to Adam before the flood and to Noah and his three sons after the flood. And when the sons of Noah settled, having one nation and one tongue, God disrupted their one-world government in a grand display of disapproval. The LORD God supernaturally provided new tongues to the sons of God. Unable to communicate with one another, our Sovereign God then forced the nations into careers of perpetual relocation and homesteading.

I perceived that the great commission of God to go into all the world has never been rescinded. We are to be a people of destiny, establishing the glory of the LORD in one place and then moving on to establish His glory in another. But sadly, many tribes move to other places for material advantage and vainglory, not to spread the LORD's glory. That is what made Captain King Alanus so admirable, as his primary heart motivation was to spread the Way of our Righteous God to the nations and claim Tarshish and Europa for the glory of God. But sadly, what had begun in the Spirit ended in the flesh, bewitched by doctrines of demon angels.

BATTLE OF NOREIA (112 BC)

Noreia was the capital city of our Boii tribe located in the southeastern Alpine territories in Noricum and bounded by the Danube River to the north, Raetia and Vindelicia to the west, Pannonia to the east and southeast, and Italos toward the south.

In the days of King Boiorix, warfare continued as our brand. It was reported that King Boiorix was born of the lineage of King Gothus, the son of Armeno, from the Jutland peninsula, a chieftain of Gothic Cimbrian warriors who migrated south into the Albus Mountain territories. We understood that the seed of Gothus conquered the ancient Cimbri tribes and united as a warrior nation committed to conquest. As Homeros affirmed in his books, the conquerors took wives from the conquered, creating blended families and cultures.

The Teutones joined King Boiorix, and together they defeated the Scordisci Catalonians, who sojourned in the territory surrounding the confluence of the Sava, Drava, and Danu rivers of Riphath. Even our well-equipped and fearless Bavarii warriors were unable to oust the invading Catalonian sons of Gothus. King Boiorix and his warriors arrived on the River Danu in Noricum, which was also home to the Roman-allied Taurisci Catalonians. Joining the defeated ranks of the Scordisci and Boii Catalonians and unable to defend themselves, the Taurisci tribe appealed to the Roman Republic for aid to fight against King Boiorix and the advancing Teutones.

The Battle at Noreia is recognized as the first conflict of the Cimbrian War, a conflict in which Gnaeus Papirius Carbo, the Roman consul, responded to the request of Taurisci allies and directed legions of warriors to encamp in the highlands of Aquileia in northern Italia along the River Natissa.

Carbo demanded that King Boiorix and his men evacuate the territory of the Taurisci in Noreia along the River Danu. The Cimbri retreated. But Carbo was not content to allow King Boiorix and his troops to regroup, so he sent troops to ambush the retreating Cimbri forces. Aware of the impending ambush, a furious King Boiorix and his men defeated the Roman Republic and nearly killed Carbo. The humiliated Carbo escaped but was later impeached by the Roman Senate.

In those days the Roman Republic experienced defeat from the south and north from confederated Carthaginian warriors in Afri and confederated Germanic/Catalonian warriors led by King Boiorix. During this season the ancient seed of Riphath united with the seed of Alanus in opposition to Roman Republic imperialism. I understood this as a civil war among the twelve tribes of Alanus sojourning in Europa as when once-united Israel split into northern and southern kingdoms. With the aid of the seed of Riphath, many Catalonians believed they could defend their homelands and push the Romans back into Italos where they belonged. Our forefathers fought with all their hearts to defend Europa from the aggressive armies of Romanus. Everything was on the line. We had to fight for our homeland, liberty, and freedom.

BATTLE OF BURDIGALA (107 BC)

After the battle at Noreia, the Cimbri and our Catalonian allies moved westward over the Alps to Gallia Narbonensis where they defeated another Roman army under the command of Marcus Junius Silanus. It is a mystery why the Cimbri waited to attack the Roman Republic after their victory. The Cimbri tribe and the Tigurini tribe became allies and recruited 30,000 warriors.

Then, about three years after their victory in Noreia, the Cimbri under the leadership of the Gallic King Divico from the Catalonian Helvetian tribe of the Tigurini advanced toward the Roman province of Gallia Narbonensis. Lucius Cassius Longinus, Lucius Caesoninus, and Gaius Popillius Laenas led a campaign against the intruders with 10,000 warriors. Longinus and Caesoninus were killed in action. The alliance of Cimbri, Teutones, and Catalonians defeated the Roman Republic. This victory and defeat of the Roman Republic was heralded throughout Europa.

BATTLE OF ARAUSIO (OCTOBER 6, 105 BC)

Over the next two years, the new consul, Gnaeus Mallius Maximus, and the new proconsul, Quintus Servilius Caepio, assembled a massive army of 80,000 men accompanied by tens of thousands of support personnel. The Roman army was divided in two; each consul commanded a division.

Each consul marched his troops to the River Rhodanus, into an area located near the town of Arausio, named after the Galatian water god because the land is blessed with an abundance of rainfall during the hot summer months. Unwisely, and mistrusting each other, the two consuls foolishly established camps independent from the other on opposite sides of the river. Naturally, this left the two camps vulnerable to separate attacks.

Without requesting support from Consul Maximus, the overconfident Proconsul Caepio unwisely led his smaller isolated army in an attack against the substantial armies of the Cimbri and Teutones. The Cimbri and our allies easily wiped out the proconsul's legions and overran their camp. With the armies of Caepio defeated and on the run, the Cimbri-backed Catalonians aggressively attacked and defeated the demoralized armies of Consul Maximus. In the end, only Maximus, Proconsul Caepio, and a couple hundred Roman troops escaped.

It was reported that paranoia spread through the Roman Republic like out-of-control forest fires. Many were afraid and feared that the Cimbri and their Galatian allies would soon be launching campaigns against Rome. Immersed in desperation and panic, the Roman Republic found itself in a state of emergency.

With the Roman armies of Maximus and Caepio defeated, the Cimbri and their Catalonian allies withdrew their pursuit. This action was difficult for me to understand. They neglected to seize another rare opportunity to invade a weakened Rome. Instead the Cimbri advanced into Hispania; the Teutones remained in Catalonian territories.

Meanwhile, in Rome, Gaius Marius, the victor over Jugurtha of Numidia, was elected consul. Gaius took advantage of the crisis and was granted an unconstitutional and unprecedented five-year term. In a weakened state and enabled by the missed opportunity of the Cimbri confederation, Consul Marius could construct a new army on his own terms.

Recently I met a knowledgeable Hellenist historian and learned more about this Roman reformer who emerged from the ranks of the Roman Republic. The reforms under Consul Gaius were implemented because of lessons learned during the Jugurthine and Cimbrian wars. I was told that Consul Marius initiated vast changes to the army. Marius analyzed and improved every aspect of the army. He replaced the current army of land-owning gentry with professional, able-bodied, but landless volunteers. He improved the command structure to avoid fiascos such as had occurred at Arausio. He standardized the manner that volunteers were trained for battle. He improved the army's weaponry and armor. And he improved the equipment used in battle.

Consul Marius also made sweeping changes to the army divisions. He divided the legions into smaller tactical cohorts made up of approximately 480 volunteer warriors each. Each cohort had six subgroups of eighty men; a newly appointed centurion officer was designated as commander of these eighty. He established ten ranks of cohorts, the first cohort being the most prestigious, the tenth the least. He established the cohort as the tactical and administrative unit of the legion.

Consul Marius understood the value of symbolic emblems and icons, so he established the Aquila eagle to be the sole animal figure to represent the Roman Republic. A soldier under the command of Consul Marius was never to allow the Aquila to fall into enemy hands. Over time, according to Marius's plan, the emblem of the Roman Republic was revered by the troops, boosted their morale, and united the warriors and all the sons of Romanus.

Foolishly, the Cimbri and our Catalonian allies gave Consul Marius plenty of time to regroup and implement his many reforms. Marius was ready to engage the Teutones with his new army. So he erected a citadel on top of a hill near Aquae Sextiae. From this fortified camp, Marius lured the Teutones and their allies, the Ambrones, into attacking them.

BATTLE OF AQUAE SEXTIAE (102 BC)

Commanded by King Teutobod, the Teutones and the Ambrones attacked the Roman armies at the Roman city of Aquae Sextiae, which was located within a plain overlooking the River Arc in southern Gaul. During the attack, Consul Marius stole a strategy from Hannibal: he selected five cohorts to hide camouflaged in the woods, and then, at the appropriate time, ordered the camouflaged forces to ambush the Teutones and Ambrones from the rear after they had advanced.

As a result of Marius's careful planning, the Teutones and the Ambrones were caught off guard and defeated. King Teutobod was captured and placed in Roman chains. Approximately 90,000 warriors were killed and another 20,000 captured. It was recorded that only a thousand Roman warriors died in the conflict. After the battle at Aquae Sextiae, the Teutones and Ambrones were eliminated as a threat to Rome. News of the Roman victory at Aquae Sextiae on the River Arc spread throughout Europa. The Cimbri warriors, however, remained a formidable threat.

BATTLE OF THE RAUDINE PLAIN (101 BC)

Refusing to give up the fight for freedom, the Cimbri returned to Gaul and prepared for their invasion of Rome. The Cimbri, under the leadership of King Boiorix and accompanied by Lugius, led 210,000 warriors into a pitched battle with the allied forces of

Rome, which numbered just 50,000 men of war. The date of the battle was agreed to by King Boiorix and Consul Marius in the plains of Raudine in northwestern Italia. They agreed to fight the battle on the same plains where Hannibal and the Galatian allies formerly fought below Vercellae, the capital of the Ligurian tribe near the confluence of the River Sesia and River Po.

The battle in the plains of Raudine was a disaster for the Cimbri, who were all but wiped off the face of the earth by the reorganized Roman armies. Consul Marius, with the able leadership of Proconsul Quintus Lutatius Catulus and Lucius Cornelius Sulla, slaughtered 140,000 Cimbri and Teutonic warriors and captured another 40,000 who became slaves.

However, a small remnant of the Cimbri and Teutones survived and migrated north to Jutland. It was recorded that a few Cimbri and Teutonic warriors who were enslaved after the war later emerged as recalcitrant Roman gladiators. As gladiators, the slaves were forced under extremely harsh conditions to entertain bloodthirsty Roman audiences. These enslaved warrior-gladiators often met violent death, torn asunder by famished wild beasts. It is difficult for me to imagine such violence and depravity of conscious among a law-abiding people who once feared the LORD God of Captain King Alanus.

THE GALLIC WARS (58–50 BC)

In those days, the Catalonians of Europa were a confederation of various tribal nations united to defend their homeland against the eminent and aggressive enemy to the south, the Roman Republic. Forty years after the battle of the Raudine Plain, Julius Caesar emerged and was bent on subduing Europa once for all.

The reforms under Marius and his successful campaigns against our Catalonian tribes paved the way for Julius Caesar to become the sovereign ruler of the Roman Republic. Gaul was of significant importance to the Romans, as they wished to secure their northern border along the River Rhodanus. It was well known that various tribal nations attacked the Roman Republic from time to time on their northern border. Although Gaul was an immediate threat, Julius Caesar had ambitions to plunder and conquer the kingdom of Dacia located in the Balkans. He claimed that the Catalonians provoked the Roman Republic into battle. The truth of the matter was that Caesar was burdened with massive debt obligation and had selfish ambitions to advance his own financial circumstances as well as to ensure a strong political career in Rome.

According to Caesar's own biased chronicles, the Gauls were a highly civilized and wealthy nation with trade connections throughout the known world, even with Rome. For centuries, some Catalonian Gallic tribes such as the Aedui and Helvetii enjoyed political alliances and lucrative trading privileges with Rome.

Although Caesar held massive debt, he formed an alliance with Marcus Licinius Crassus, and Pompey, both men of means. Through this political triumvirate, Caesar was appointed proconsul of two Roman Republic provinces. Caesar was the governor of Cisalpine Gaul, where Galatian tribes sojourned in northern Italos along the River Po, and Illyricum, where Galatian Illyrian tribes sojourned along the coast of the Adriatic Seas, and in the western regions of the Peninsula of Haemus and north as far as the River Danu.

Later Caesar was assigned to govern the province of Transalpine Gaul where Galatian tribes sojourned beyond the Alps. It seemed to me that Caesar's five-year term of service as proconsul was a rare political appointment in those days.

THE BATTLE OF MAGETOBRIGA (63 BC)

Another battle took place near the Sequani town of Magetobriga. The Sequani and Arverni Catalonians enlisted the aid of Suebian King Ariovistus, who crossed the River Rhodanus with 15,000 warriors. With aid from the Suebi, the Aedui who allied themselves with Rome were defeated and massacred by our allied Catalonian armies.

After the successful campaign against the Romans, the Aedui tribe became a tributary to the Sequani tribe. The Sequani and Arverni tribes granted land to King Ariovistus for their contribution to the defeat of the Aedui. King Ariovistus settled and colonized the land gifted to him, doing so with 120,000 of his people. This colony greatly concerned the Roman Republic.

Following the massacre near Magetobriga, the Aedui tribe sent envoys to their ally, the Roman Republic, and appealed to Caesar for help. An apostate Catalonia chronicler from among the Aedui named Diviciacus was a guest of Marcus Tullius Cicero, a Roman philosopher with great understanding and wisdom.

I learned from a copy of the writings of Cicero that I obtained from the Academy that Diviciacus was an educated man knowledgeable in divination, astronomy, and philosophy. This request for aid articulated by Diviciacus and the other Aedui ambassadors provided Caesar the opportunity to move troops into central Gaul.

After Caesar defeated the Helvetii, a majority of the Catalonians congratulated him and sought to meet with him in a general assembly. Diviciacus emerged as the head of the Aedui tribe and was spokesman for the newly established Gallic confederation of Roman sympathizers. The Gallic delegation expressed concern over the hostages taken by King Ariovistus. Caesar, on the other hand, was eager to protect his allies in Gaul and defeat the Suebian king Ariovistus.

THE BATTLE OF BIBRACTE (58 BC)

In our day, Julius Caesar, the son of Gaius Julius Caesar III and the nephew of Gaius Marius, emerged as a great leader with six Roman legions under his command. I learned that Rome made allies with the Aedui tribe who settled the territory between the River Arar, a right tributary of the Rhodanus, and Liger, the largest river in Gaul, one well situated to provide needed supplies to the Roman armies.

Preparing to attack the Suebian warriors, Caesar moved to Bibracte, the capital citadel of the Aedui tribe in the territory of Burgundus, about eighteen miles from their camp, and there he received the promised supplies from the Aedui. While stationed in Bibracte, the Helvetii Catalonian warriors harassed Caesar's rear guard. Shrewdly, Caesar sent his cavalry to delay the attack.

Caesar marshaled six legions. He led the First, Second, Third, Fourth, and Fifth legions along with the Eleventh and Twelfth, which occupied the top of the hill. Then he organized the Sixth, Seventh, Eighth, Ninth, and Tenth legions in a triplex formation at the foot of a nearby hill. The baggage carts, along with all his auxiliaries, were also stationed at the top of the hill.

While Caesar was stationing his troops, the Helvetii warriors drove off the cavalry. At noon they engaged the Romans in battle. Armed with javelins, Caesar's soldiers resisted the onslaught of the Helvetii warriors running up the hill. Then the legions of Caesar counterattacked the Helvetii and drove them back to their hill, where the Helvetic baggage train sat.

Then, coming to the aid of our tribal cousins, our Boii warriors from the east joined with the Tulingi warriors in the west, 15,000 warriors in all coming to the aid of our Helvetii kinsmen, and now flanking the Romans on one side. Fortified by Catalonian warriors from the east and west, the Helvetii warriors returned to battle with a vengeance. From the Helvetii tribes, there were 263,000 warriors. From the Tulingi tribes, there were 36,000 warriors. From the Latobrigi tribes, there were 14,000 warriors. From the Rauraci tribe, there were 23,000 warriors. And from our Boii tribes, there were 32,000 warriors. In all, this came to 368,000 courageous warriors, noncombatant and combatant, resisting the legions of Julius Caesar in battle.

The battle lasted deep into the night, but Caesar finally captured the Helvetii baggage train along with the son and daughter of Orgetorix, the wealthy aristocrat who encouraged the Helvetii tribesmen to migrate toward Gaul to defend Suittes-Land. The Helvetii and our Albus Mountain warriors who survived fled into the night and took refuge with our allies, the Lingones, who sojourned near the headwaters of the Seine and Marne rivers in Gaul, a four-day journey from Bibracte.

THE BATTLE OF VESONTIO (58 BC)

Although Julius Caesar had aspirations to conquer King Ariovistus and the Suebi warriors, the Roman Senate had declared Ariovistus "a king and friend of the Roman people." Concerned about the welfare of the Aedui tribe, Caesar delivered an ultimatum to the Suebian king, demanding that he not cross the River Rhodanus and that he return the Aedui hostages he had captured.

King Ariovistus responded to the demands of Caesar by arguing that the Roman Republic had no jurisdiction over the Suebian territory. He asserted that his people were a warrior nation just like the Romans and that the Aedui hostages would be safe and secure as long as the Aedui maintained their annual tribute.

Germanic Charudes warriors from Jutland, who were also known as Harudes, joined King Ariovistus in securing land in Gaul. So in total defiance of the demands of Julius Caesar, the Suebi and Charudes warriors united and crossed the River Rhodanus, commenced to plunder, and then sought to settle into the best territories in Gaul. Plans were drafted to capture Vesontio, the large town of the Sequani.

Informed of the Suebian and Charudes aggression, Julius Caesar felt justified to protect his Aedui allies and wage war against King Ariovistus. When Caesar received reports about the Suebian campaign against Vesontio, he was angered by their disobedience and reacted by marching his troops north toward Vesontio. It was reported that Caesar arrived in Vesontio before King Ariovistus.

King Ariovistus requested a meeting with Caesar. Caesar agreed and, while en route, learned that Suebian horsemen were throwing stones at his mounted escort. Caesar, suspecting an ambush, felt violated and returned to camp.

A second time King Ariovistus requested a meeting with Caesar. King Ariovistus was insulted when Valerius Procillus, a trusted friend of Caesar, and Caius Mettius, a merchant who traded with the Suebi, arrived to meet with him instead of Caesar himself. The Suebian king was angry and shackled all friends of Caesar in chains.

King Ariovistus was furious, marched his men for two days, and camped behind the Roman warriors, successfully cutting off communication and supply lines with allied tribes in the region. In response Caesar baited King Ariovistus by building a smaller camp of warriors between their two encampments. King Ariovistus took the bait and attacked the smaller camp.

The next morning Julius Caesar marched five legions of warriors in triplex formation toward the camp of Ariovistus. King Ariovistus responded, commanding 60,000 warriors into battle against the Romans. On the verge of defeat, Publius Licinius Crassus, the son of Marcus Licinius Crassus, came to the aid of Caesar with his cavalry and pursued Ariovistus back to the River Rhodanus. Thirty-five thousand Suebi and Charudes warriors were killed in the battle. Again, Julius Caesar had become the victor.

THE BATTLE OF THE SABIS (57 BC)

One year after his victory at Vesontio, Julius Caesar intervened in another inter-tribal Catalonian conflict. On this occasion it was the Belgae tribes, principally the Nervii, who sojourned northeast on the River Rhenos, south of the territory of the sons of Francus, the son of Hessitio.

Fearing and anticipating attack by Caesar, the Belgae tribes united under the leadership of King Galba of the Suessiones.

The Belgae confederation included fifteen Catalonian tribes: the Aduatuci, the Ambiani, the Atrebates, the Bellovaci, the Caeroesi, the Caleti, the Condrusi, the Eburones, the Menapii, the Morini, the Nervii, the Paemani, the Suessiones, the Veliocasses, and the Viromandui. The Belgae were prepared to defend their territory against Roman imperialism.

As expected, Caesar marched his imperial army toward the Belgian territory. While setting up camp on the River Selle, the Belgae warriors ambushed the Romans, taking them by surprise. Caesar's army suffered many losses in the well-engineered surprise attack.

The Nervii cavalry led by Boduognatus were said to be fierce in battle and well equipped. It was reported that the Nervii warriors skillfully captured Roman javelins in midair and threw them back at the Romans! Caesar himself engaged in the battle against the confederacy until he was aided by the arrival of rein-forcements. The Romans came close to being defeated by the league of Belgian tribal nations, but were able to surround the Nervii and put them to flight.

Caesar persuaded the Remi tribe to join the Romans. In response, the Belgae and Galatian tribes attacked Alaudanum on the River Aisne. Caesar counterattacked the confederation and won yet another victory. Low on supplies, the Belgae tribes returned to their villages. Caesar was relentless and pursued the Belgae until they were defeated.

At this point Julius Caesar and his legions had subjugated all the Catalonian warriors on the mainland of Europa.

With success on the mainland, Caesar set his ambitions on the Britons.

THE CAMPAIGN AGAINST ARMORICA (57 BC)

With most of the Catalonian tribes of continental Europa in check, Caesar set his gaze on Armorica, a British colony in northern Gaul and an anti-Roman confederation of tribes led by the Veneti tribe. Armorica was the part of Gaul between the Seine and Loire rivers, including the Brittany peninsula on the coast of the Sea of Atlas. The Veneti had well-established trade routes to the Great Isles of Javan and to the Mediterranean.

The Catalonian Veneti built a large fleet of ships in the Gulf of Morbihan. I learned that the ancient territory surrounding the gulf had been inhabited since the days of Tarshish. Since the Veneti were a skilled seafaring people, Caesar had to launch several campaigns on land and sea to conquer the sons of Brutus. Ceasar eventually defeated the British confederation on the mainland.

After a punitive tour on the River Rhodanus in the territories of the Belgae and Suebi, Ceasar lead his legions to Brittany and waged war against and defeated the Catuvellauni tribe on the British Isles; these were led by their fearless chieftain Cassivellaunus. In the end, the Catuvellauni joined the ranks of those defeated Catalonian tribes who were forced to pay tribute to Rome.

THE BATTLE OF GERGOVIA (52 BC)

I was informed that a leader, Ambriorix, arose among the discontented Eburones of northeastern Gaul. The Eburones were ruled by two kings. King Ambriorix was king of half; King Cativolcus led the other half, a people who settled between the River Meuse and the Italos River Rhodanus. These two kings and their territories united under the leadership of Ambriorix and rose up against the Roman Republic. King Ambriorix was outraged with news that Caesar set up a camp nearby and had forced the scarce food supply of the Eburones to be rationed to his warriors.

At first, fifteen Roman cohorts were defeated by the Eburones. A garrison under the leadership of Quintus Tullius Cicero narrowly survived the attack. Caesar arrived with reinforcements and led the Romans to victory against the Eburones in a series of successive punitive campaigns. It was reported to me that the Roman armies nearly wiped the Eburones from the face of the earth.

However, a much larger uprising was incubating in the town of Gergovia in central Gaul. King Vercingetorix, chieftain of the Arverni headquartered in Gergovia, successfully united several Catalonian tribes under his leadership. The king understood that the Roman armies were superior in a pitched land battle, so he decided to establish a blockade against the Roman warriors to cut off their food and supplies.

Hearing of the blockade, Caesar rushed to the aid of his armies and captured the town of Avaricum. However, the Roman armies suffered a rare defeat in Gergovia. Following his defeat at the hand of King Vercingetorix in Gergovia, Caesar retreated, relocating his legions in the territory of the hospitable Aedui.

THE BATTLE OF ALESIA (52 BC)

In the same year as the victory in Gergovia, during the winter, when Roman armies were dormant, violence among the Carnutes broke out in the city of Cenabum. The Carnutes killed all Roman settlers in their city. This ethnic purging proved contagious, and several large Catalonian cities followed suit, slaughtering all Roman settlers, citizens, and merchants.

When Julius Caesar heard of the violence expressed toward Roman citizens, he navigated his armies over the snow-covered Alps into central Gaul and surprised our Catalonians. While Caesar commanded six legions in pursuit of our confederacy under the command of King Vercingetorix in Gergovia, four legions under the command of Titus Labienus were instructed to fight against the Senones and the Parisii.

When the cavalries collided, the confederate armies of Vercingetorix held a strong defensive position in Gergovia. Suffering heavy losses, Caesar and his warriors were forced to retreat to avoid total annihilation.

King Vercingetorix was reluctant to meet the Roman armies in a full land battle, so he bunkered down near the town of Alesia on the hilltop at Fort Mandubii. Surrounded by rivers, Fort Mandubii was an excellent defensive position; 80,000 men were stationed there.

Discouraged by his circumstances and unable to execute a frontal assault on the Galatian cavalries, Caesar decided to borrow King Vercingetorix's strategy from the Battle of Gergovia and siege the fort. Like Vercingetorix, Caesar reasoned that in the course of time he could be victorious by starving his enemies garrisoned at the fort.

In order to guarantee a successful blockade, and with a bit of genius, Caesar constructed a circumvallation with fortifications around the entire town of Alesia and the hilltop fortress. Deep ditches were dug to connect the fortifications; water was diverted from the many nearby rivers to fill the ditches. Deep holes and mantraps were dug in front of manmade streams to make trespassing even more dangerous. Several watchtowers were erected as batteries to house artillery.

In desperation King Vercingetorix and our confederation made every effort to stop the Romans from building the blockade. Our cavalry seized every opportunity to thwart construction, but this was ultimately unsuccessful as the Roman cavalry kept our raiders in check.

Nearly two weeks into the building project, our cavalry escaped through an unfinished and weakly guarded opening in the surrounding circumvallation. When Caesar realized that the breach had been successful and reinforcements would soon be at their back, he ordered that a second line of fortifications be constructed exactly as the first. Caesar completed his project and was prepared for his reinforcements.

Meanwhile, conditions within the circumvallation deteriorated. The area within the rounded blockade was overpopulated and food resources scarce. King Vercingetorix was unable to sustain both the warriors and the families of those who sojourned there. So the Mandubii gathered all the women and children and sent them out of the citadel with hopes that Caesar would be magnanimous and allow the civilian women and children to pass through the blockade. King Vercingetorix reasoned that this action might provide another breach to the surrounded area.

But Caesar maintained his position and prevented the desperate women and children from exiting the barricade. Without food, the deported civilians starved to death. The Catalonians within the surround watched as their kinsmen fell in the fields without battle. Morale among the Catalonians inside the barricade weakened. With great mourning within the camp, some among the warriors appealed to King Vercingetorix to surrender. While waiting for reinforcements, Vercingetorix made every effort to encourage the men within the citadel. When the barricaded Catalonians were about to lose all hope, reinforcements arrived in their desperate hour.

Led into battle by King Commius of the Belgic nation, the Atrebates joined the resistance. Commius attempted to advance to the citadel by breaking through the wall. King Vercingetorix ordered a simultaneous attack from the inside. The first attempt to penetrate the wall was unsuccessful, though the battle raged until sunset. Before the crack of dawn, in the darkness of night, King Commius and his warriors were able to breach the outer wall. Had it not been for the rapid response of the cavalry led by Mark Antony and Gaius Trebonius, the Romans may have been defeated altogether.

The inner wall also was attacked, but King Vercingetorix's men were delayed in battle by having to fill in the trenches the Romans had dug. The Catalonians attacking from within the walls were unable to surprise the Romans as their counterpart armies had done on the outside.

By this time the Roman armies were near the point of physical exhaustion. They found themselves besieged, and food was being rationed to Caesar's legions.

The morale among the Catalonians heightened when the

army received news of the arrival of 60,000 warriors led by Vercassivellaunus, a cousin of Vercingetorix. The reinforcements launched a massive attack on the outside through a heavily wooded area that was used by the Romans as a natural barrier in the circumvallation. Caesar attempted to keep the area a secret, but the Catalonians eventually discovered it.

While the armies of cousin Vercassivellaunus waged war on the outside, King Vercingetorix and his men attacked from every angle within. Caesar ordered his men to simply hold the lines of the inward press as he rode through the perimeter cheering and encouraging his men. Meanwhile, Labienus's cavalry was defending the area of the breach from the outside armies of Vercassivellaunus.

Unable to hold the lines, Caesar launched a counterattack on the advancing Catalonians inside the wall. Caesar and his legions pushed back the armies of Vercingetorix.

Meanwhile, the Roman cavalry of Labienus was on the verge of collapse as the armies of Vercassivellaunus persisted in breaching the outer wall. Wisely, and with the interior battle managed, Caesar ordered 6,000 men and thirteen cavalry cohorts to attack Vercassivellaunus and his warriors from the rear. This strategy invigorated the Roman warriors in conflict and discouraged Vercassivellaunus and his men, who panicked and attempted to retreat. The experienced, disciplined, but exhausted Roman armies pursued and slaughtered the forces of Vercassivellaunus. It was reported that the Catalonians avoided annihilation only due to the weariness of the Romans.

With news of the defeat of the relief armies and facing starvation, King Vercingetorix surrendered without a final conflict. The Galatian king presented his arms to Caesar the next day. The gallant king was captured and imprisoned by the Roman Republic. The Catalonian sons of Romanus were successful under the leadership of Julius Caesar, who defeated, annexed, and lorded over their European cousins.

The Catalonians of Wean and Istropolis

In the latter days of Julius Caesar, I was king of the Boii tribes sojourning in the ancient town of Istropolis. Istropolis is located at the intersect of the Danube and Morava rivers and, according to our tradition, had been inhabited since the days of Noah by native sons of Morava, the son of Riphath, the cherished younger brother of Regen. The Carpathian mountain range is birthed in Istropolis. From Istropolis I was able to facilitate trade with the Catalonian tribes in Anatolia and in the Mediterranean world.

I also understood from our tradition that the neighboring city of Wean, on the Danube, a short distance to the west from the Istropolis oppidum, was settled by Catalonians centuries earlier. The legacy of the ancient pfeifers lived on in the town of Wean, which is known as "the city of music."

As the reigning king, I revived the sounds of music, the mining of precious metals, and cattle ranching. Although I wrote extensively about the battle strategies of kings, I never had an appetite for war, preferring the merriment of Wean. I visited the jubilant whistle city often. Although I enjoy history and the stories of our ancestors, I occupied my latter days with numismatic projects minting coins of silver and gold.

I was a literate, God-fearing Catalonian schooled in linguistics, history, and many other arts and sciences. I sought the LORD God of Noah for understanding when interpreting the ancient *Book of the Chronicles of Bohemian Kings* that passed forward to my estate.

My coinage was minted with a bust of Japheth. The Galatian god, Bussumarus, also known as "the Great Voice," was the same as Jupiter, the Roman god. I argued that both Bussumarus and Jupiter bespeak of Japheth, the Great Voice, progenitor of both Roman and Galatian tribes according to our Catalonian traditions and ancient chronicles.

I frequently argued that our Catalonian chronicles accurately recorded our ancestry back to the days of Japheth. But I am challenged by many a fickle foe, especially among the new order of Catalonian chroniclers, who categorize our connection to Japheth and Noah with the likes of Danaoi mythology and catalogues of Achaean ships, with warriors preparing to destroy Troy and sleep with their enemies' wives. The debate raged on among philosophers as many questioned, "How can such prose and chronicle be proven right or wrong, nonfiction or fiction? Who among men has seen with his own eyes or lives to judge the circumstance of the ancients!"

It was amazing to me to learn that after so many thousands of years, I was privy to our well-written tradition, which spoke of the great descent from the Kaucasus Mountains, where we sojourned at Endon Lake after the flood of Noah. Patriarch Japheth taught our ancestors to fear the LORD God of Noah and keep his seven commandments. I was well aware, however, that having begun in the Spirit, the Catalonian sons of Captain King Alanus had fallen into the desires of the flesh. The objective faith of Noah and Abraham—through which we had stood firm for thousands of years—had been replaced with the subjective philosophies of ignoble men who had little respect for history and the historical tribal chronicles of their ancestors.

RETURN TO ANGORA

After being severely defeated in Alesia by Julius Caesar, some Galatian tribesmen with historical perspective retreated beyond the Hellespont. They established a base camp in the ancient territory of Dodanim and Iobaath to the east of the Sea of Marmara and Marmara Island and what was once Ox-ferry of Ashkenaz, the son of Gomer. A remnant of Catalonians that survived the Gallic wars settled along the southern coast of the once hospitable Blach See in the land between the Kaucasus Mountains in the east and the Balkans in the west.

Although our Catalonian ancestors lost many brave men in the causalities of war defending against Roman aggression, our people continued to grow large in numbers across Europa, from

Anatolia to the British Isles. The Catalonian nations expanded across central Europa and were the dominant tribes living amidst the Belgi tribes, Helvetii tribes, Cisalpini tribes, Pannoni tribes, and Scnoni tribes sojourning on the northeast coast of Italos.

Sadly, many Catalonians living in Anatolia lost their connection with the LORD God of the Patriarchs Noah and Japheth. Having begun in the Spirit of the LORD under the principled leadership of Captain King Alanus, the Catalonians, like many other tribal nations, devised their own paths of righteousness in their attempts to please God. Through a complicated set of circumstances, the Sovereign Ruler of the Universe returned a remnant of Catalonians back to the land of their forefathers in the territories of Panphylia, Lukka, and Kilikia, back to the great city-states of Ephesus, Corinth, Thessalonica, and among all their ancient tribal cousins on the Chief Sea, and back to the holy lands of Abraham, Isaac, and Jacob on the coast of the Levantine Sea.

Largely unaware of being sent forth from Iopolis by King Fetebir to populate Europa, a remnant of the sons of Captain King Alanus occupied the very same land where they settled after the flood of Noah and after the LORD God gave tongues to the nations of Shem, Ham, and Japheth in Babylon. Our ancient homeland in Iopolis was renamed by the Seleucid rulers as Antioch.

Our people in Galatia remained a God-fearing Catalonian people who regularly attended the Jewish synagogues to hear the preaching of the Oracles of God. A few men and women among the Galatian tribes became proselytes, converting to Judaism, and were circumcised according to the Law of Moses. Others remained God-fearing Gentiles who believe God just as Noah and Abraham did. Our people there attend synagogues in Pessinus toward Asia in Phrygia, as well as synagogues in Ancyra, Tavium, Iconia, Lystra, and Derbe. Many intermarried with Jewish men and women who also settled in Galatia.

Just like the sons of Javan, the Jewish synagogues read from a register and maintained *The Book of the Generations of the Sons of Abraham.* We were encouraged that the Hebrew nation maintained its connection to our Creator as our ancestors have done for thousands of years. Their Hebrew scribes did not give up this important work, accurately maintaining their record of ancestry.

I was curious and secured a copy of the sacred document. It read:

Abraham was the father of Isaac, and Isaac the father of Jacob, and Jacob the father of Judah and his brothers, and Judah the father of Perez and Zerah by Tamar, and Perez the father of Hezron, and Hezron the father of Ram, and Ram the father of Amminadab, and Amminadab the father of Nahshon, and Nahshon the father of Salmon, and Salmon the father of Boaz by Rahab, and Boaz the father of Obed by Ruth, and Obed the father of Jesse, and Jesse the father of David the king.

And David was the father of Solomon by the wife of Uriah, and Solomon the father of Rehoboam, and Rehoboam the father of Abijah, and Abijah the father of Asaph, and Asaph the father of Jehoshaphat, and Jehoshaphat the father of Joram, and Joram the father of Uzziah, and Uzziah the father of Jotham, and Jotham the father of Ahaz, and Ahaz the father of Hezekiah, and Hezekiah the father of Manasseh, and Manasseh the father of Amos, and Amos the father of Josiah, and Josiah the father of Jechoniah and his brothers at the time of the deportation to Babylon.

And after the deportation to Babylon: Jechoniah was the father of Shealtiel, and Shealtiel the father of Zerubbabel, and Zerubbabel the father of Abiud, and Abiud the father of Eliakim, and Eliakim the father of Azor, and Azor the father of Zadok, and Zadok the father of Achim, and Achim the father of Eliud, and Eliud the father of Eleazar, and Eleazar the father of Matthan.

I noticed that many of the names in the Hebrew chronicles were spoken of in our tradition. Our people were unaware of the document, but we were not totally surprised. We understood from our tradition that Shem and Eber were chroniclers committed to preserving a record of generations for princes not yet born.

I recalled the words of the Hebrew, Jeremiah, who prophesied:

> *Thus says the Lord: "Stand by the roads, and look, and ask for the ancient paths, where the good way is; and walk in it, and find rest for your souls."*
> *(This passage would become part of the Hebrew Bible, book of Jeremiah, 16:6.)*

So, pondering the "ancient paths," I felt compelled to provide a copy of *The Book of the Chronicles of the Bohemian Kings* to the remnant of our people sojourning in Galatia. So I spent many years creating the Galatian copy from the original Greek text. Of course, I added the recordings of the king's chronicles since King Fetebir. My great hope is that the Catalonian Galatians cherish the ancient chronicles as I do here in Istropolis.

The literate Latin sons of Romanus prevailed with their large government bureaucracy, dominating military muscle, and burdensome taxation. On the backs of the people that they conquered, the Roman Empire emerged as the most powerful kingdom the world has ever known. *Pax Romana*, a season of Roman Peace, had begun. All the nations benefit from Roman rule, but as Joshua, the Hebrew, said, "As for me and my house, we will serve the LORD." I am persuaded that the government is upon His shoulders. And this is what Isaiah, another great Hebrew prophet, prophesied: "The Way of Peace, they do not know."

God ended the time of war in all the earth as predicted by the Hebrew prophet Jeremiah. The whole world, including the Romans and Catalonians, was chastised and disciplined by God for their man-centered idolatries. Hundreds of thousands of European and African warriors lost their lives in battle.

The discipline of the LORD God displayed His care and affection for all nations, both Jew and Gentile, for all those He had created. My soul yearns for the Seed of Abraham who is to come with His righteous kingdom.

Come, Prince of Peace! Come, King of Kings!

After many years of research, I, King Biatec, the chronicler for the germ of Boguarus, sojourning in Istropolis in the days of Julius Caesar, hereby preserve a record for future generations in *The Book of the Chronicles of the Bohemian Kings:*

Nicolas was the son of Niall. Niall was the son of Sionn. Sionn was the son of Guaire. Guaire was the son of Biatec. Biatec was the son of Brianan. Brianan was the son of Maon. Maon was the son of Eicheard. Eicheard was the son of Bearach. Bearach was the son of Luag. Luag was the son of Ailean. Ailean was the son of Ceallach. Ceallach was the son of Oscar. Oscar was the son of Fearghas. Fearghas was the son of Diarmad. Diarmad was the son of Taog. Taog was the son of Wilton. Wilton was the son of Rheticus. Rheticus was the son of Arbor Felix. Arbor Felix was the son of Aalen. Aalen was the son of Hagano. Hagano was the son of Ewald. Ewald was the son of Raetus. Raetus was the son of Boius. Boius was the son of Daedalus. Daedalus was the son of Telmun. Telmun was the son of Amphare. Amphare was the son of Hercle. Hercle was the son of Boguarus. Boguarus was the son of Negue. Negue was the son of Alanus. Alanus was the son of Fetebir. Fetebir was the son of Ougomun. Ougomun was the son of Thous. Thous was the son of Boib. Boib was the son of Simeon. Simeon was the son of Mair. Mair was the son of Ethach. Ethach was the son of Aurthach. Aurthach was the son of Ecthet. Ecthet was the son of Oth. Oth was the son of Abir. Abir was the son of Rea. Rea was the son of Ezra. Ezra was the son of Izrau. Izrau was the son of Baath. Baath was the son of Iobaath. Iobaath was the son of Rhodanim. Rhodanim was the son of Javan. Javan was the son of Japheth. Japheth was the son of Noah. Noah was the son of Lamech, Lamech was the son of Methuselah, Methuselah was the son of Enoch, Enoch was the son of Jared, Jared was the son of Mahalaleel, Mahalaleel was the son of Cainan, Cainan was the son of Enos, Enos was the son of Seth, Seth was the son of Adam, Adam was the son of God.